THE LOST ORPHAN

THE LOST ORPHAN

STACEY HALLS

WHEELER PUBLISHING
A part of Gale, a Cengage Company

LIBRARY OF CONGRESS CIP DATA ON FILE.
CATALOGUING IN PUBLICATION FOR THIS BOOK
IS AVAILABLE FROM THE LIBRARY OF CONGRESS

ISBN-13: 978-1-4328-8279-2 (hardcover alk. paper)

Published in 2020 by arrangement with Harlequin Books S.A.

Printed in Mexico
Print Number: 01   Print Year: 2020

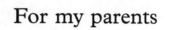
For my parents

■ ■ ■ ■

Part One:
Bess

■ ■ ■ ■

CHAPTER 1

Late November 1747

All the babies were wrapped like presents ready to be given. Some of them were dressed finely — though their mothers were not — in tiny embroidered sleeves and thick shawls, for winter had arrived, and the night was biting. I'd bound Clara in an old blanket that had waited years to be darned, and now never would be. We stood clustered around the pillared entrance, thirty or so of us, like moths beneath the torches burning in their brackets, our hearts beating like papery wings. I hadn't known that a hospital for abandoned babies would be a palace, with a hundred glowing windows and a turning place for carriages. Two long and splendid buildings were pinned on either side of a courtyard that was connected in the middle by a chapel. At the north end of the west wing the door stood open, throwing light onto the stone. The gate felt a long

9

way behind. Some of us would leave with our arms empty; some would carry our children out into the cold again. For this reason we could not look at one another, and kept our eyes on the ground.

Clara was clutching my finger, which neatly slotted into her tiny palm as a lock does a key. I imagined her reaching for it later, her hand closing around thin air. I held her tighter. My father, whom Ned and I called Abe because Mother had, stood slightly behind me, his face in shadow. He had not held the baby. Earlier, the midwife — a wide woman from a neighboring court who was as cheap as she was discreet — had offered her to him as I lay beached on the bed, shimmering in pain, and he shook his head, as though she were a hawker proffering a peach.

We were shown inside by a slim, bewigged man with reedy legs, and through an entrance hall unlike anywhere I'd been. Everywhere surfaces gleamed, from the walnut banister to the polished long-case clock. The only sound was our skirts rustling, and our shoes on the stone — a little herd of women swollen with milk, bearing their calves. It was a place for hushed, gentle voices, not hawkers' ones like mine.

Our little procession made its way up the

claret carpet of the stairs, and into a high-ceilinged room. Only one skirt and bundled infant could pass through the doorframe at a time, so we lined up outside, like ladies at a ball. The woman in front of me had brown skin, and her black hair curled beneath her cap. Her baby was unsettled, making more noise than the others, and she bounced him with the unpracticed air we all had. I wondered how many had their own mothers to show them how to swaddle, how to feed. I had thought about mine fifty times that day, more than I had in the past year. I used to feel her in the creak of the floorboards and the warmth of the bed, but not anymore.

The room we had entered was papered green, with elegant white plaster piped below the ceiling. There were no flames in the fireplace, but it was warm and brightly lit with glowing lamps and pictures on the walls, framed in gold. A chandelier shivered at the center. It was the finest room I had ever stood in, and it was crowded with people. I had thought we might be alone, perhaps with a fleet of nursemaids who carried off the babies that would stay, but a score of faces lined the walls — mostly women who were certainly not nursemaids, fanning themselves and smiling curiously.

They were very well dressed and interesting to look at, and they were very interested in us. They might have climbed out of the paintings on the walls; their necks flashed with jewels, and their hooped skirts bright as tulips. Their hair was pinned up high and cloudy with powder. There were half a dozen men scattered about, too, silver-buckled and potbellied — not like Abe, with his drab coat like a bag of horse feed. The men appeared more stern, and many of them were eyeing the mulatto girl, as though she were for sale. They held little glasses in their gloved hands, and I realized for them this was a party.

I was still bleeding. Clara had been born before daylight that morning, and every part of me felt torn. I had not been her mother a day, yet I knew her as well as myself: the smell of her, the little patter of her heart that had beat inside me. Even before she was pulled from me, red and squealing, I'd known what she'd feel like and how heavy she would be in my arms. I hoped they would take her, and I hoped they wouldn't. I thought of Abe's lined face, his eyes on the floor, his calloused hands holding the door for me. He was the only father in the room. Most of the others were alone, but some had brought friends, sisters, mothers, who looked on miserably. Abe would not meet my eye, and had not spoken much on our slow, sad walk from where we lived at Black and White Court in the city, but his being there was as good as a hand on my shoulder. When he had reached for his coat at home and said it was time for us to leave, I had almost cried with relief; I had not thought he would come with me.

A hush fell over the room as a man standing before the huge fireplace began to speak. His voice was as rich and thick as the carpets. I stared at the chandelier as he told us how they drew the lottery: that a white ball admitted a child, a black one did not and a red one meant we had to wait for an admitted child to fail the medical examination. It took all my energy to listen.

"There are twenty white balls," the man was saying, "five red and ten black."

I shifted Clara at my breast. The swells at the edges of the room were looking on us more boldly now, wondering which of us would be lucky, which of us might leave our babies on the street to die. Who among us was unmarried. Who was a whore. A nurse began moving about the room with a cloth bag for us to reach inside. By the time she came to me, my heart was stomping around my chest in boots, and I held her indifferent

13

gaze as I shifted Clara to one arm and put a hand in the bag. The balls were smooth and cool as eggs, and I held one in my fist, trying to feel its color. The nurse shook the bag impatiently and something told me to let the ball drop and take another, so I did.

"Who are the people watching?" I asked her.

"They were invited," was her bored reply. I clutched another ball, let it go, and she shook the bag again.

"What for?" I asked in a low voice, aware of the many pairs of eyes on me. I thought of their sons and daughters in their grand houses in Belgravia and Fitzrovia and Mayfair, lying beneath warm blankets, brushed and washed and full of milk. Perhaps they would visit the nursery before going to bed tonight, grown sentimental at our plight, dropping a kiss on sleeping cheeks. One woman was staring hard, as though willing me a particular color. She was large and held a fan in one hand, a little glass in the other. She wore a blue feather in her hair.

"They're benefactors," was all the nurse said, and, feeling as though I couldn't ask another question and knowing I must choose a ball, I settled on another, weighing it in my palm. I drew it out, and the room fell silent.

The ball was red. I would have to wait.

The nurse moved to the next woman, while the rest watched her journey around the room, their jaws set in tight, anxious lines as they tried to work out what had been drawn, and what was left. We had been told at the gate that our babies must be two months old at most, and in good health. Many of them were sickly, starving things that their mothers had tried to nurse. Some were six months at least, swaddled so tightly to look smaller they cried out in discomfort.

Clara was the smallest of them all, and the newest. Her eyes had been closed since we arrived. If these were her last moments with me, she would not know. All I wanted was to curl around her in bed like a cat and go to sleep, and come back the next month. I thought of Abe's silent shame. Our rooms at Black and White Court were thick with it; it stained like coal smoke and rotted the beams. I thought of taking her to Billingsgate, sitting her on my father's stall like a miniature figurehead on the bow of a ship. A mermaid, found at sea and put on display for all to see at Abraham Bright's shrimp stall. Briefly I fancied taking her hawking with me, bundling her to my chest so my hands were free to scoop shrimp from my hat. I'd seen some hawkers with their babes strapped to their fronts, but what happened when they were no longer the size of a loaf? When they were fat little things with fists and feet and hungry, empty mouths?

A woman began wailing, a black ball clenched in her fist. Her face and her child's were the same unhappy masks of despair. "I cannot keep him," she cried. "You must take him, please." While the attendants calmed her and the rest of us looked away for her dignity, I yawned so widely I thought my face would crack. I'd not slept for more than an hour since two nights ago, when Clara began to come. This morning Ned sat with the baby before the fire so I could shut my eyes, but I was in so much pain I could not sleep. Now, every part of me ached still, and in the morning I had to work. I could not walk home tonight with Clara in my arms. It was not possible. But neither could I leave her on a doorstep for the rats. As a girl I'd seen a dead baby by a dung heap on the roadside, and had dreamed about it for months.

The room was very bright, and I was very tired, and suddenly I was aware of being led to a little room off the side, and told to sit and wait. Abe followed and closed the door behind him, shutting out the sobs and the tinkle of sherry glasses. I wished for a cup of warm milk or some beer; I did not know how to stay awake.

A nursemaid appeared from nowhere and removed Clara from my arms, but I had not been ready, and it was too soon, too sudden. She was telling me there was a space for her, because a lady had brought an infant of at least six months, which was far too old, and did she think they could not tell the difference between a babe of two months and one of six? I thought of the woman and her child, and wondered idly what would happen to them, then pushed away the thought. The nursemaid's frill cap disappeared through the door again, and I felt delirious, too light without Clara in my arms, as though a feather could knock me over.

"She is not yet a day," I called after the nurse, but she had gone. I heard Abe shift behind me, and the floor creaked.

A man was now sitting before me, writing on a ticket with a fat feather, and I forced my eyes open, and my ears, too, because he was speaking. "The doctor is inspecting her for signs of ailment."

I unstuck my mouth. "She was born at quarter past four this morning."

"If she shows signs of ill health she will be

refused admission. She will be examined for venereal disease, scrofula, leprosy and infection."

I sat in dumb silence.

"Do you wish to leave a token with the memorandum?" The clerk finally looked at me, and his eyes were dark and solemn, at odds with his eyebrows, which sprouted from his head in a rather comic way.

A token: yes. This I had prepared for, had heard how the babies were recorded with an identifier, left by the mother. I fished in my pocket and brought out mine, placing it on the polished desk between us. My brother, Ned, had told me of the Foundling — a hospital for unwanted babies, on the edge of the city. He knew a girl who'd left her child there and cut a square from her dress to leave with it. "And if you leave nothing and go back?" I asked him. "You might be given the wrong one?" He'd smiled and said perhaps, but the idea had chilled me. I imagined a room piled high with tokens, and mine being thrown on a heap of them. The man took it between his finger and thumb, and examined it with a frown.

"It's a heart, made from whalebone. Well, half a heart. Her father had the other." I flushed furiously, my ears scarlet, aware of

18

Abe still standing silently behind me. There was a chair next to mine but he had not taken it. Until now he'd known nothing of the token. The size of a crown, I had the right-hand side, smooth at one edge and jagged at the other. A B had been scored into it, and below it, more roughly, I had scratched a C, for Bess and Clara.

"What will you use it for?" I asked.

"A record will be made should you wish to reclaim her. Her number will go in the ledger as 627, with the date, and a description of the token." He dipped the feather in ink and began to write.

"You will put that it's half a heart, won't you?" I said, watching the words spill from his quill, but not understanding them. "In case there's a whole one, and they get mixed up."

"I will put that it's half a heart," he said, not unkindly. I still did not know where my baby was, or if I would see her again before I left. I was afraid to ask.

"I will reclaim her, when she's older," I announced, because saying it aloud made it true. Behind me Abe sniffed, and the floorboards creaked. We had not yet spoken about this, but I was certain. I straightened my skirt. Streaked with mud and rain, on washing day it was the milky pewter of an

19

oyster's shell, and for the rest of the month the dirty gray of a cobbled street.

The nursemaid came to the doorway and nodded. Her arms were empty. "She's fit for admission."

"Her name is Clara," I said, feeling overcome with relief.

A few months before, when my belly was small, on one of the more genteel streets around St. Paul's, where the townhouses stretched up to the sky and jostled for space with the printers and the booksellers, I'd seen an elegant woman dressed in a deep blue gown, glowing like a jewel. Her hair was golden and shiny, and one plump, pink arm held a little hand, belonging to a child with the same yellow curls. I watched as she tugged at her mother, and the woman stopped and bent down, not caring that her skirts were brushing the ground, and put her ear to the little girl's lips. A smile broke out across her face. "Clara, you are funny," she had said, and took up her daughter's hand again. They moved past me, and I rubbed my growing stomach, and decided if I had a girl I would name her Clara, because then, in a very small way, I would be like that woman.

The man was unmoved. "She will be christened and renamed in due course."

So she would be Clara to me and no one else. Not even herself. I sat stiff-backed, clenching and unclenching my fists.

"And how will you know who she is, if her name changes, when I come back?"

"A leaden tag is attached to each child on arrival, bearing a number that refers to their identifying records."

"Number 627. I'll remember it."

He regarded me, and his eyebrows fell into stern furrows. "If your circumstances change and you do wish to claim your child, the fee for her care will be payable."

I swallowed. "What does that mean?"

"The expenses the hospital incurred caring for her."

I nodded. I had no idea what sort of cost that might be, but did not feel as though I could ask. I waited. The nib scratched, and somewhere in the room a clock ticked patiently. The ink was the same color as the night sky in the window behind him; the curtains had not been drawn. The quill danced like some strange, exotic creature. I remembered the large woman outside with the blue feather in her hair, and how she had stared.

"The people in the room," I said. "Who are they?"

Without looking up he replied: "The

governors' wives and acquaintances. Lottery night raises funds for the hospital."

"But do they need to watch the babies be given over?" I asked. I knew my voice did not sound right here; it made him sigh.

"The women are very moved by it. The more moved they are, the more donations are made." I watched him come to the end of the paper and sign it with a flourish. He sat back to let it dry.

"What will happen to her, when I go?"

"All new admissions are taken to live in the countryside, where they will be cared for by a wet nurse. They return to the city at around five years old, and live at the Foundling until they are ready to work."

I swallowed. "What do they work as?"

"We prepare girls for service, and set them to knitting, spinning, mending — domestic pursuits that will make them attractive to employers. The boys work in the ropeyards making fishing nets and twine to ready them for naval life."

"Where will Clara be nursed? Which part of the countryside?"

"That depends on where there is a place for her. She could be as near as Hackney or as far as Berkshire. We are not at liberty to reveal where she will be placed."

"Can I say goodbye?"

The governor folded the paper over the whalebone heart, but did not seal it. "Sentimentality is best avoided. Good evening to you, miss, and you, sir."

Abe moved toward me and helped me from my chair.

The Foundling Hospital was on the very edge of London, where pleasant squares and tall houses gave way to open roads and fields that yawned blackly into the distance. It was only a mile or two from Black and White Court, where we lived in the shadow of Fleet Prison, yet it may as well have been two hundred, with its farms and cows to the north, and wide streets and townhouses to the south. Coal smoke choked the courts and alleys I was used to, but here there were stars, the sky like a large velvet drape, covering everything in silence. The moon was pale, illuminating the few remaining carriages of the wealthy guests who'd watched us give up our children. Sated with the evening's entertainment, they were now home to bed.

"You'll be wanting something to eat, Bessie," Abe said as we walked slowly toward the gate. It was the first time he'd spoken since we arrived. When I didn't reply, he said: "Bill Farrow might have some

23

meat pies left."

I watched him trudge beside me, and noticed the defeated slope of his shoulders, and how stiffly he moved. The hair that spilled from under his cap had turned from the color of rust to iron. He squinted at the quays now, and the younger boys had to point out the boats from Leigh that brought the shrimp from among the hundreds swarming on the water. For thirty years my father had sold shrimp from a shed in London's fish market. He sold it by the basket to costermongers and bumerees, to hawkers and fishmongers, alongside two hundred other shrimp sellers, from five in the morning to three in the afternoon, six days a week.

Each morning I took a basket to the boiling house at the end of Oyster Row and hawked it from my head in the streets. We did not sell cod; we did not sell mackerel, herring, whiting, pilchards, sprats. We did not sell roach, plaice, smelt flounders, salmon, shad, eels, gudgeon, dace. We sold shrimp, hundreds of them, thousands, every day, by the double. There were plenty more fish that were nicer to look at, nicer to sell: silver salmon, rosy crabs, pearly turbot. But our living was made, our rent paid, from the ugliest of all, looking as they did like unborn creatures ripped from the belly of a giant insect, with unseeing black eyes and curled little legs. We sold them, but we did not eat them. Too many times I'd smelled them spoiled, and scraped the little spidery legs from my hat, the eyes clumped together like spawn. How I wished my father had been a Leadenhall market man instead, and I a strawberry seller, smelling like a summer meadow, with juice and not brine running down my arms.

We'd almost reached the tall gates, and a cat mewed nearby. My insides were empty and aching, and I could think only of a pie, and my bed. I could not think of my baby, and whether or not she had woken to find no comfort. If I did that, I would fall to my knees. The cat wailed again, and did not stop.

"It's a baby," I realized aloud in surprise. But where? The grounds were dark, and the sound came from somewhere to our right. There was nobody else around — I turned to see two women leaving the building behind us, and ahead the gates were closed, manned by a stone porter's lodge with a glowing window.

Abe had stopped, looking with me into the darkness. "It's a baby," I repeated as the noise started up again. Before all this, before

I grew Clara and gave birth to her, I'd never noticed infants crying in the street or wailing in our building. But now, each little mew was as impossible to ignore as if someone was calling my own name. I left the path to go along the dark wall that hemmed the hospital grounds.

"Bess, where you going?"

In a few strides I saw it: a small bundle left on the grass, pressed against the damp brick, as though for shelter. It was swaddled as Clara had been, only a tiny, ancient face visible, with dark skin and fine black wisps of hair at its temples. I remembered the mulatto woman. This was surely her child, and she must have picked a black ball. I gathered the baby in my arms and shushed it gently. My milk had not yet come, but my breasts were sore, and I wondered if the child was hungry, and if I should feed it. I could hand the baby to the porter at the lodge, but would he take it? Abe looked openmouthed at the bundle in my arms.

"What shall I do?"

"It ain't your trouble, Bessie."

A noise came from the other side of the wall: people running and shouting, a horse neighing. Outside the city everything was darker and louder, as though we were in some strange land at the very edge of the world. I had never been to the countryside before, had never even left London. The baby was settled in my arms now, its tiny features creasing into a sleepy frown. Abe and I went to the gate. In the road beyond, people were gathering, and men were running with lanterns toward a coach-and-four, and trying to calm the sweating, bucking horses that had worked one another into a panic. Several white, shocked faces were looking down at the ground, and I slipped through the gate to move closer, still holding the baby. Two feet poked out from beneath the shafts. I saw a muddied skirt, and elegant brown hands. There was a low, guttural moaning, like an injured animal. Her fingers moved, and instinctively I turned to shield the baby from the sight.

"She came from nowhere," the coachman was saying. "We was only going slow and she jumped out."

I turned and walked the short distance to the porter's lodge, which was unlocked and abandoned; he was likely at the scene. Inside it was warm, with a low fire burning in a grate, and candle flickering at a small table set with an abandoned supper. Finding a spare buff coat on a peg, I wrapped the child and left it on the chair, hoping the porter would understand whose it was, and take pity.

In the distance, several windows in the Foundling were yellow, but most were black. Inside, perhaps in their beds, were a hundred or more children. Did they know their parents were outside, thinking of them? Did they hope they would come, or were they happy in their uniforms, with their hot meals, their lessons and instruments? Could you miss somebody you didn't know? My own daughter was inside, her fingers closing around thin air. My heart was wrapped in paper. I had known her hours, and all my life. The midwife had handed her to me, slick and bloodied, only this morning, but the Earth had turned full circle, and things would never be the same.

CHAPTER 2

If I wasn't woken by the sound of my brother pissing into a pail, it was because he hadn't come home. The next morning Ned's bed was empty, and I leaned over to see he was not lying on the floorboards next to it, which he sometimes did when he'd fallen out in a tangle of sheets. The bed was made, the floor bare. I rolled back, wincing. I felt bruised on the inside; filleted, I'd be purple and blue. Next door, I could hear Abe's footsteps creaking on the bare boards. The windowpanes were still black, and would be for hours.

My breasts had leaked in the night, and my nightgown was wet, as though my body was crying. The midwife had warned me this would happen, and said it would stop soon. My breasts had always been the first thing people noticed about me, often the only thing. She'd told me to bind them with rags so the milk wouldn't come through my clothes, but all that had was a clear, watery liquid. The pump in the court felt a long way away when I was this sore, but it was down to me to fetch the water. I sighed and reached for the slop pail, and from the other room heard Ned clatter in through the front door.

Our rooms at no. 3 Black and White Court were on the top floor of a three-story building, overlooking the murky depths of the paved court below. It was here I'd been born, and where I'd lived all my eighteen years. I learned to crawl and then walk on the sloping floor, tucked as we were under the eaves, which creaked and sighed like an old ship. There was no one above us, only birds roosting in the roof and shitting on the chimneys and church spires that jabbed into the sky.

Our mother had lived here with us, too, for the first eight years of my life, before she left us. I cried when Abe opened the window to let out her spirit; I wanted it to stay, and ran over to watch it fly up to heaven. I didn't believe in all that now. They took her body away and Abe sold her things, keeping only her nightgown for me to sleep with, which I did until it didn't smell of her anymore — of her thick, dark hair and milky skin. I didn't miss her much, because it had been so long ago. I expected to need her less the older I got, but when my belly grew and the pushing began, it was her hand I wanted to hold. I'd been envious of the girls with mothers last night, who'd worn their love on their faces.

Ned came stumbling into the bedroom we shared, crashing open the door and tripping over the slop pail I'd left on the floor, tipping my piss all over the floorboards.

"You clumpish fool!" I cried. "Bit of warning next time."

"Shit." He stooped to pick it up from where it had rolled.

In the two rooms Ned, Abe and I called home, there wasn't a straight line anywhere — the roof slanted and the floorboards tilted. He didn't stumble as he set it back on the floor. He wasn't too soaked with booze, then, merely dampened. I wouldn't return from the market with sore feet and an aching neck to find him pale and groaning in bed, smelling of vomit.

Ned flopped on the bed and began pulling off his jacket. My brother was three years older than me, with pearly skin, red hair and enough freckles for the two of us. He spent what little money he earned as a crossing sweeper in gambling kens and gin houses.

"You going to work today?" I asked, knowing the answer.

"Are you?" he said. "You only had a baby yesterday. The old man ain't making you go on the strap, is he?"

"Are you in jest? Think I'd be tucked up in bed with a pot of tea?"

I went into the other room to find that Abe had mercifully fetched the water while I was asleep, and was warming it in the kettle. The main room was sparsely furnished but homely, with Abe's narrow cot against one wall and Mother's rocking chair before the fire. Opposite that was another chair and a couple of stools, and all our pots and plates piled up on shelves by the small window. As a girl I'd stuck pictures to the walls, reproductions of bonny farm girls and buildings we knew: St. Paul's, and the Tower of London. We had no frames, and time had made them curl and fade.

I liked being at the top of the house: it was quiet and private, far from the shrieks of the children who played below. I soaked a rag and scrubbed the floorboards in my room, wincing at the smell but not made sick by it. When I'd been pregnant with Clara, the smell of everything on the market made me heave. Perhaps now it wouldn't.

Once I'd finished and set the pail by the

door to take down, Abe passed me a cup of small beer and I took a seat opposite him, still in my nightgown. The events of yesterday went unspoken between us. I knew we would talk of it one day, but for a long time it would lie like a frost between us.

"They took the baby then, Bess?" Ned's voice came from the bedroom.

"No, I put it under the bed."

He was silent but after a while said: "And you ain't gonna tell us whose it is?"

I glanced at Abe, who stared into his cup, then drained it in one.

I began to pin my hair up. "She's mine," I said.

Ned appeared in the doorframe in his shirtsleeves. "I know she's yours, you halfwit."

"Oi," Abe said to Ned. "Why you getting undressed? Ain't you going to work?"

Ned fixed him with a superior look. "I'm starting later," he said.

"The nags ain't shitting this morning then?"

"Yes, but I need somewhere to shove my broom. Know of anywhere?"

"I'll get dressed," I announced.

"You're making her work after yesterday?" Ned went on. "Are you her father or her master?"

"She ain't afraid of work, unlike some as live under this roof."

"You're a fucking slave driver; let the girl lie in for a week."

"Ned, shut your arse and give your face a chance," I said.

I washed our cups in the water over the fire and set them on the shelf, then brushed past Ned to get dressed, taking a candle with me. Ned swore and kicked the bed frame, sitting down on it with his back to me. I knew we'd come home later to find him gone.

"Go to sleep, will you? Stop ragging him," I said, standing briefly naked, pulling on my shift and wincing.

"Listen to yourself — you should be lying in."

"I *can't*. I didn't work yesterday."

" 'Cause you was birthing a baby!"

"Didn't care about that then, though, did you? Where were you?"

"As if I want to be around to see that."

"Right, well, shut your bone box. Rent day tomorrow." I could not keep the scorn from my voice. "You got your share, or are me and Abe gonna pay it again? It would be nice if you contributed once in a while. This ain't an inn."

I blew out the candle and set it down on

the dresser. Abe had buttoned up his old coat and was waiting for me at the door.

Ned's voice came through from the bedroom, hard and spiteful. "And you ain't the Virgin Mary. Don't be pious with me, you little whore."

Abe's mouth was set in a grim line, and his light eyes met mine. Without a word, he passed me my cap and motioned me into the cold, bare corridor that always smelled of piss and last night's gin, and the door swung shut behind us.

To the river, then. Each morning, by the time the clock face hanging off St. Martin's reached half past four, Abe and I had already left Black and White Court, keeping the high walls of Fleet Prison on our right and going south through Bell Savage Yard to the thoroughfare of Ludgate Hill, before turning east toward the milky dome of St. Paul's.

The road was wide and lively even at that time, and we'd pass crossing sweepers and delivery carts and sleep-soaked wives queuing outside bakeries with their bread for the ovens, and messengers bouncing between the river and the coffeehouses with news from the water. The traffic thickened toward the bridge, and the masts in the wharves bobbed and drifted beyond the sheds crowding the river's edge. Men making for the quays and piers yawned, still half dreaming of their beds and the warm women they'd left there. Even though it was black as pitch — here and there oil lamps burned above some doorways, but in the November fog they were like pale little suns behind a heavy cloud — Abe and I knew the way with our eyes shut.

We passed the Butchers' Hall and moved down toward the river, which lay low and glittering before us, already choked with hundreds of vessels bringing fish, tea, silk, spices and sugar to the various wharves. The going was steep this way, and not easy in the dark. When the clock struck five a few minutes after we arrived, the porters would begin shoring in, moving baskets of fish from the boats in the hithe to the stalls. From six, the city's fishmongers and costermongers and innkeepers and fish fryers and servants would descend with barrows and baskets to haggle over the price of three dozen smelt or a bushel of oysters or a great fat sturgeon, moving up in price as the sellers came down, meeting somewhere in the middle. The sun would rise, weak and watery, so the cries of the merchants — "Cod, alive, alive-oh!" and "Had-had-had-

haddock" and "Getcher smelt, flounder, shad, gudgeon, dace" with a low and deep emphasis on the last word — were no longer disembodied, but belonged to the red-cheeked merchants and their wives. Each cry was as distinctive as the next, and I knew without looking who had called it.

There was a kind of magnificence to Billingsgate, to the morning sun on the creaking masts in the hithe, the iron-necked porters with four, five, six baskets piled on their heads sliding through the crowds. By seven o'clock the ground was a churning mass of mud, studded all over with fish scales like glittering coins. The stalls themselves were a jumble of wooden shacks with leaning roofs that dripped icy water down your neck in winter. Willow baskets lay bursting with stacks of silver sole and crawling crabs, and handcarts groaned with shining shoals. There was Oyster Street in the wharf, called for its row of boats parked nose to tail, piled high with gray, sandy shells. Or if it was eels you were after, you had to get a waterman to take you out to one of the Dutch fishing boats on the Thames, where curious-looking men with fur hats and jeweled rings balanced over great tureens of the serpent-like creatures, writhing and stirring in their murky broth.

Blindfold me and I would know a plaice from a pilchard, a Norfolk mackerel from a Sussex one. Sometimes the fishermen caught a shark or a porpoise and strung it up for all to see; once a high-humored porter put a dress on one and called it a mermaid. Then there were the Billingsgate wives, themselves porpoises in petticoats, with their fat red hands and prow-like bosoms pushing through the crowds, shrieking like gulls. They carried flasks of brandy to nip in the cold months, and wore gold hoops at their ears. I decided from an early age I would not become one of them, would not marry a Billingsgate boy for all the shrimp in Leigh.

Vincent the porter brought our first three baskets piled with gray shrimp, and Dad and I tipped them into ours. We had to work quickly, as the other shrimp sellers would be doing the same. After we'd unloaded, I took a basket to the boiling house, where it would be cooked by a ham-armed Kentish woman named Martha while I went to fetch my hat from the storehouse. Martha was uncommunicative but not unfriendly; we'd wordlessly agreed a long time ago the hour was too early for chatter, and when the shrimp was the same color as her red face, Martha would pile it onto my hat, clattering and steaming. I was used to the weight by now; it was the hot water that hurt, running as it did down my neck and scalding me, but it was nothing compared to Martha's raw pink hands that were stripped of all feeling.

"All right, Pidge?" Tommy, one of the pox-scarred porters, paused on his delivery of Thames smelt. "Might I see you in the Darkhouse later on?"

"Not tonight, Tommy." It was our daily ritual. I told him the same every time, and he replied in kind. Sometimes I wondered for how long I'd be obliged to take part in this performance, and would feel relieved if I missed him on his deliveries. He called me Pidge on account of my large chest. One afternoon a long time ago, Tommy had caught me on his way back from the Dark-house, the roughest pub on the north bank, and pushed me against one of the sheds, pawing at my breasts as he pumped himself with one hand, trying to get me to touch him before shuddering gratefully onto my skirts.

"How about we find a dark house of our own, then, Pidge?"

"Not today, Tommy."

He winked, and went on his way to Francis Costa's stall.

39

I began the climb from the river to the city. London was waking up properly, washed with a low tide of clerks and businessmen on their way to their counting houses and coffeehouses. Often their wives or servants made their breakfast — smoked mackerel or eggs or porridge in china bowls. And I could count on one hand the sailors and mariners who'd bought from me, sick to their stomachs as they were of seafood. No, I was looking for the mousetrap makers, the blacking boys and plasterers having a tobacco break, the lavender sellers and street sweepers pausing to stretch their backs. Knife grinders, wig sellers, market gardeners on their way back to the country having sold their wares. Harried mothers who'd buy a handful to divide between their screaming kids; drunks who had not yet been to bed. Once I'd emptied my hat, which could take one hour or three, I'd go back to Billingsgate and do it again.

Summer was the worst, when the city stank, and I with it. In those months, by midday most of our stock was only good for the cats. Winter was terrible, but at least it kept fresh until sundown, when the market closed.

Left, right, left, right; each day I walked to my own pattern, calling: "Fresh shrimp, straight off the boat, tuppence a third for you, sir, for you, madam." It was difficult to compete with church bells and carriage wheels and the general din of a winter morning. I moved up Fish Street, past the pale column of the Monument, and into the city, stopping to rub my hands together at the corner of Throgmorton Street and kicking a dog from sniffing at my skirts, but only for a moment, because to stop was to freeze and feel the weight of my hat. And that's when I saw the bone shops.

There were four or five of them, supplying bones for all of London's waists. Symbols sat over their doorways: a wooden whale, an anchor and sun, a pineapple. Wicker baskets stacked with skeletons stood outside. The bone made its way downriver from the warehouses at Rotherhithe, selected by merchants, cut slender as a blade of grass and wrapped in linen, silk or leather, or whittled by a scrimshander into horns and handles. Into hearts.

I put an instinctive hand to my stomach; my stays had sat in a drawer for months now, and it would be a while until I could wear them again. If anyone had seen my globe of a belly at Billingsgate, they'd never mentioned it, just as they wouldn't now as it slowly disappeared. Even Vincent and

41

Tommy said nothing. Soon it would be flat again, and I'd forget how big it had been. I'd never forget, though, what it felt to be a home to someone.

"Are you gawking or hawking?"

A woman who couldn't have had more than three teeth in her head had stopped before me. I felt around for the little pewter tankard, filled it and tossed the contents into her grubby hands. She threw the lot into her rotten mouth, and fished in her pocket for another coin.

"I'll take a handful for me son as well. He's an apprentice at a milliner's. He'll be hungry by now, he will, so I shall take this to him at his place of work."

I unloaded another tankard into her palm. "I shall look forward to buying a hat from him one day," I said.

"Got a little one at home, have you?" She indicated my swollen stomach pushing through my cloak.

"Yes," I lied.

"A little cherub, is it? Or a darling angel?"

"A girl. Clara. She's with her father, before he goes to work."

"Lovely. You look after yourself," said the woman, and she limped away into the crowd, clutching her shrimp.

I turned to face the morning once more.

"Fresh shrimp," I called, as the sun finally, slowly, climbed into the sky. "Straight off the boat."

CHAPTER 3

Six years later
January 1754

Keziah had delivered on her promise. She came through the door with a sack in one hand and a bottle of beer in the other, and a smile that reached from ear to ear. I cleared a pile of washing from Abe's chair, dusted the low stool we used as a table free of crumbs and poured the beer into two chipped mugs, handing one to my friend and taking the seat opposite her.

"Let's see what you got."

I exclaimed in delight as she began pulling bundles of frocking out — clouds of linen striped red and blue and white, frothing petticoats, linsey blankets, flannel jackets, drawers, stockings . . .

"Oh, Keziah!" was all I could say.

My friend, who sold secondhand clothes and frippery on Rag Fair to the east of the city, had been saving things for Clara for months, taking them home and mending them, storing them away in a trunk for the day I could collect her. I had saved and saved for six years, and at last I'd added the final shilling to the wooden domino box I kept under my mattress. With two pounds saved, I finally had half a year's wage to pay for Clara's care at the Foundling, without which they might not release her. Sometimes, if sleep did not come, I would take the money out and rattle it to settle my thoughts. I pulled the box now from its hiding place and shook it, and Keziah grinned and clashed her mug with mine as we cackled like wenches.

I settled on the floor to rummage through her loot, made giddy with it. The sun slanted in through the high windows, which were open to let in the fresh air, and the sounds of the court drifted in. A Saturday afternoon, it was one of those blindingly bright winter days, and I'd finished work an hour earlier and come straight home with three currant buns — one for me and Abe to share, one for Keziah and one for Clara.

"I love them, all of them," I said.

"I washed them for you," Keziah said, beginning to fold them. "Where shall I put them?"

I held up a particularly smart red jacket,

slightly faded with wear but otherwise in good condition. I wondered if my daughter would have hair like mine — dark brown, with a hint of red. If she did, it would look splendid against the scarlet linen, and I smiled, picturing a dark, solemn little girl in her red coat.

"I've got caps as well — indoor, outdoor . . ." Keziah said. "Almost made me want a girl, it did, collecting all this." She had left her two boys, Moses and Jonas, at home as she usually did, as she didn't like them to be out on the streets. It wasn't through fear of them turning to a life of crime and vice. Keziah Gibbons was a blackamoor, as was her husband, William. Though the Gibbonses were born free, owned by no one and able to work within the limited trades available to them, young black boys went missing every day in London. At eight and six, Moses and Jonas could at any moment be plucked from the street like two ripe plums, spirited to the mansions of Soho and Leicester Fields and Fitzrovia, gilded with turbans and made into pets. So Keziah said, anyway. I had never known it to happen, but she was very cautious, so bright and beautiful were they, and so desirable to many. It meant that, until they were a little older and Keziah could be certain they had their wits about them, they were mainly confined to the family's two rooms on the ground floor of a boardinghouse in Houndsditch, in the East End of London. They were cared for mostly by a Jewish widow who lived on the first floor.

Keziah's husband, William, was a violinist who had learned to play in the house of his mother's master. He performed now with a modest arrangement of musicians in the very households that would cage his sons like songbirds.

I met Keziah one cold morning five years ago when I was looking for new shoes, going through a pair every six months as I did in my line of work, and we'd become fast friends. At twenty-six, she was two years older than me, and she had what I wanted most: a husband and two adoring children, who looked upon her as though she was a goddess and an angel both.

I took the pile of clothes into the bedroom and knelt on the floor by the chest that kept my own, and began folding them neatly away. Keziah sat on the end of my bed with her cup, kicking off her shoes and folding up her legs beside her.

"She'll sleep in here with you now Ned's left home?"

"Yes." I smoothed a maize-colored skirt, printed with blue flowers, and patted it on top of the others.

"Are you excited?" I could hear that she was, how it burned inside her.

"Yes."

"You don't sound so sure."

"I am!"

The bed creaked as she moved. "I wonder if you'll know her to look at her. Being her mother . . . I wonder if you will pick her out from a room of girls."

"Mmm."

There was a beat of silence. "Bess?" she said. "Are you having doubts?"

I closed the lid of the chest carefully — my mother's chest, carved with roses. It was a cumbersome, old-fashioned thing, but I would never sell it. Her nightdress sat in the very bottom, musty with age. I remembered her wearing it when she warmed milk on the fire, and padded barefoot about our rooms, moving piles of laundry. She died in it, but she had lived in it, too, and when I was younger I used to drape it across my back like a cloak and wrap the sleeves around myself.

"Bess?"

In a small voice, I said: "What if she's dead, Kiz?"

48

"Oh, I'm certain she ain't. They're well cared for there, with doctors and medicine and all that. She has a better chance there than here."

I took a breath. "I suppose I'll find out tomorrow. How much do I owe you for the clothes?"

"Nothing."

I smiled at her. "Thank you."

She winked. "Pleasure's all mine. Why don't you go now, to the Foundling? You're ready, ain't you? You've been ready six years."

"Now?"

"What you waiting for? A carriage? A Tuesday? You got the money."

My stomach felt like one of the Dutchmen's eel tanks, slithering and sliding. "I dunno."

"What does Abe say?"

I took a swig of beer. "He ain't beside himself with the idea, but he's promised to stick with the story: that she's our apprentice, come to live with us and work with me hawking. She's old enough, just about."

Keziah did not reply. I knew she thought six years old was too young to work, that she would keep her boys at home as long as she could. But she had a proper family, and I did not. Still, I would try and make the

49

best of it. Tomorrow, after I collected her, I would take her to see the lions at the Tower of London, like Abe had done with us when we were children, when Mother was ill or tired. But I would not search the streets for a dead dog to feed to the lions as payment, as Abe had done — I would hand over a coin, and in the bright winter sunshine Clara would take my hand and tremble with fear and delight at the golden beasts. Perhaps she would dream about them at night, and I would smooth her hair and tell her not to be afraid. No, a dead dog would not do — that was not the type of mother I wished to be.

"You'll bring her by the rag market, won't you?" Keziah asked, draining her cup.

I nodded, and brushed at my skirts. I hoped the odd feeling in my stomach was hope, not dread. But if it was, why did I feel like weeping? I imagined coming home to a chest full of clothes that would never be worn, and a currant bun on the shelf that would never be eaten, and felt sick with anxiety.

"Bess." Keziah came to meet me on the floor, kneeling on the rag rug. "She will be there, and you will be a mother again. You've been waiting for this for so long, and she's out of danger now. She ain't a baby no more; she's ready to come home and work with you, and be loved by you. Everything she needs is here."

I felt my face fall. "I thought it was, Kiz. But what if it ain't enough?" I tried to see our two rooms as a child might for the first time: the slanted shelves stacked with dented tinware, the darned bedclothes, the sloping ceiling and patchy rugs. I should have bought her a toy, or a dolly — oh, why had I not bought her a dolly? — and set it on her pillow, ready for her homecoming.

Keziah took my hands, and fixed her large brown eyes on mine. "Bess," she said. "It's more than enough."

And now the day was here, and the clock was striking eight outside, and another hour had been wasted with fretting and tidying. Abe had been driven from the house by it, and said he was going to the docks to hear the newspapers read. I moved the currant buns, wrapped in cloth, to a higher shelf so the mice couldn't reach them, swept my eyes around the room a final time and closed the door behind me, locking it with a trembling hand.

"Fine morning it is, Bess." Nancy Benson was standing on the stairs. She took up the width of them, so I could not slip past

51

without making conversation. Nancy did not even live on this floor, though nowhere was off-limits to her; she clambered up and down like an overweight mouse.

"It is that, Nancy. Good day to you."

"Off to church, are you, in your best frock?"

I stood three or four steps above her, and waited for her to move. She knew I did not go to church. "I'm out to collect our new apprentice."

Nancy's eyebrows rose. "For Abraham's stall, is it?"

"No, for me. She'll help me hawking."

"Will she now? A girl, eh? Well, I never. You don't see many girl apprentices."

"You don't see many boys selling food from their heads, either." I moved to pass her on the stairs and she turned her wide back against the wall. The floorboards creaked as I passed. Nancy had lived in Black and White Court ten years, and been a widow most of them. She made broom heads for a living, and her hands were red raw from it.

"She'll stay with you, then? The girl?"

"Yes." I could rely on Nancy to sweep the news about the court, piling it in little corners and letting it settle. She knew I'd had a baby — it was impossible to hide as my stomach grew. She'd shivered with glee at the shame of it, and tried many times to trick me into telling her who the father was, but I'd been tight-lipped, taking pure pleasure in the frustration it gave her.

"How's your Ned?"

I stopped at the foot of the stairs and held the knob of the banister that Ned would always knock off and send clattering down the hall. It was still loose, and I spun it around and around. "He's well."

"And Catherine and the little ones?"

"All well, thank you, Nancy."

"Lovely." Nancy was disappointed. She always held a candle for my brother, even though he treated her like a particularly dim mongrel. She'd been useful to him, before the gin laws arrived. When she'd realized his weakness, she'd opened a shop in her single room, distilling grain and selling it, and Ned was her most loyal and most credited customer. At one point, he was in her lodgings more than ours. I'd feel him sink into the bed next to mine and begin snoring, reeking of turpentine, and knew on the floor below, Nancy would be tossing and sighing in hers.

The way she looked at me, I had no doubt she knew about Clara, knew she would have drawn the tale of my shame from his mouth

53

like a silk kerchief from a pocket. The smell of her sulphuric jars was enough to make your eyes water, but nothing was too neat for Ned. Madame Geneva, he called it, which I hated, as though it was an exotic, fragrant thing.

When he met Catherine, I thought his life might take a turn in the right direction. She was a butcher's daughter from Smithfield, thin as a splint and sharp-tongued enough to whittle him into shape. But a family wasn't the making of him. First their girl, Mary, came along, then two babies in between that died, then they had their boy, Edmund, just a few months ago. But becoming a father seemed to have taken something vital from Ned, as if by creating them he'd lost part of himself, and was fading around the edges. He often disappeared for days; the longest had been two weeks. I'd been hopeful for him, once.

"You seen him lately?"

"Not lately."

I replaced the knob and smacked it in with the flat of my hand. "I must be going, Nancy."

"I'll say a prayer at St. Bride's for the baby. Edmund." Her wide, flat face loomed above me.

"Very kind of you."

"And his father, that the Lord may deliver him from his demons."

The demons that you conjured in a jar.

We were silent for a second.

"Very kind. Good day to you, Nancy."

Many times I'd approached the Foundling, but only got as far as the gates. The porter's lodge was still there, its round window like an eye looking over the street. The flat gray sky pressed down on the sand-colored stone, and the clock face in the chapel told me it was a quarter past nine. I stood for a moment on the dusty road, remembering that night: the darkness and the soreness between my legs. The muddied skirts beneath the carriage wheel, and the poor woman's twitching fingers.

The porter's face appeared at the door. I stood up a little straighter, smoothed down my dress, hoped I looked respectable. "I am here to collect my child," I told him.

He looked warily at me. "You got the collection fee?"

My stomach flipped. "Yes," I said, more confidently than I felt. Surely half a year's wage was enough; I hardly dared ask him, in case it was not and he refused to let me in. If it was not . . . . it did not bear thinking about.

Suddenly I imagined what it would be like to meet my daughter after all this time, with her thinking I'd come to get her, and being led back through a door, pleading and crying, and reaching for me. What if they wanted *twenty* pounds? I could not save that in a lifetime. A faraway ringing noise started in my left ear, and I began to feel dizzy.

"This way, miss. All the way to the end; go in on your left."

I thanked the porter, then walked stiffly through.

The driveway was wide and empty, and in the distance I could hear singing. My legs were shaking. My daughter was inside these very grounds. *Unless she is dead,* came that little voice that lay buried like a worm in my mind.

The lawns in front of the Foundling were occupied with little groups of boys sat in rows, making ropes and nets. They wore a uniform of plain brown jackets with white shirts and red scarves tied at their necks, and they glanced briefly at me as I passed, before going back to their work. They did not look as though they minded it, and talked easily with their legs crossed as their hands busied themselves.

Among the white faces was a brown one, and I stopped and watched him for a moment, recalling the baby I'd taken from the grass and put in the porter's house, wrapped in his coat. He looked a little like Moses Gibbons, with closely cropped hair and slim hands. He was around the same age as Clara would be. I wondered if he knew her. He felt me looking and stared at me with round, curious eyes. Perhaps every child wondered if a woman walking up the drive was his or her mother. I smiled at the boy, and he turned quickly back to his work.

I hesitated outside the large black door that led into the wing on the left before pushing it open and stepping inside. There was that familiar smell of furniture polish and cooked food. My stomach groaned, and my legs weakened again. I leaned back against the door, my ears ringing in the quiet. I could barely believe I was there, ready to collect my daughter after so long. But would she want to come? Was it not better for her that she stay here, where she surely had friends, and hot meals, and slept under a roof that did not leak? She would go into service soon, and might stay in a fine house, and have a kind mistress. But then I thought of the one or two girls I'd heard of from the neighboring courts who had gone to work at the houses in the west of the city and were never heard of or spoken of again. Likely they'd been made mothers by their masters and turned out with no reference, swallowed up by the city. At least that fate had not befallen me, though was I really so different?

A short woman in an apron approached me. "May I be of assistance?"

"I am here to collect my child."

There was more warmth in her small eyes than in the porter's. "How lovely," she said with sincerity. "Let me take you through where someone will see you."

There were no children around, other than the disembodied singing; had I not seen the boys making the nets on the lawn, I might have wondered if there were any here at all. Children lived loudly; they sneezed and shouted and ran — at least in the city they did. Only this morning I'd heard some shrieking, dragging a grisly bone around the courtyard for a dog. Perhaps the Foundling children were refined; perhaps they stepped elegantly and sat quietly, like little swells.

I was shown to a small room off the corridor that smelled of cigar smoke. My heart was racing, and I was glad to sit down opposite a large, gleaming desk. The window behind it overlooked the fields stretching out of London. Clara would be used to the same view, with all the trees and sky. What would she think of our rooms, which looked out on chimneys and rooftops?

I heard the door close behind me and a small, slight man in a neat wig edged around the desk to take a seat opposite. "Good morning, miss."

"And to you."

"My name is Mr. Simmons; I am one of the clerks here. You have come to remove your child from the hospital?"

"Yes," I said, and swallowed. "My name is Bess Bright. I am here for my daughter. I brought her in on the twenty-seventh day of November, six years ago."

He nodded once, showing the top of his wig. "Six years, you say? Then she should be here at the hospital, all being well. Now, did you leave a token?"

All being well. "Yes," I faltered. "A piece of whalebone, it was, cut in the shape of a heart. Half a heart. The other piece . . . Well, her father had it. The piece I gave had two letters engraved in it: B and C."

"And you have the fee for the care and maintenance she has received?"

"How much is it?"

"Well, you say she was brought in November of . . ."

"The year of our Lord 1747."

59

"So that makes it six years and . . ."

"Almost two months to the day."

He nodded obligingly, drawing his quill and doing some sums. "That would make the sum total six pounds and, let me see . . ."

"Six *pounds*?" I'd raised my voice, silencing him. "I do not have six pounds."

He blinked, considering me. His quill trembled. "When you gave your daughter into the Foundling's care, it should have been made clear that a reimbursement of one pound per year of accommodation was payable."

"I . . . I do not . . . I cannot . . . How does anyone get their child back?" I thought of the measley bag of coins in my pocket, made up of pennies and tuppences and threepennies, two pounds in total, that had grown heavier so slowly. I felt as though I was sinking very slowly into the ground.

He scratched beneath his wig, setting it wriggling like a live animal.

"I shall fetch your daughter's papers, and we can speak on the terms of agreement once I've reviewed her case." He looked a little uneasy; his eyes were not unkind, but his mouth was glum, as though he was not used to delivering good news.

I understood what he was leaving unsaid: *Let us not get carried away with ourselves, for she might be dead.* Many women must come here, only to be told their children had died. I tried to smile back at Mr. Simmons, though my nerves were getting the better of me.

"Before I do," he said. "May I ask if your circumstances have changed, Miss Bright?"

"My circumstances?"

"Indeed." He waited.

"I am unmarried, if that is what you ask. And I have not changed my work since I brought her."

"You are not a burden on the parish? And keep a good home?"

"As well I can."

"With whom do you reside?"

I was so unused to his language, it took every effort to scrape together my wits and understand him, and my head swam. Six pounds!

"My father. My mother died when I was a child, so I know how it is to want for a mother."

The old man looked meaningfully at me. "And you could guarantee that the burden of her care would not fall to the parish until she reaches adulthood?"

"I can guarantee it, though I must confess I do not understand. I've told you I don't have six pounds. I have two, and it's taken me all these years to save it."

Mr. Simmons continued to look at me for a moment, pursing his thin lips. "Miss Bright, not very many children are claimed at the Foundling. Only about four a year, from four hundred. Which is why we do what we can when their parents do come back, within reason, you understand. Do you design to have the child work?"

"Alongside me."

"In which profession?"

"I'm an hawker. I sell shrimp from my father's stall at Billingsgate. She wouldn't leave my side."

Why had I not lied? All her lessons and learning would go to waste — her sewing skills, if she had started, would be as useful as a butter teapot. This was all going badly. I would not be allowed to take her home, not now.

Dismay must have been written on my face, for Mr. Simmons leaned in slightly and said: "While it's not conventional, at the hospital we aim to reunite as many children with their families as possible. It is not our position to judge circumstances. So as long as you are prepared to take responsibility for your daughter's needs, we are prepared to sign her guardianship over to you, for whatever sum you have. To take her away you will sign a receipt for her care, and leave a name and address. It is a kind of contract, you understand. Now, if you could remind me of the day she was brought."

"The twenty-seventh day of November, 1747. And the token was half of a heart, made from whalebone."

He bowed, then he left the room.

Every part of my body was tense. I moved my neck, stiff from work, and rolled my shoulders, then got up and went to the window, looking out for something to distract me. Surely country people did not enjoy such views: it was like looking at a picture, for nothing moved. I rubbed my arms beneath my cloak, feeling cold. There was a noise in the corridor, and I heard children's voices, and the sound of boots on stone floors. I went to the door and opened it a crack.

A procession of girls was passing in pairs — eight or ten of them — in brown dresses and white caps. I peered into their faces, looking for my own. A few of them glanced at me, then away, absorbed in their chatter. And suddenly they were gone, closing a door behind them, their absence ringing in my ears.

I went back to my chair and lowered myself slowly into it. I had hoped when I saw her I would know her at once, that we would be connected by an invisible thread, fine and strong as a spiderweb. I thought of the ropes the boys were making outside, knotting and twisting with their small hands. A slick white rope had attached her to me after she came out, that I'd made inside me. It was grotesque, slick as an eel and milky as a pearl, with a slab of meat at the end of it, like a sheep's lung. The midwife had severed it, then thrown them both on the fire.

Mr. Simmons had been gone for a long time. He had said he was fetching her papers, but what if he came back with Clara? I was not expecting him to, and was not prepared. When the door began opening I clutched the sides of the chair, thinking I might pitch forward. But Mr. Simmons entered alone, with some documents in his hand, a blue ribbon trailing where he had unwrapped them. I remained where I was, for he did not sit down, and his face was puzzled. He took an eyeglass from his desk, set the sheaf down and examined the top item for a long moment.

"You say your daughter was brought in on the twenty-seventh of November, 1747."

I nodded.

"The token you left was a piece of scrimshaw. Half a heart, you say, with a B and C engraved."

"Yes."

He frowned, and looked very hard at me. "You are Elizabeth Bright?"

I stared at him.

He pushed the bundle of papers to me across the desk. "Miss, have you seen these documents before?"

"I can't read except for recognizing a few letters." I plucked at the blue ribbon. Fear was rising in me, filling me like a rain bucket. "Are these hers? Is she dead?" Elegant script curled meaninglessly over the heavy cream paper, but I saw the numbers six and two and seven, which, to me, was like reading her name.

Mr. Simmons looked at me for what felt like a full minute. Then he blinked, and pulled the papers back to his side of the desk. The ribbon lay splayed between us, and inexplicably all I could think was what a waste it was, that something so fine should be shut up in a drawer.

"Mr. Simmons, I don't understand," I said. "Has she died?"

The governor shifted uneasily in his chair and put his eyeglass down carefully. "Child 627 was collected many years ago, by her mother."

There was complete silence, but for a pounding in my ears. I opened my mouth, then closed it and swallowed. "Her mother? I'm sorry, sir, I don't understand. Are we talking about my daughter, Clara?"

He scratched at his wig, at a loss for words. "We do not record children's names; they are baptized and given new ones. Privacy reasons, you see."

My head hurt, as though I was wearing my shrimp hat, piled with thoughts and riddles. "But this is the first time I've come to take her home. Child 627, are you sure?"

Mr. Simmons's eyes shone with concern and alarm. "Might you be mistaken about the date on which you brought her?"

"No, of course not. That's her birthday, I'll remember it the rest of my life. Every year I light a candle for her. And 627 — they told me that was her number. I remember it as well as my own name." A clock was ticking somewhere in the room, and I felt as though I was watching the scene from above. My fingers were still gripping the sides of the chair, and I let go and sank down into it, using the desk as support. My knuckles were white.

"Might her father have —" he began.

"Her father's dead."

There was a long pause.

66

"So what you are telling me," I said slowly, "is someone has claimed Clara? My daughter?"

The fear had gone, replaced by a dull kind of awareness that sat heavy on me and made me stupid. Something terrible, beyond my worst imaginings, had happened, but . . .

"Hold on," I said. "What was her name? The name of her mother?"

Mr. Simmons held the eyeglass to the paper. "It says here: *'Child 627 was collected on the twenty-eighth day of November, 1747, by her mother, Elizabeth Bright, of number three Black and White Court, Ludgate Hill, London.'*"

He held the paper toward me and showed me a signature by the words: a shaky, hasty X. The room tipped to one side, but oddly the glass paperweight, the candle and the papers sitting on it did not roll to the floor. I waited for it to stop moving, which it did, after half a minute or so. I reached out and touched the X, which marked the neat page like a burn.

"That's me," I whispered. "This can't be happening." Then something made me look up suddenly. "But the twenty-eighth day of November. That's . . . That was . . ."

"The day after she was brought to the hospital. Miss Bright, I am afraid we have not had your daughter in our care for more than six years."

CHAPTER 4

It had been a long time since I'd thought of Clara's father. Even longer since I'd seen him. No more could I recall his face than my mother's. Like hers, all that remained was an impression: a blue coat, the height of him, his light eyes — were they blue, or green? — and the way he grinned behind a cloud of pipe tobacco. He had given me his clay pipe — a small, smooth thing with his initials carved into the side. But it wasn't a sentimental gesture — he'd passed it to me to look for something in his pocket, and I'd been so admiring of it that he told me I could keep it. No doubt he had several more at home — wealthy people did. I used to lie in bed tracing the D for Daniel, the C for Callard with a fingertip — I could not read, but I knew those letters — and when I could not find him, I threw it into the Thames. I regretted it when I found out he'd died.

Now I had nothing of his: not his child,

69

nor his pipe. People tossed all sorts into the river, including themselves. It was something I'd thought about, too, for less than a moment, when I found out he was gone, and I was growing his child. But the river was the busiest street in London, and drowning would not be quick, nor private, with hundreds of boats choking the water from the Middlesex to Surrey banks, as far as the eye could see. Likely I'd be struck by a packet boat or severed by a prow. For an even briefer moment I had thought about the alternatives — jumping from a high window, or drowning myself from the inside with gin like the bloated creatures outside the shops. None were particularly appealing. Besides, I had felt the growing life inside me, and knew I could not snuff two out at once.

Perhaps death brought peace for people like Daniel Callard, where the sun dappled the quiet churchyard through leafy boughs, and flowers were left at their stones. But I knew how crowded the dry and shallow burial yards for those like me were. I'd smelled their rotting mass, and did not wish to join their unhappy slumber just yet.

Once, when we were very small, Ned had told me that at night the dead climbed from beneath their thin blanket of soil and

70

crawled the streets and courts, looking for children to take to their graves. They waited, he said, in alleys, and clung to the shadows. I had been too afraid to leave the house, attaching myself to Mother's skirts and screaming for us to stay inside. When I told her why, Abe smacked Ned about the head. A while later, when Mother died and Ned and I had been lying in our narrow beds, I'd asked him if she, too, would crawl the streets in the dark, looking for us. He pulled me close and told me no, and when I rolled away his face in the moonlight had frightened me — he looked very grown-up and sorrowful.

Back then, our mother dying was the worst thing in the world, and we'd clung to one another night after night while Abe retreated into his own silent grief. How green we were.

Walking back from the Foundling, my feet had brought me to Russell's coffeehouse, somewhere I had not been able to bring myself to stand outside for a long time. Russell's was set above a chandler's shop and flanked by a large golden lion outside, its jaws locked midroar. I had never stepped foot inside, because I was a woman. But if the day was a slow one, in the hours between

71

breakfast and luncheon, I sometimes lingered in the streets by the Exchange with my brimming hat, waiting for men to spill out of the meeting houses onto the street, their teeth dark with coffee, their heads full of business and shipping news and other pursuits, and their bellies empty.

Sometimes they'd take a handful of shrimp from me; sometimes they wanted a handful of something else. I saw what coffee did to their eyes — it made the pupil blacker, and larger, as though they were looking not at me but inside their own minds.

I met Daniel in 1746, on a dark morning a month or so after Christmas. It had been very cold, and the doorway he had come from had looked very warm and bright and friendly, and my gaze had lingered on it and, I suppose, got lost in it. I realized he was staring at me, his own gaze soft as ash in the thin gray light. A slim piece of lead was tucked behind his ear.

"Penny for them," he had said, and I'd come out of my reverie, closing my mouth and standing straighter.

"I beg your pardon, sir?"

"Penny for them," he said again, nodding at my hat, and I reached blindly for the little tankard, and began scooping.

"Tuppence, actually, for a third pint, sir," I'd said, and he'd laughed and shook his head.

"No, for your *thoughts.*"

I had looked so surprised he fell about laughing, and the air between us turned warmer. From him came the scent of coffee, and sawdust, and something else pleasant — was it wool? Or horsehair?

After that first meeting I went back to the coffeehouse again and again, hovering around the golden doorway like a moth, greedy for the sight of him. Dusk came early, and in the middle of a gray afternoon, when snow had threatened from the sky all day and clouds had been a queasy yellow, I saw him among a small group of men in front of the chandler's shop. They might have been arriving or leaving, but they were very splendid in their blue wool coats and hats, standing upright with outturned feet and easy smiles, for they had been warm, and would be warm again. I walked up the street and felt overcome, unable to speak or look at him, so I hid in a doorway, and after gathering myself, began back the way I'd come, making sure I caught his eye. Our gazes caught like a tinderbox, and I was aflame. I was done for.

"Shrimp girl," he'd said. "Where's your hat?"

I have no memory of what I'd mumbled — something stupid, not sparkling, because he made my head feel full of cotton. He put an arm around me, making me feel small and dainty. I'd hoped I did not smell of shrimp. We'd gone into a tavern — a low, smoky place by the hide market, and I'd had my first taste of wine. It was sweet and sticky, like melted fruit on a summer's day, and had burned my throat. His companions had come with us — three or four officers and merchants, like him, who called him Cal, and I sat dumbly as they roused and rabbled, speaking loudly over one another and rolling their tobacco.

Women were allowed in taverns, and several whores moved freely about, touting for customers. One or two sat with us for a time, joining in with the men and making me feel like a little girl, like a daughter. I learned small things about him: that he was a whalebone merchant who spent a lot of time in Rotherhithe, down the river, and Throgmorton Street, where I knew the bone shops to be, and they spoke of a man named Smith, and another named Tallis. Meanwhile, I drank another cup of wine straight down, and after a while, when the noise and the smoke was almost too much for me, he found my eye and gave a private smile, then asked if I wanted to go somewhere more quiet. I nodded, cotton-headed again, and we moved out to the street.

It had been dark then, and I didn't know properly where we were, for the walls were so narrow, full of inky corners and buildings that buckled over the street, blocking the moonlight. I hardly remember what was said, except he asked me if I was cold. I said yes, and he gave me his coat — a fine, warm thing that reached my knees — and then he kissed me. He tasted of liquor and pipe tobacco. My back found a wall, and he moved his hands to either side of my head, leaning into me. Before long they moved south, finding my body and then my skirts, and I moved him toward me and inside me. I had seen couples in the street before, young lovers and old lovers and men emptying themselves into whores. I had never thought I would become one of them, never thought a man — no, a merchant — would want to go with me in the dark. It was the wildest thing I'd done. I had not gone with a man before, though I'd come close once or twice with some of the bolder Billingsgate boys — Tommy not being one of them.

After we were finished, I put my hands in

the pockets of his coat, which I was still wearing, and drew out what was inside: the short wooden pipe, with which the tobacco smell grew stronger, a few coins, which I put back hastily, and something odd-looking. I held it toward the stingy moon-light and saw it was two pieces of a heart, which fit perfectly together.

"This from your sweetheart?" I asked him.

"Don't have one," he said, and took one of the pieces, leaving me with the other. "Something to remember me by."

"What's your name?" I asked.

He took it back from me, smiling from the corner of his mouth, and reached for a penknife from inside the coat that I was still wearing, brushing my breast with his hand.

He asked me what my name was, and when I told him "Bess Bright," he carved a letter on it and handed it back to me, gesturing for his coat, which I took off, feeling the February chill rush in again.

"It ain't fair if you don't tell me yours," I said shyly.

"Callard."

"Your first name."

"Daniel. I'll be seeing you, Bess Bright."

And with that, he made for the light and noise spilling from the tavern doorway, while I stood shivering, feeling the wine slowly wear off and clutching his gift tightly. I was still holding the pipe in my other hand. I'd almost followed him back in, but could not face that bright, crowded room, and turned instead for the river, and home.

I'd gone looking for him a few times after that. It had been a Wednesday when I first saw him, and I went every Wednesday after that, floating up and down Gracechurch Street like a spook, waiting once for two hours in a doorway. But Daniel Callard had been swallowed up by London. Like the Thames tide, the city had a temperament, and it could give or take away.

When winter warmed to spring and I knew I'd have his child, I intensified my search and found the man I'd heard spoken of in snatches, Tallis. He was the owner of one of the Throgmorton Street bone shops, who looked like a bone himself, with paper skin that clung to sunken cheeks.

He told me the merchant Daniel Callard had died the month before, very suddenly and unexpectedly. He was a fine merchant, and his funeral had been very well attended. He'd noticed my stomach then, and his expression darkened, and I'd staggered from the shop into the quiet street, and vomited in an alley.

I stood looking now at the lion, then

moved toward it and reached inside its gaping mouth, leaving my hand suspended between its jaws. I had wanted to take our daughter to the lions at the Tower, to show her how they roamed and padded. I thought of the currant bun at home, waiting on the shelf, and Abe, home by now and sitting in his chair, expecting us. "Where is she?" he would say. *Where is she?*

I thought of Daniel, sleeping in the soil. I'd paid a boy to find me the death announcement from April and read it aloud to me in the street. It was very short — one or two sentences — with the church for the funeral named: one I did not know, and had missed besides. I wished I had not thrown his pipe in the river; wished I could press my lips to it once more.

On the eastern edge of the city, beyond the old wall, was the Rag Fair — a quarter of a mile of stalls selling clothes second-, third- and fourthhand, even on a Sunday. It was busiest in the mornings, with people browsing after church, so when I arrived in the middle of the afternoon the crowd had thinned, plus the bite of winter at people's collars and fingers meant only a few idle souls drifted about — those without families, picking at pawned frippery instead of a glistening roast bird. In the warmer months the tables were a riot of color — blood reds and sky blues and foamy frills as far as the eye could see — but at this time of year people wanted warm coats, thick drawers and sturdy boots.

Keziah's stall was halfway down Rosemary Lane, and I saw her crouched over her jumble of ladies' jackets and coats. She carried everything in her barrow from Houndsditch each morning, and was one of the few traders who took care of her stock, dabbing at stains with lye and mending holes and tears. A woman was examining her items, extracting sleeves here and there before discarding them. By the time I reached the stall she had ambled off, and Keziah sat down, rubbing her hands together and blowing on them.

"You've no reason to be cold with all them coats," I said, trying to sound cheerful. My own wool cloak was one of Keziah's, bought a few winters ago. If business was quiet and we were passing time, we'd make up stories about the people who'd owned them before. My cloak, we'd said, belonged to a beautiful woman who fell in love with a sailor and moved with him to the West Indies; she'd sold her warm things because she wouldn't need them in her new life.

Keziah made a face, and got up to embrace me. "Seems everyone's got one this time of year. And those who haven't are in the ground by now."

She saw my face then, and understanding flooded my friend's features. She looked around, as though I might have been hiding Clara under my skirts. "Where is she?"

"She wasn't there."

My friend's face collapsed. "Oh, Bess. She died."

I shook my head. "No. She's already been —"

"Penny a dip!" the wig seller behind me bellowed, making me jump. He repeated himself in Yiddish, then three more languages, and I moved around the table to speak more quietly.

"She's already been claimed," I said.

Keziah blinked. "By who?"

"This is the strangest part. By *me.*"

She shook her head, and I wrapped my cloak tighter around myself. "The person who took her gave my name, and my address. I don't understand, Kiz. My mind's in a spin. I came straight here, I haven't even told Abe. He'll be —"

My voice died in my throat, and I had to whisper. "Whoever took her did it the day after I left her there. All these years and she wasn't never there, all this time."

"*What?* But who could it be? Daniel is . . ."

"Dead, I know."

Keziah's brown eyes grew even larger. "But what if he ain't?"

"He is. It was in the newssheets."

"You can't read."

"I paid a boy to read it. He's dead, Kiz."

"Penny a dip!" cried the wig seller.

"But why would someone take her? And in your name as well?"

"What I don't understand is how they know who I am in the first place — at the Foundling you don't give your name, or your address, or nothing, to protect your identity. But whoever it was knows where I live, and who I am. *How?*"

Keziah adjusted her bonnet, tucking her woolly black hair inside. "You've made me all nervous now."

"I know."

"And they wouldn't tell you this to cover up that she'd died?"

"I imagine plenty of babies that go there die. It's not the Foundling's fault — most of them come in half-dead. Besides, they send them out of London, like I said, to be nursed in the countryside."

"What if it is their fault? What if there was

an accident, or —"

"Kiz, why would they lie?"

"What if they sold her?"

"To who? Who would buy a day-old baby? Abandoned children are ten a penny, you can get one from anywhere: the gutter, the poorhouse . . . Half the families in this street would sell theirs if they could."

Keziah shuddered. At that moment, two small figures hurtled toward us, skipping and tripping over themselves. Moses, Keziah's eldest, leaped over a pile of boots in a basket, arriving in a heap at our skirts, and his younger brother, Jonas, copied, falling short and clipping the table leg, making it collapse and sending half of Keziah's clean clothes to the ground.

"Jonas, you filthy scrap! Look what you've done," she scolded, lifting him by one scrawny arm. "Why aren't you at Mrs. Abelmann's? I pay her to watch you, not let you out to crawl like lice over my clothes."

She righted the table and I set about lifting and folding.

"She let us take the bread to the oven," Jonas said with pride.

"Le-khem," said Moses. "That's Yiddish for bread. And *ta-nur* is oven."

"And where is the bread?"

"Being baked!"

"You go and get that bread and take it straight back to Mrs. Abelmann's, you hear me? Do not speak to anyone, do not stop and do not leave the house again, even if the king himself comes down Rag Fair on a sedan."

They scampered off past the boots and petticoats, and Keziah watched them until they disappeared down an alley behind a stall. In their merriment, I had forgotten my own troubles — children would do that for you. I brushed off a set of stays and placed them on top of the pile.

"You are too protective," I told her.

"There is no such thing."

We stood for a moment looking up and down the market. People were huddled against the icy wind with their hands and heads wrapped. Only those who had to be were out in this weather, but plenty had no choice. Dusk was falling already, and no one bought clothes when it was dark. Keziah's finer things — flowered cotton and striped satin and colored ribbons — hung on pegs from the cooper's shop behind. These garments looked better in the half-light, when you could not see the hems stitched a different color, or the sweat stains at the armpits that no amount of lye would get out.

"What will you do now?" she asked me, rubbing her hands together.

I pulled on a length of violet ribbon. "I don't know. I will go home alone, and Abe will ask where my child is, and Nancy Benson will, too, and I will look like a fool. I told Nancy we were getting an apprentice; I told everyone at Billingsgate. I don't know how I'll bear it."

Keziah was silent for a time, during which it seemed to get darker, so that when I looked at her again I could no longer make out the finer details of her face, the gentle wrinkles at the corners of her eyes.

"Perhaps she has a better life than you can give her," she said quietly.

"Yes," I said with a hollow laugh. "Perhaps a duchess has taken her in as her own, and teaches her to draw and play the pianoforte. Oh, Kiz. I don't know what to believe. I don't trust those men at the Foundling, with their wigs and quills. They look at you through their eyeglasses. We're all the same to them, us and our children."

"I'm sure that's not true. Did Daniel know where you lived, even?"

"No, of course not. I only met him twice! I don't know, Kiz. It's like I'm feeling around in the dark."

I looked down Rosemary Lane toward

Black and White Court, where I knew Abe would be sitting in his chair, thinking he was going to meet his granddaughter, and fretting about money. "How will we keep her?" he'd asked more than once, and I reminded him we'd managed fine when we had three mouths to feed, before Ned left home, and would again. He would be listening for two sets of feet on the stairs, and getting three bowls down from the shelf for supper. The idea of telling him that I did not know where she was . . . it was *careless*. It was the opposite of what a mother should be. I could not bear the vastness of it all. Was she in London, or even England? Had she been put on a ship? At worst I had thought she might be dead, but knowing she could be anywhere instead of nowhere at all was a torture even more exquisite.

"Help me pack up and come to ours for supper," said Keziah.

I accepted gratefully, and helped her bundle all her clothes into sacks, which we piled into her barrow, laying the table and baskets on top. We walked north, along the wide thoroughfare of the Minories, where two drays could pass one another, and turned into the dingy passageways that led to Broad Court, where Keziah lived with her family.

Flanked on both sides by synagogues, this pocket of London belonged to the displaced — blackamoors like the Gibbonses, Spaniards, Huguenots, Jews, Irish, Italians and lascars — all crowded into the little courts and boardinghouses. The lodgings here were more respectable than the rookeries, where thieves and prostitutes laid their heads and three families slept to one room, but a rung or two below Black and White Court, with its water pump and one or two rooms per family. Keziah's two rooms were at street level, and when I visited I had to tap on her window, for her landlady — an irritable French woman with a hooked nose and beady eyes — spat forth an angry, rapid torrent if visitors knocked on the front door, and sometimes slammed it in their faces.

It was dark by the time we arrived, but there was a gentle glow at the edges of the curtain, which meant her husband, William, was home. We let ourselves in to find him mending a violin string at the large scrubbed table, while Jonas and Moses huddled on the bench reading the bible aloud. Only one candle was lit, but William had not seemed to notice, so Keziah lit another stump, giving it to Jonas and telling him his brother would go blind if he tried to read such tiny words in the dark.

I helped her prepare supper: bread, cold roast beef and beer, and we ate all together at the table, with William setting down his instrument on a chair, as though it was dining with us. The boys had a story about Mrs. Abelmann's canary, which had flown inside the chimney and refused to come down, and amid the chewing and chattering I forgot for a very short time, just a minute or two, what had happened that morning.

It was only when I looked around at my friend's simple room, with its russet-painted walls and clothes piled and baskets and on every surface, and the happy faces of their boys as they chattered, and the tired, loving way she and William looked at one another, that I remembered, and the shadows seemed to grow, and the little room seemed chillier. I must have looked sorrowful, for Jonas, the more bashful of the two, caught my eye, and I tried to smile for him.

After supper Keziah told her sons to go to bed, which they did obediently, leaving the door ajar so she could hear they were asleep. We washed the supper things while William went stoically back to his violin. When we were finished and the plates and cups put away, Keziah took off her apron and we sat in the two comfortable chairs before the fire. I longed to put a cushion behind my head and close my eyes. I did not want to go back to Black and White Court without Clara and see her bed empty.

"You should go back to the Foundling," Keziah said.

"What for?" I said. "They will only tell me what they already have. I swear they think me a liar. Or, worse, mad: What sort of mother forgets she's taken her own child? They'll send me to Bethlem."

As Keziah told William the events of the morning, which already felt a year ago, I watched the flames dancing, undeterred by the icy gusts that shuddered down the chimney. William listened, cleaning his violin with a rag and a small bottle of turpentine oil, and after a long pause, said: "The Foundling Hospital . . . I have played there."

I sat up. "You have?"

He nodded, frowning hard in the dim light but not looking up. The care he showed that instrument was unlike anything I'd ever seen in a man. "A few months ago. September, I think. They had a service in the chapel. Did you know Handel composed a song for the hospital?"

"Who's that?"

Now he looked at me. "The composer Handel. Handel's *Messiah*?"

I shook my head.

"How does it begin . . . ? *'Blessed are they that considereth the poor and needy —'*"

Keziah interrupted him. "If you ain't talking about music, you're talking about sermons, and we're talking about neither."

William ignored her. "It's a remarkable place. The children who are taken in are very lucky. Your daughter will be in safe hands."

"But she isn't there, that's the point."

"*Listen,* William!"

The room went quiet, and the only sound was the crackle of the fire.

"You know," I said after a while, "I could have married years ago, and had more children. I was waiting, I suppose, to get her back, before I would let myself start a life with someone else. I wanted to be able to tell them the truth, because if I'd married without them knowing, what husband would have agreed to take her in? And now I don't suppose I'll ever see her again. I've waited all this time for nothing. Soon I'll only be good enough for the widowers."

"There's still time," Keziah said, as though reading my mind. "You're no old maid; you've years in you yet. Ain't that right, William?"

He placed his violin under his chin,

propped it on his left shoulder and played a long, sorrowful, beautiful note. Then he played a popular wedding march, which made us smile.

I knew I could tell Keziah anything, yet part of me wondered if deep down she'd thought I would never take my daughter back. That I would change my mind, meet a husband, have a fat bouncing baby, then another, and forget about my firstborn. That I would come to imagine Clara better off where she was, raised by nurses and servants, with laundered linen and plum pudding and a chapel in which to sing. Perhaps Keziah imagined Clara was safer away from the freezing sheds of Billingsgate and the damp walls of Black and White Court. But would my friend have left her sons to be raised like orphans, no matter how comfortably? I doubted it very much.

CHAPTER 5

I lingered in front of the gates for five minutes before announcing myself at the porter's lodge, knowing he had probably seen me wandering back and forth as I rehearsed what to say. I'd worn my best dress — of the three I had — a cream cotton frock printed with flowers that Keziah had set aside for me a few years ago. She'd said the dark red of the flowers set off my hair, and brought out the color in my cheeks. I'd also cleaned my bonnet, borrowing some starch from Nancy downstairs in exchange for a needle and thread. At half past three I'd locked my shrimp hat in the storehouse and hurried home ahead of Abe to change before making the walk across town to the Foundling. It was as cold and dark as the November night I'd first come, and I felt as I had then: determined, and just as frightened.

The porter admitted me and I walked

91

alone up the drive. The lawns on either side were black and empty — the children would most likely be eating, or else in their beds. In Black and White Court the children went to sleep when their parents did, but here I imagined they were washed and brushed, lined up like dolls in the candlelight. I mounted the three steps and went in, closing the door behind me. The stone corridor was quiet, and I wondered if I ought to have shut it with force to announce myself. I tidied my hair and waited, but no one came.

A minute, two minutes, three passed, each second measured by two beats of my heart. I walked toward the staircase and stood at the foot of it. Hanging on the first landing was a vast portrait of a man. He had large eyes, and was wearing a cap and sable-colored coat. There was a prominent scar on his forehead, and a little dog sat to his left. I examined his face and found it to be alert, and so lifelike I should not have been surprised had he reached through the frame to unhinge it from the wall and let himself out.

A voice startled me. "Can I help you?"

The speaker was a woman coming down the stairs, large and piglike in a frilly apron and cap. Her face was pink with disapproval. I looked down and realized I'd trodden on the immaculate claret-colored carpet, leaving very faint marks. "We take no infants in from the street. You must apply the proper way and we're full to capacity at present," she said, without taking a step farther.

"I don't have an infant. I mean, I do, but she's not here." The woman waited, her dark eyes little shards of coal, and I felt my cheeks go hot. "Can I speak to a governor?"

"A governor?" A cackle escaped. "I needn't think they oughter be troubled by you."

"Who can I speak to, then?"

"You're speaking to me, ain't you?"

I felt my temper rise. I looked down at my shabby boots, and my shawl that needed darning. My best dress was no disguise here.

"Six years ago," I said, matching her tone, "I left my daughter here to be cared for, and the next day she was collected by someone who claimed to be me."

The woman was very still, and a frown drew her beady features together. Her eyes hardened even more.

"I don't know who it was, or why they did it, but . . . I'm her mother. I want to find out what happened, and speak to someone who might remember what they looked like, or . . . anything."

There was a pause, and I heard a door

close somewhere. Then a horrible noise; I realized the woman on the stairs was laughing. It was too loud and brash in this quiet, carpeted place, too much like what I'd come from, and not where I was. I wanted to stride up the stairs and slap her bacon face.

"We've a mad one here!" she cackled into the empty hall. "A live one! Have you escaped from Bethlem?"

Before I could speak, a voice came from behind me. "What is this?" A young man was leaning out of a doorway near the clock. He was small, for a man, and slim, a few years older than me, with straw-colored hair. He was hatless, wearing only his shirtsleeves — we had clearly disturbed him at work. In the slice of the room behind him I could see the glimpse of a desk and papers and the soft, inviting glow of an oil lamp. He was staring at me.

"Sorry to bother you, sir," I said. "I didn't mean to disturb you."

"Is Marjery assisting you?"

"No."

"Can I?"

I stood in dumb silence. They were two simple words, but I was not used to hearing them.

"I don't know, sir."

He glanced briefly at Marjery, and turned

to me again. "Would you like to come into my office?"

Leaving the unhelpful woman trembling like a vexed jelly, I followed him into his little room, and he closed the door. It was not unlike the other rooms I'd sat in here — warm and bright and purposeful. The ceiling was high, but the walls close and comfortable, and a marble fireplace framed a cheerful little fire. Pictures hung on the rail, of seascapes and farmland, and a carpet stretched to all four corners. I could hardly believe such fine rooms were made to work in; I would have lived there happily.

The man went behind his desk and sat down. "I am Doctor Mead," he said. "I work here at the hospital as a physician for the children. My grandfather is one of the founding governors."

I had never met a doctor before, but thought it would be an ignorant thing to say. "I am Bess," I said.

"Are you a mother of one of the children here?"

"How did you know?"

"Well, you aren't with child, and you don't work here, and it is a Tuesday evening, and nobody has taken your coat, so . . . an educated guess."

I smiled. "I was last here on Sunday, sir," I said.

"Let me get you a drink, and you may sit down and tell me who you are here to collect. Do you have your child's number?"

"I know it," I said, my tongue sticking to the roof of my mouth as I realized how thirsty I was. "But the thing is, sir, she's already been claimed."

Doctor Mead blinked, and I tried to put my words together. "I brought her here six years ago, when she was not even a day old, and I have just learned the next day she was taken by someone pretending to be me. I know it sounds false, like I'm lying. And I ain't mad," I added firmly, realizing too late that saying this was in itself a sign of madness. "I want to find out where she might have gone."

The doctor's eyes were blue, which might look cold in some people, but not him. He narrowed his eyes as Marjery had, but not in mistrust. It was as though he was trying to see me properly.

"Will brandy do?"

Before I could reply, he went to a low cupboard beside the fireplace and brought out a decanter and two glasses. Setting them on his desk, he poured an inch of golden-brown liquid into both and handed one to me. I sniffed; it was rich and spicy and powerful. It was a man's drink, but not for men I knew — it was for doctors and lawyers and captains. It was for men like Daniel.

I looked at it for a moment, as though I might find a clue there. Then I swallowed it down, and felt it scorch my throat and warm my empty stomach. My eyes stung, and I blinked.

"I presume you have already told someone here what you have told me?" Doctor Mead said.

I nodded. "Mr. Simmons, sir. I was told I was mistaken."

"And he sent you on your way?"

I nodded.

There was a thoughtful silence. Then Doctor Mead said: "The child's father? Might he —"

"He's dead."

"You know that for certain?"

"Yes."

"You weren't married?" There was no judgment in his face.

"No. He died before she was born."

"Do you have family? Could a relative have taken her in?"

"There's only my dad and brother; my

mother's dead. And it weren't neither of them."

"Grandparents?"

I shrugged. "All dead."

Doctor Mead ran a hand through his hair and propped an elbow on the table. His hands were small, like a woman's. He was calmly expressive: I could see him thinking in a neat, contained sort of way, and lighting on a suggestion or an idea, then dismissing it. "Do you have any . . . How do I put this? Anyone who might wish to seek revenge? Any enemies, let's say."

I stared at him. The drink had done something funny to me — where I'd been warm, I now felt cold all over. I set the glass down on the desk. "Enemies?" The word felt strange in my mouth; I don't think I'd said it aloud before. I'd had no reason to. "Like who?"

He exhaled loudly. "A feud with a neighbor or . . . I don't know . . . an old friend."

Nosy Nancy Benson appeared in my mind's eye, and I almost laughed. "No one who'd do something so wicked, I'm sure. I've never offended no one, or at least I never meant to."

"Could it be extortion? You aren't . . . wealthy, or expecting an inheritance?"

Now I did laugh. "No," I said, and then I

said it again, more kindly because his cheeks had gone pink. I flushed in turn: not once had he laughed at me, or not taken me seriously. "I'm not. In fact, I saved two pounds, thinking that would be enough to get her back. It wasn't. Not that it matters now. So perhaps I am for the moment. Well, more wealthy than I've ever been, and likely ever will be in my life." I drained the drops from the brandy glass for something to do.

"I suppose there is only one question remaining: You're *certain* it's the same child?"

"I can't read, but yes. Child 627. They changed her name, but it was Clara. Same token as well. And like I said, the person who collected her knew all about me. I can't understand that part. That means it weren't a mistake."

Doctor Mead nodded. "I will see what I can find out. Do you have time to wait, if I fetch her papers now?"

I almost smiled again, and nodded. He left, first checking the date again, and I sat by myself in the comfortable little room. I was curious to realize I felt calm, where half an hour before, pacing outside the gates, I had felt so full of dread I was almost crippled with it. Within minutes Doctor Mead returned with the little bundle of papers I had seen a few nights ago, wrapped in the blue ribbon. He untied it with gentle fingers, scratched his head and examined the contents with a frown. I watched him carefully, and when he'd finished he put it down before him and clasped his hands.

"When a child is returned to its family, a memorandum is made and signed by both parties — the mother, usually, and the secretary. The secretary present at your daughter's collection on the twenty-eighth day of November was Mr. Biddicombe." He sighed, and his shoulders sagged. "He passed away just last year."

"Oh," I said in a small voice.

"Oh, indeed. We might have been able to ask him if he remembered anything about Elizabeth Bright, of Black and White Court, Ludgate Hill. That is your full name, and address?"

I nodded, and he sighed again, and drew his lips into his mouth. My crystal glass was empty now, and I wondered if he would pour more. I wondered how much I'd get for the glass if I pocketed it without him noticing.

"Well," he said after a silence. "I daresay this has never happened before. My grandfather would have told me."

"Who is your grandfather?"

"He is Doctor Mead, too. He was the doctor when the hospital opened; he's retired now, but still involved. He would be astonished at what you have told me."

"He wouldn't believe me."

"I am certain he would. But I'd like to find out as much as I can first before I go to him. And, of course, we need to make certain this never happens again — new measures may have to be introduced. Aside from the person fraudulently claiming to be you, what's to say more children couldn't be claimed this way? Or indeed have been. But there's the token —" He was thinking aloud, his eyes moving rapidly. "The person must have correctly named your token. What was it?"

"It was one side of a heart, made of whalebone."

"Whalebone. How unusual. Most women leave fragments of fabric from their dresses. Extraordinary." He threw the rest of his liquor down his throat in a gallant way, not greedily like Ned, and put the glass down with a determined smack. "Tell me, are you able to come back on Sunday? The governors will be here for the church service, and we can appeal to them when they are all in one place. They will be very interested to hear your story, no doubt. In the meantime,

101

I will look into this." He looked at me directly, his blue gaze clear, and there was a beat of silence, during which I held my breath. "My sincere apologies."

I opened my mouth, then closed it. Words failed me. After a pause, I said: "It's not your fault."

"Sunday," he said. "I will meet you outside the chapel at half past nine, and you will be my guest."

My belly was warm with liquor, and something else that I had felt only days before, and had thought lost altogether. My belly was warm with hope.

Ned was sitting in Abe's chair when I arrived home, his legs spread wide. One hand dangled over the arm, the other rested on his belly, as though he'd eaten too much. But that was not it: he had been pale and thin for a while now, and complaining of pain in his stomach. He only visited to ask for money. Occasionally I gave it to him. At some point he had stopped promising to pay it back. He never brought his wife, Catherine, with him, never brought their children, never brought a hot pie or a custard tart to share with us. He didn't invite us to his house, or save room for us on a church pew next to his young family.

His children were the only reason I gave him money, if I had it to spare.

I looked more closely at him now. His jaw was tight, his face flushed.

"Come to wish us a Merry Christmas, have you?"

"That was last year."

"I know. We haven't seen you."

"I been away."

"Catherine's thrown him out," said Abe from the other side of the room, where he was sitting on his cot, removing his boots.

"She ain't. I left."

"Left her for Madame Geneva, have you? Your cruel mistress?"

He said nothing, and I looked between him and Abe; they both had the glum appearance of men who'd lost badly at a card game. There was no fire built, and I glanced around at the muddy footprints, the dirty bowls and laundry strewn around the room that took twice as long to dry in the cold. Empty ale bottles on the side needed washing, next to a pile of clothes that needed mending. Every surface was filled with some task or other that would fall to me.

"Any news, Bessie?" Abe asked.

I shook my head.

"About what?" Ned was looking at me now. At seven and twenty, he had the face of a much older man, with broken red threads beneath his skin and a dry, gray complexion.

The liquor Doctor Mead had given me had lightened my head and made my tongue sharp. "If you ever asked after me, you'd know I went back to the Foundling to collect my daughter."

"Oh," he said, softening, and looked around in surprise. "Where is she?"

"Not here and not there. Not anywhere." I had missed supper, and there was no food left. The effort of going back downstairs and onto Ludgate Hill for something hot seemed too great. I began tidying the room for something to do, while Abe knelt creakily to build a fire. I would clean the plates and cups, wipe the coal smoke from the windows and then go to bed.

"Eh? What'd you mean?"

"She was collected. By Elizabeth Bright, of Black and White Court, six years ago."

"What you leaking on about?"

"She's gone, Ned, and I don't know where. Someone pretended to be me — what's the word he used? — *fraudulently.*"

"Queer thing to do, ain't it? Who would do that?"

"Your guess is as good as mine."

"The dad's gone to peg, ain't he?"

"Last time I checked."

Ned was thoughtful, and watched Abe's hunched shape at the fireplace without offering to help. He sat like an aristocrat at leisure, as though the labor and hardship we were forced to endure did not interest him at all. I supposed he would stay for a night or two — he did, sometimes, snoring next to me in his old bed that was now supposed to be Clara's. How disappointed Catherine must be that she'd married him.

He ran a hand over his unshaved chin. "What an head-scratcher, eh?" he said.

He did not care. His mind was elsewhere. I watched him, with his boots planted on our floorboards, planted in our lives, wondering when he'd get around to asking for money. I felt myself slowly fill up with hatred. I turned away and flicked a roach off a dirty plate. The room was freezing, and all the pleasantness I'd felt just an hour earlier in that warm, comfortable little room had disappeared at the doorway as soon as I'd seen my brother.

"What you gonna do, then?" he asked after a while.

I moved things about with my back to him. "I'm gonna try and find her, of course."

He laughed, a short, sharp note of mirth

that made me want to smash the dish I was holding over his head. I imagined the pleasurable crack it would make. But we couldn't spare it.

"And how you gonna do that in a place like London?"

"Don't pretend you care. Don't sit there and pretend you're paying a call to see how we are, because you're not. Come on then, out with it — why have you really come? How much do you need? A shilling? Three?"

"Ten."

Abe gave a low whistle, wiping his coal-streaked hands on a rag and getting to his feet with difficulty. "I think you're mistaking us for bank clerks, my lad."

"He mistakes us for a lot of things. Fools, mainly."

"That ain't fair."

"No, it ain't. What do you need it for, then?"

"The baby needs medicine."

I folded my arms and looked hard at him. "If you tell me what you really need it for, I'll give you a crown."

His eyes flicked away and back again, landing somewhere near my shoulder. "I have a debt to pay. I'm already behind on it and they won't wait no more." There were dark shadows beneath his eyes, but they might have been blackened with a fist.

I went to the bedroom to fetch my domino box from beneath the mattress.

"This goes to your debt, nothing else. Do I need to come with you?"

He shivered. "No. I ain't having you near any of it." I dropped the crown into his hand, and he closed his fist around it. "I'll add you to my list of creditors. Only you'll need to lend me paper and a quill, too. Oh, and I can't write."

If he thought he was being funny, we didn't laugh. Nor did he move to go, and it was a moment before I realized he was looking at me peculiarly. Abe was sat on a stool, brushing his boots into the waste bucket, absorbed in his task.

In a low voice, Ned said: "Why are you still here, Bess?" He gestured at the sorry state of our neglected living quarters. The water Abe had set over the fire had warmed, and I tested it with a finger before removing it with a cloth and setting it on the shelf before me. Through the dark window, I could see the Irish family, the Riordans, who lived across the court. They were moving around their room in a complicated sequence, setting out their supper while their father held a large orange cat to his chest. He was telling a story, and smiling, and the boys laying the table were smiling, too, though I could see their bowls were chipped and didn't match, and their tiny room was strung with drying sheets. I realized I was still wearing my shawl, which was damp, and took it off and hung it before the fire, where it began steaming.

"Bess," Ned said again as I moved past him. I felt his fingertips brush my arm, and I was overcome by a rush of powerful sadness and love for my brother, as though he had stained me with it. Was this the boy who pushed our beds together and made foolish voices from behind the red curtain that hung in between? Who would put on a puppet show, making mouths in the fabric with his hand? He used to make me laugh, once.

"You take my money and ask why I'm still here? That's why." I kept my back to him, and dunked our cups once, twice, drowning them, relieving them, drowning them again.

After a moment, he said: "I'm sorry about your daughter. I'm sure you'll find her. Let me know if I can help."

I closed my eyes, and opened them, and the Riordans were blurred in their window. I sniffed, and dunked, and wiped, and set the things on their shelf, and a minute or two later heard Ned speak to Abe, the creak of the floorboards and the door closing. I looked at the rooftops and the spires, and thought of the steady flow of the city moving darkly below them. How easy it would be to slip into its depths, and be swept away.

CHAPTER 6

There was no market on Sundays. We were not churchgoers — the last time we had been as a family was my mother's funeral at St. Bride's — so Abe looked at me a beat longer than usual when I came out in my printed cotton dress. I went to church only at Christmas with Keziah and William and the children — we packed ourselves into little pews with the Spanish and the Irish and the blackamoors, and sang and listened and recited, and tried to hush the children impatient for their roast goose and plum pudding. I didn't eat Christmas dinner with them, though, always buying a chicken on the way home to eat with Abe.

"Church?" Abe said when I told him where I was going. "What for?"

"I'm going with Keziah," I lied, swapping my indoor cap for my outdoor one so I didn't have to look at him. "Why don't you visit Catherine today? You could see the baby; he'll be getting on now."

He stared at me with cloudy eyes. Was he growing thinner? It was difficult to tell; I saw his face more than my own. He shifted in his chair, not yet dressed for the day. It was so cold we needed the fire lit all the time.

"I ain't going out in this weather," was his reply. "Fetch my blanket, would you?"

I covered him with it and tucked it around his shoulders. At home he was not the Billingsgate man; he took up less space, and seemed less capable.

"I wonder if the Fleet River will freeze like it did last year," I said, busying myself with covering him in blankets. He'd eaten half his toast and I finished it off. "Do you remember the dead dog that was frozen in it? And all the little ones were poking it with a stick?"

His eyes were closed; he nodded to show he was listening. He was always tired on Sundays. I had no need to worry — he spent six days outside, shivering in a shed, plunging his hands into icy buckets of shrimp. Of course he didn't want to go outside. I tucked the blanket more firmly around him, tossed a few more coals on the fire and left.

On Sundays the Foundling Hospital opened

111

up like a country mansion, throwing its black gates wide for all of London's finest. The road was choked with carriages, and glossy horses tossed their manes, puffing steam into the cold air, while blank-faced coachmen waited to turn through the left gate as empty ones came through the right.

I slipped through behind a well-dressed couple and walked alongside the splendid painted traffic, noticing house crests stenciled on the side and velvet curtains at the windows, and wondering how many people sat in them who lived on neighboring streets, who wished to sit in a queue just to be seen arriving. Ahead, at the farthest building with the large clock face, I watched them disembark, with their straight backs and tall wigs and gloved hands. I remembered the way the same people had pressed themselves against the walls on lottery night to watch, with their fans and sugary smiles.

Doctor Mead had told me to meet him outside, so I stood a little way off the drive to wait for him. It was a clear morning, more like spring than winter. A few young trees were planted at the edges of the lawns, and behind the chapel there were large manicured gardens and an orchard farther on. Today there were children everywhere: some belonging to the hospital in brown uniforms, while the rest, who had parents, were very finely dressed. Swells I saw often enough, even on the city thoroughfares, for they liked to be seen, trotting in and out of the haberdashers and confectioners and toy emporiums. But their children: hardly ever. Several looked to have never been outside at all, and were pale and plump as doves. I watched two young boys striding alongside their mother, wearing silver wigs like little gentlemen. Their drawers were white as flour, and the gold buttons on their frock coats shone.

Another carriage had drawn to the front of the queue and was unloading its cargo — a tall woman dressed in green Spitalfields silk and her daughter in butter yellow. The little girl held the layers of her mother's skirt in her fist and jumped to the ground, then reached for her hand, but her mother was talking to the coachman and had not noticed.

"Miss Bright."

Doctor Mead was standing behind me. I might not have recognized him; his hay-colored hair was hidden beneath a cocked hat, and his shirtsleeves under a smart blue coat. I had only seen him quite intimately; now he was just one gentleman in a sea of them. But he had found me, all the same.

"Shall we?"

He gave me his arm, and after a moment's hesitation I took it. I had seen wealthy couples do this in the street, as though the woman could not walk without help.

"Is this a chapel or a pleasure garden?" I asked.

Doctor Mead laughed. "It would seem they are one and the same. This excursion, however, will cost you more than a shilling, so naturally it's even more desirable."

I stopped, and my arm slipped from his. "I have brought no money."

He smiled and shook his head. "There is a collection plate, and no obligation. You can give nothing or you can give a pound; whatever you are able."

We began walking again, joining the trickle of cuffs and cravats and cocked hats narrowing toward the chapel doors.

"Who are all these people?" I asked.

"Benefactors. Governors and their familiars. Wealthy Londoners, and some from the country, too: Middlesex, Hertfordshire."

"They have no chapels in Middlesex and Hertfordshire?"

Doctor Mead smiled very easily, I noticed. "Evidently not."

A woman in front of us was wearing one of the tallest wigs I had ever seen. Piled and plaited, with ribbons strewn about in it, it was the color of bare branches and reached a foot off her head. Doctor Mead and I were attracting curious little looks, and many people said good morning to him, fixing their smiles determinedly on him and avoiding me. Some of them cast pointed looks at my cotton frock, peeking from beneath my plain cloak, but my head might have been covered with a feedbag. No one looked me in the eye.

Inside, the chapel was modern, only a few years old, and had none of the soaring ceilings and ancient spires of St. Bride's. It was more like a theater than a place of worship. At the top of the high walls, the sun poured in through stained-glass windows the height of three men, and there was a balcony wrapped beneath the ceiling, supported by marble pillars. The pews did not face toward the front, but inward, with an aisle running through and a pulpit at one end, so everybody would have to turn to the right or left to watch the preacher deliver his sermon.

I followed Doctor Mead to a pew in the center at the front, and he indicated for me to step in. I felt like a chop on display at a butcher's, and wished we had sat at the back. But he did not seem aware of the looks we attracted, or rather the meaning

115

behind them, meeting them with his easy smile. It made me like him all the more. Across the aisle, two tall-wigged women regarded me openly; I met their stares with my own, until they looked away, and whispered behind their fans. My cheeks felt hot, my mouth dry. I wished to be at home, eating a sugar mouse with my stockinged feet on the stool and Abe dozing in his chair. Sunday was a day of rest — our only day of rest. Surely these people did nothing but rest, and so much that it grew dull to them, so they brushed on their powder and laced their stays and polished their shoes to come here. This chapel was a hall of mirrors: they were not here to see one another but rather themselves, through the gaze of others.

A troupe of Foundling children came down the center aisle, dressed smartly in their brown outfits. I knew Clara could not be one of them, but I peered into their faces anyway. They were smooth and untroubled, with none of the pinched, tired expressions of the infants at Black and White Court, who were like tiny old men and women.

"Elliott," said a deep, rich voice. A large man with heavy jowls and an elaborately curled wig was standing before us, leaning on a gold-topped cane.

"Grandfather." Doctor Mead was delighted. "Will you sit with us?"

"I am with the countess — her family are visiting from Prussia — but do come to Great Ormond Street for luncheon afterward. There will be a gathering." His dark eyes were fine and friendly, and I felt their effect when they turned to me. "Who is your companion?"

"Grandfather, this is Miss Bright. She is a friend whom I am endeavoring to help. And you might be able to help us, too. May I bring her to Great Ormond Street after the service?"

Before I could protest, the old man waved a large hand covered with rings, as though he had pasted his fingers and plunged them into a jewelery box. "All friends welcome," he said. "A pleasure to meet you, Miss Bright." He nodded at us both and moved swiftly along, only to be stopped two or three yards away by some other wigged creature.

In the close air of the chapel, with the smells of hair and bodies and perfume all around, sweat and musk and floral and tobacco clamoring all at once, I felt quite light-headed, and the knot in my stomach tightened.

"Have you found out anything since last week?" I asked Doctor Mead in a low voice.

He withdrew Clara's papers from his jacket, bound in the blue ribbon. "I have brought the memorandum, to show it to the governors, and ask if any of them might remember the person who collected your daughter. So few children are reclaimed, you see — only about one in a hundred — so there are not many women to remember, which is a great shame, but may mean fortune is on our side."

I took the parcel from him. The paper smelled old and dusty, and I traced with a finger the only part I could make sense of: the numbers six, two and seven, turning them to see the other side, as if the words might suddenly make sense.

Somebody else approached Doctor Mead and began speaking. If only we had gone to a public house or a chophouse, or his house or mine — here we might as well have been standing on the Strand.

I sat on my ungloved hands while he exchanged pleasantries with the woman before him. He did not introduce me this time, and she did not ask. She was tall and pale and elegant, with slim, ungloved hands and yellow hair beneath her hat. There was a movement at her skirts, and a moment later a little girl emerged to stand before me on the other side of the wooden balustrade.

She fixed me with large, dark eyes, and I recognized her as the girl in the butter-yellow dress I had seen jumping from the carriage earlier.

I wondered if I should speak, to tell her I liked her dress or ask her name, but before I could her expression grew furtive, and I fell into silent surprise as she brought something out of a pocket at her waist. In the palm of her hand sat a tiny, curious creature I had never seen before. It had a wrinkled head and ancient neck that reached from a hard shell of green and brown, so intricately patterned I thought she might have painted it. It might have been a toy, had it not withdrawn its head and four spiky feet, disappearing altogether, and leaving only its pretty shell. My mouth fell open in astonishment. The little girl put it back inside her dress and turned her mouth up at the corners in a shy, private smile. I could not help but smile back.

"Charlotte, come." Her mother, who had not noticed our exchange, placed a firm hand on her shoulder. A ruby ring glittered on her hand.

"A pleasure seeing you, Mrs. Callard," said Doctor Mead.

It took a moment for me to understand what he had said. The words traveled slowly through my ears, thick as pea soup, congealing somewhere in my mind and making me dumb. The woman and the little girl moved away — I saw green and butter yellow steering through the crowd, and the backs of their heads, fair and dark. I craned my neck to see where they would go, and they moved into a row of seats at the end of the chapel, behind us, out of sight, their faces eclipsed by hats and wigs.

I had dropped the sheaf of papers, and Doctor Mead leaned to pick them up. "We will go to my grandfather's after the service — he only lives a few minutes' walk, at Great Ormond Street," he was saying. "There will be Foundling governors there, of course. I went to visit him myself yesterday, but he was at some surgeons' dinner or other. He still works, at eighty! Would you believe? I said to him: 'Grandfather, it would not surprise me if somebody sneezed at your funeral and you sat up in the coffin to prescribe a tonic.' " Doctor Mead was smiling, but I was not listening.

"Who was that?"

"Who?"

"The woman you were speaking with just now."

"Mrs. Alexandra Callard? Do you know her?"

120

"No. Is that her daughter?"

"Yes. Charlotte."

"And is she . . . Is she married?"

"Widowed. Her husband died some years ago. He was a friend of mine."

I thought of the child's private smile, and her dark eyes. Had her hair a tint to it? Did it shine red in the sun? My voice would not rise above a whisper. "What was his name?"

"Daniel. He had an interesting job: a merchant. I forget now what he dealt in. Ivory, was it? No, I remember now. It was whalebone. Ah, here is the chaplain. Do you have a hymn sheet?"

I barely remember the service. I sat through all of it somehow, though it wasn't difficult, for I felt numb, and let the sermons and hymns wash over me. For an hour all I could think was three things in turn, over and over, around and around: Daniel was married. That was his wife. And with her was my daughter. She was the right age and size, with those dark, dark eyes and hair like mine. Her mother was fair, and older than me. Older than Daniel, even, who had been, I supposed, twenty-five or six, though of course several years had passed. She had called her daughter Charlotte.

I was vaguely aware of Doctor Mead's

121

hand on my arm, and people rising from the pews and surging toward the doors. He might have spoken, but I could not hear him; my ears were muffled, filled with a rushing sound, and my limbs were heavy and slow. I felt frozen, like the dead dog in the Fleet.

"Miss Bright?"

Clara was returned to me the day after I brought her, the papers said. Perhaps Charlotte *was* Alexandra Callard's daughter, and we'd had daughters around the same time? But Daniel had been fair, like his wife, with sand-colored hair and light eyes. In Black and White Court there'd been a litter of redhead children, and one sibling had stood out like a raven among doves, with brown skin and sullen features. They said his father beat him.

"Miss Bright?"

The chapel was emptying, save for some women chatting and tossing their wigs, and a group of men standing like painted peacocks, clucking around Doctor Mead's grandfather. There were no children anywhere.

"Miss Bright!"

I was startled back to life. Doctor Mead was staring at me, his eyes burning with concern. "Are you unwell?"

I leaped from my seat, almost colliding with him, and peered around the chapel, twisting so that I could see every corner and bench, craning up at the balcony and then pushing past him and fleeing down the aisle to the doors, holding my bonnet on my head with one hand and the neck of my cloak with the other.

Blue, red and white: dark coats and black hats and cloud-colored hair everywhere, but no green, no yellow. I pushed my way through the little groups congregating in the weak sunshine, and felt my throat closing. The carriages had begun collecting their owners, and out of the corner of my eye I saw a flash of butter yellow disappearing through a door, and a little stockinged foot clad in a black shoe. A sleek coachman closed the door and climbed up to his seat. As he tidied his coattails and reached for the reins, I rushed toward the carriage, and was ten or twelve yards away when I felt a hand, firm on my arm.

"Miss Bright." Doctor Mead's cheeks were pink. "Where are you going?" His breath came in little puffs, turning the air between us to smoke. He must have run after me. I must have appeared mad. I could not appear mad before a doctor. He was waiting for an explanation, distress clouding his usually cheerful face.

"I'm unwell," I said. "I needed some air."

"Then I will take you home; my house is a few streets away. We can walk in five minutes, or I can send for the carriage."

"No, thank you. I should go home. Please tell your grandfather I'm sorry."

I turned from him and walked briskly away.

Mrs. Callard's carriage was already nearing the gates; I'd have to hurry if I was to see them again. I was vaguely aware of attracting glances — chins turned sharply over shoulders, and eyes following me down the drive — but as I gathered speed I did not look back, letting them bounce from me like hailstones.

Beyond the gates the road was straight for a quarter of a mile, and I followed on foot past the open fields on either side, where curious cows lifted their heads at the procession. At the end of the road I watched it turn right and roll west, toward Bloomsbury. I kept it in my sights, walking on the roadside, sidestepping horse dung, as any woman might after a church service on a bright winter's day. My pace was purposeful, but I felt as though I might burst apart at any moment. I focused on putting one foot before the other, and keeping my cloak from turning around my neck, and followed the glossy black carriage as it rolled through the Sunday traffic.

After only a few minutes it slowed and turned left down a street stacked with townhouses so identical it was enough to make you feel drunk. My head spun, and my mouth was dry, so certain was I that my daughter was sitting yards away from me, dressed in silk the color of sunshine, with a strange shelled creature in her pocket. She had shown it to me, a secret in her palm, and smiled.

The carriage was drawing to a halt. We could not have been more than two streets away from the Foundling. I stood for a moment, blinking stupidly like a mouse on a dinner plate, before sense took over and I moved to stand against the black iron railings of a house across the street. I pulled my cloak tighter, and my bonnet farther down over my face, and watched the coachman climb down and drop gracefully to the ground before a four-story townhouse.

Steps led up to a wide front door painted black. There was no space between the house and the others on either side, standing as they were like soldiers shoulder to shoulder, and so similar that if I looked away and back again, I might not have been able to tell it apart. I peered more closely, searching for a feature to know it by. The shutters in the first-floor windows were red, and there was something funny about the brass doorknocker. I squinted, and took as many steps closer as I dared. The door-knocker was a whale.

A green dress appeared, and with it the woman who wore it. Her face was turned away, so I could only see gold hair piled high beneath a hat. I realized I was shaking, my legs threatening to buckle beneath me. Two little feet appeared, and the hem of a yellow dress. She held her skirts and jumped again, and though I'd only seen it once before, it was so dear and familiar it made me ache. The woman was already moving into the house without a backward glance; she did not offer her hand to her daughter.

My daughter.

The little girl skipped onto the doorstep, and I saw the creamy curve of her neck, and dark ringlets falling from her cap. She gave a cursory glance up and down the street, as though wishing to remember it on that bright winter morning, and then the black door was opening, and they were vanishing through it, and I leaned back against the railings, feeling for them behind me, and watching as with a flash of glossy paint and

a thud the door closed, and the house shim-
mered into stillness.

■ ■ ■ ■

PART TWO:
ALEXANDRA

■ ■ ■ ■

CHAPTER 7

Every day at three o'clock I took tea in the withdrawing room with my parents. Before that, I would sit in my parlor at the back of the house, and when the slim gold hand on the mantelpiece clock reached fifteen minutes to the hour, I would fold my newspaper and set it on the table next to my chair. On it was a little dish of water and a handkerchief for me to wash the ink stains from my hands. I did this very carefully, removing my rings and cleaning each finger one by one, polishing the nail until it shone and listening for Agnes's tread on the stairs and the jangle of the tea service. At a minute before three I would examine myself in the glass between the two windows and tidy my hair, brushing down my skirts and pinching my jacket sleeves straight where they had creased. Then I would cross the landing and go in.

The withdrawing room overlooked Devonshire Street below and the terrace opposite in a mirror image. The view from every window front and back was more houses, identical to our own — four stories, with two windows on each of the floors and one on the ground by the door — and so close to one another that when we moved in I saw a delft jug sitting on a washstand in the house opposite, where a family of five lived, with three children. From the way the husband dressed and the hours he kept, I expected he worked as a lawyer or doctor. They were very social creatures, and often had all manner of guests at the table, going through five or six sets of candles, and sometimes not getting up from dinner until supper was served at ten or eleven o'clock. At first it seemed strange, as though we were all living behind eyeglasses. But quickly I'd got used to it, finding comfort in the proximity and the false intimacy it created. I did not know my neighbors, but I watched them, and no doubt they watched me, too.

No. 13 Devonshire Street was one of my father's houses. The street was just wide enough for two small carriages to pass one another, which they did with great ceremony, each coachman being territorial about his space. At both ends of our street were large, handsome squares with young plane trees and wide green lawns around which the houses sat, looking in at one another like diners at a table. Of course I had only seen one, and studied the other on Mr. Rocque's map. I lived on the very edge of London, before the houses fell away and the countryside began. The city sprawled south, east and west from Devonshire Street, but not north, where brick and roads gave way to grass and fields. Daniel had not liked living in a townhouse at first, likening us to horses in a stableyard peering out at one another. I'd reminded him that if he wished to work as a merchant he had to be in London. Gradually, life here seduced him, and his business grew, and after a year he said he would rather live the rest of his days as a merchant than a marquess.

Agnes was setting out the tea things when I went in. I kissed my parents hello and took my usual chair opposite them by the window. As it was winter, the room was dim, and it would be dark soon — our faces were already half in shadow. I lit a splint in the fire and took it to the lamps before throwing it back on the flames.

"The linkboys will have less work soon," I said. "The nights are shortening by two minutes a day."

In firelight, Father's dark eyes were kinder,

133

and the years were ironed out of Mother's pearly skin. I poured three cups and stirred in sugar for Father and me; Mother had none, complaining it hurt her teeth.

My hands were clean, at least — they did not like to see me reading the papers, which is why I washed them, but Father was always interested to hear the shipping news. I read those parts just so I would have something to talk to him about. As a girl I would sit on his lap in my nightgown as he read the parts of the *Evening Post* he thought I'd find interesting, squinting in the candlelight. That's how I learned to read: as his eyes deteriorated, mine grew more useful, and I knew the words consignment, insurance and speculation just as other children were learning cat, apple and boy. Once or twice Charlotte had sat on my lap to do the same, but quickly tired of the long words and dull topics. Agnes was much better than I at telling stories, and more often Charlotte sat by the kitchen hearth with the cat on her lap and a biscuit in her hand while Agnes rolled dough and invented tales. Sometimes I stood behind the kitchen door, listening myself.

"Did you hear about the new bridge at Blackfriars?" I asked them. "Why we need *three* across the river I do not know. Surely one is enough."

My mother smiled placidly; my father was benign. I was older than them now. It was a strange thought. We passed half an hour with idle chitchat, and once I had finished my tea, I put the lid back on the sugar box and extinguished the lamps, for the room would be unused until the same time tomorrow. Before I left I polished their frames with the handkerchief I kept in my sleeve: Father first, on the left alcove of the fireplace, and Mother on the right.

Charlotte was standing on the landing when I closed the door quietly behind me. I rarely heard her soft feet on the carpets, and she often startled me, which caused me to scold her.

"Who were you talking to?" she asked, not for the first time.

"Nobody," I replied, not for the last. Sometimes she would go into the room after me and look around, crouching to peer beneath the dresser, behind the curtains and once even up the chimney breast. Her curiosity was boundless; it filled the house, pressing at the windows and flooding the rooms, finding its way into cracks and corners, drawers and cupboards. Soon it would spill over altogether. There would come a day when the things I'd bought to keep her entertained — instruments, pets, books, dolls and her once-weekly outing (five minutes in the carriage, an hour in the church, then five minutes home) — would no longer be enough. I knew the time would come when she would want to feel the sun on her face and walk through a park among strangers like an ordinary person, and I dreaded it. For now, though, she knew we lived this way to stay safe.

I ran through all the locks in my mind, counting them on my fingers. There were three doors — front, kitchen and basement stairs — and sixteen windows, fastened at all times. My modest townhouse was no palace, but there were two rooms on every floor — the kitchen and scullery with the pantries and storehouse in the basement, the dining room and what used to be Daniel's study on the ground floor, my parlor and the withdrawing room on the first, and all the bedrooms above that. Charlotte slept in the chamber opposite mine, and Agnes, my maidservant, and Maria, the cook/housekeeper, were in the attic.

Instead of a garden there was a small courtyard, enclosed by a brick wall about five or six feet high, in which Agnes hung washing and Maria took deliveries from the narrow alley, accessed from a passage at the side of no. 10. Beyond the alley were the backs of the houses on Gloucester Street, identical to mine but for their outbuildings and window dressings.

My sister, Ambrosia, used to suggest I'd be more comfortable in the countryside, in a house with gates and a long mud drive. She had no memories, though, of our old life. She did not know what it was to lie awake listening to the wind tearing at the windows, groaning to be let in. Our house in the Peak District had felt on the edge of the world. The darkness so black you could touch it. The unsettling silence. London knew neither. And that was how I liked it.

The doorknocker echoed through the house, and Agnes shuffled up from the basement to answer it while I waited on the turn of the stairs, out of sight. It was Ambrosia, announcing herself loudly and dripping all over the hallway like a parasol. It was a hideous night, and she had paid a call only two days before, so I did not expect her. She came to see me once a week, sometimes bringing her children, more often bringing her dog. Tonight she'd brought neither, as the streets were already dark, and the weather foul. I was even more surprised to see what she was wearing.

"What *have* you got on?"

My sister was what the periodicals would call a beauty. She was a large woman, and everything about her spilled over like champagne from a saucer: her breasts, her laughter. She was loud as a fishwife, could smoke like a skipper and outdrink any man. At thirty-three, a woman's best years were behind her, but not my sister's: somehow she only grew more dazzling. She and her husband, George Campbell-Clarke, were as indulgent, narcissistic and wasteful as it was possible for two people to be, and I was remarkably fond of them. They lived in a large house on St. James's Square, when they were not at all the most fashionable assembly rooms and drawing rooms, often coming home at six or seven in the morning and meeting their servants on the stairs.

She pulled her muslin cap from her head and wrung it out on the stone floor. "Agnes, the mangle might be necessary, I'm afraid," she announced in her singsong voice.

"Your coat . . ." I said.

"Is George's, yes. It's a dreadful night and I didn't want to spoil my things." It was a masculine, gray thing, sleek and warm and perfectly suited to a wet winter shower, but it made her look like a dray horse.

"But you might have been *seen*. Wearing your husband's clothes!"

"By whom?" Ambrosia teased. "I assure you the sedan I hired was very discreet."

I raised an eyebrow. Ambrosia took lovers, and sometimes it got her into trouble — not with George, who was just as adulterous as she — but with her paramours' wives and mistresses. She loved to regale her adventures in my parlor, even with her children present. Her two sons and two daughters were wan-faced, disappointing things, more like me than their mother. Just one of her exploits could entertain me for a week; when she left I would be half-startled not to see half-smoked cigars smoldering in an ashtray, and stockings trailing from the furniture. I knew of the ballrooms and parties at the mansions in Grosvenor and Cavendish Squares, but the places themselves were as unknowable to me as Nazareth and Jerusalem, though they existed fully formed in my mind, and of course on Mr. Rocque's map. For I had seen some of the world a long time ago, and could easily recall the vast carpets, the brocade drapes and silver dishes circulating beneath glittering chandeliers, the roaring men with fetid breath and powdered women with patches of sweat at their lips and armpits. I had seen enough of it for a lifetime.

"So why have you come?" I asked.

"Agnes." Ambrosia spoke to my maid, who was caught in a scuffle with the monstrous coat. "If I were to find a hot buttered crumpet and a glass of sherry at my elbow, I would not be vexed."

"Yes, madam." Agnes beamed. Ambrosia was always a welcome guest at Devonshire Street — a cat among the pigeons — and provided all the joy of a roadside spectacle to the servants. "I shall hang this afore the kitchen fire for you, madam, to dry it off."

"You are an angel. Oh, and do something with this, would you? Though it may be beyond mercy." She passed Agnes the sodden cap, which, off her head, had all the glamour of a dishrag. Beneath George's coat was one of her usual splendid ensembles: a sack-back of pale gray, with violet skirts the color of storm clouds.

We went up to my parlor, where the lamps were lit and the fire built. The *London Chronicle* lay folded on the table beside the little dish I used to wash my hands, and I saw Ambrosia appraise the arrangement with an amused glance. She went straight to the looking glass and peered into it.

"My, my." She spoke to her reflection. "Aren't I quite the muse tonight?"

The parlor on a winter's night was my favorite place. With the drapes drawn and the fire lit, it was cozy as a nest. Agnes brought a plate of hot buttered crumpets and a crystal decanter of sherry with two glasses, and I poured us both a measure and watched Ambrosia eat with relish, wiping butter from her chin.

Father had been enthralled by the classics, and in Greek my sister's name meant "food of the gods." There was more than a touch of the deity about her; lounging with her feet on a stool and a sherry in her hand, it was easy to imagine grapes instead of a glass, and a cloud for a chair, and a sheet to preserve her modesty, of which she had none. I did wonder what our parents' design was, giving a baby such a sensual name — it could have been a glaring irony, but instead had been a prophecy.

"No dog today?" I asked.

"The children were dressing him up in the baby's gowns so I left them to play."

"I presume you have not come all the way from St. James's for crumpets?"

"No, I have not. I have come to tell you we will be going to the country tomorrow, George and I, and the children. George has got himself into a rather compromising situation, shall we say, and it's necessary for us to *sortie* for a season or two."

I fixed her with a stare as she licked her

fingers. "A compromising position of the financial or carnal sort?"

"The latter. It involves a viscount's daughter and a miscommunication in age, and now one very furious viscount, who challenged George to a duel, of all things. No matter, the girl will be sent to the continent and be back by Whitsun."

Ambrosia treated George's infidelities as she did one of her children breaking a vase. Anything else would have been hypocrisy.

"For how long will you be away?" I asked, trying to hide my disappointment.

"A few months, I suppose. I told George it wasn't necessary and everyone will have forgotten in a week, but he has recently discovered a passion for horse racing and says there are two courses in the northeast he wishes to visit." She sighed. "I would stay in London but it would appear unsupportive."

"The northeast?" I swallowed. "How far north?"

"Durham, I think, or Doncaster. He might have mentioned somewhere else, too, but the provinces elude me."

I went to my bookcase and found the relevant book of maps. "Doncaster is in Yorkshire, and Durham is farther north. So you are to stay in two counties?"

She sighed. "I am not certain. Maria really does make the most marvelous crumpets; I may have to steal her from you."

"You will find out before you go, though, so I can follow your journey?"

"Yes, of course. I'll send a message and I'll write once we are there." She smiled, as if that settled it.

"And the stopping places on the way?"

"It's not always easy to know . . ." Ambrosia looked at me, then nodded. "Yes, and the stopping places on the way."

I opened the well-thumbed pages of my map book at Skipton. "I expect you will be on the road between a week and ten nights, with all your things. How are the roads up to the north at this time of year?"

"They are much better these days."

"Because snow will slow you. And ice could be dangerous."

"I know, my dear."

"I wonder if the mail coach for the northeast leaves from the Bull and Mouth at St. Martin's Le Grand? The mail goes from there to Edinburgh and York, I think, so perhaps Doncaster is on that route."

"I will endeavor to find out."

There was a noise at the door and Ambrosia broke into a smile. "Is that a quiet little mouse I hear snuffling around the skirting?"

she said.

Charlotte was standing in the doorway, twisting her hair and grinning shyly, no doubt hoping her cousins had come to play.

"Oh, it's you! I was wrong, I thought I heard the tiniest creature searching for a crumb of cheese. Come here and give me a kiss at once."

Ambrosia's news had sent me into a flurry of anxiety, and I paused my finger somewhere in the West Riding. "Charlotte, why are you not dressed for bed?"

She hovered at the threshold. There was a beat of silence, and Ambrosia gave Charlotte a friendly wink. "Is it bedtime for little mice?" she said.

The child smiled, and I asked her to close the door. With a glance at me and a fonder, more lingering look at Ambrosia, she did as I bade, and a moment later I heard her running up the stairs.

I sighed, distracted. "Where were we? Ah yes, Yorkshire."

"I shall go and give her a kiss before I leave," Ambrosia said, settling back into her chair.

I went to the bureau to fetch a quill, ink and paper and seated myself at the little writing table beneath the window. It had belonged to our mother, and was pitted all over where her quill had nibbled the wood.

"Now," I said. "Do you think you will stop first in Stevenage, or will you go all the way to Cambridge?"

The next few days passed uneventfully, excepting a mix-up with the butcher's boy, in which he delivered next door's meat order and we cooked the mutton before the error was noticed. My sister and her family loaded up their carriage and went north, promising to write but leaving me in London quite alone. The months of Ambrosia's absence would drag, no doubt, without her weekly visits. With the excess of Christmas behind and spring a way off, it was a dull, dead period, a time of hibernation and renewal, in which to reintroduce good habits, turn mattresses and repair wigs.

The day after Ambrosia left, it began to snow. I watched it from the large windows in the withdrawing room that first night, Mother and Father and me and a glass of sherry, with the lamps unlit to better see the flakes falling in the moonlight, landing softly and knitting together in their great white blanket. After I'd checked all the doors and windows, I went up to bid Charlotte good-night and found her doing the same thing — sitting in a chair at her bedroom window, looking over the quiet street. Her dark hair was loose down her back, and her arms were wrapped around her knees. I watched her silently for a moment, framed in the night sky, and then I noticed she only had on a nightdress.

"Charlotte, come away from the window and get into bed. You'll catch your death of cold."

Catch your death. What a ridiculous phrase, as if it was a ball to be intercepted. Mother, Father and Daniel had all caught it, and now it was airborne again, soon to land in an unwitting palm. There were only two people left in the world now who I loved. Charlotte I could keep close, but Ambrosia was no budgerigar, content to chirrup in a cage, no matter how grand and gilded. She was a tiger, or a comical elephant. I smiled to myself and went to my own room across the tiny landing to undress for bed, counting again the locks in my head.

CHAPTER 8

She snow melted to slush, and by Sunday morning was like a glossy layer of goose fat pressed along Devonshire Street. I spent the morning anxious that our carriage wheels would not turn in it, then resigned myself to the idea of not going to church, so by the time the brougham I hired once a week drew up at the front door to take us the short journey to the chapel, I was quite vexed. More so when Charlotte came down the stairs wearing an ermine cape and an incongruous straw boater.

"Charlotte," I said crossly. "It is February. We are not having a picnic in Lamb's Conduit Fields."

She stared at me, her dark eyes wide. Having never been either on a picnic or to Lamb's Conduit Fields, my remark was lost on her, and I sighed. "Take your boater off, and quickly go and find a smart bonnet. The blue one, with the wide brim. Now!"

She scurried away and thudded up the stairs. I stood in the quiet hall and fastened my cloak at the neck with fumbling fingers, trying to ignore the urge to check the kitchen door a final time. Charlotte would be a minute or two, and by that time the paranoia would be buzzing in my consciousness like a fly, so I hurried toward the stairs at the back of the house and went down to the basement. Maria was scrubbing turnips at the wide wooden table, chatting to Agnes, who was ironing by the range, one of her hands bound tightly in linen. A kettle simmered on a trivet. The kitchen was the only room where my authority was superseded. I did not know the order of the platters loaded in the high dressers, or what time the milkmaid came. It had all the purpose of a small business, one I had no role in, apart from once a week when Maria showed me the bills, and I paid them.

I went straight to the back door and pulled the handle, and it opened into the cold morning. Maria and Agnes stopped talking at once. I stood like that for a moment, with my hand on the door, my ears ringing with anxiety, my throat closing, then turned slowly to look at them. There was a gentle hiss as the iron was placed on the cloth pinned to the table, and Maria spoke first.

"I am sorry, madam," she said. "I was washing the turnips and threw the water out into the yard. I was about to lock it."

The key stuck out of the keyhole. I drew it out and held it between two fingers. "Anybody could have come in when your backs were turned, copied this and then returned in the dead of the night with us all dreaming in our beds." My voice was measured, though I could feel it begin to tremble. The brass key was as long as my first finger, and I returned it to the lock and turned it once, twice, three times, feeling the satisfying movement of the mechanism falling into place. Then I put it in my pocket. Agnes and Maria watched in unhappy silence, their mouths slack. "I will take this with me to church," I said.

"Madam," Maria began. "We need to use the —"

"I need to be able to trust you." I stared at her across the scrubbed table. "I am trying very hard."

There was an awful silence, and I glanced at the turnip heads on the table, and saw the knife resting on its side. On my left, the iron sat gently sizzling next to a pile of linen. Weapons were everywhere, if only you looked for them. The thought made me feel defiled, corrupted, and once again I found myself wishing I could scrub my mind with lye, starch the stains from my memories. Without another word I went from the kitchen to find Charlotte, who was waiting for me at the door.

We made our careful way down the steps to the brougham, and I felt the outside air for the first time in a week. The snow had made it colder, and it quickly reached down my neck and found the tender place between my gloves and my sleeves. Charlotte scrambled into the carriage holding her blue hat, and I followed her. Henry shut us inside, and I could not breathe until we were locked in, and the little curtain was drawn. Charlotte lifted the curtain on the other side, peeking out at a group of young women — servants, in plain brown cloaks — walking good-naturedly together despite the cold.

"Where are they going, do you think?" she asked.

"Charlotte," I said, and she closed the curtain.

We journeyed the short way to the chapel in silence. I felt the carriage turn its familiar way right into Great Ormond Street, and left at the tip of Red Lyon Street, sailing toward the Foundling's gates. Henry helped us out, and we stood for a moment, blinking in the bright light.

The time of year meant there were no groups standing outside the chapel, and Charlotte and I followed an elderly couple across the courtyard, half-bent against the wind. Charlotte's hat blew off before we reached the doors, and she went running after it, chasing it along the ground with outstretched arms until a great gust blew it upward and straight into the chest of Doctor Mead. He captured it with both hands, laughing easily and passing it back to Charlotte before removing his own. I did not hear what he said, but they walked toward where I stood at the large cedar door, clutching their hats close to them like kittens.

"Mrs. Callard," he said as he drew close. "You show great command over your bonnet. I am afraid mine and Miss Callard's require more discipline."

Charlotte grinned toothily.

"We may not go inside until you have your head covered," I told her, and she stuffed it over her hair in a manner unbecoming, but there was no time to say so.

Doctor Mead held the door for us, but before I could hurry us to our usual pew, he stopped me. "May I pay a call on you later this morning?"

I blinked in surprise. "You need no permission to call, Doctor Mead. You are always welcome at Devonshire Street."

"I'm glad to hear it. If I can't find you after the service, I expect I'll arrive before noon, if that does not interrupt your day?"

I smiled. He knew the way I lived, yet always spoke as though my Sundays were filled with calling cards and invitations.

"Not at all. You are very welcome to join us for Sunday luncheon."

"I would be delighted, thank you."

We parted and went to our usual pews, and I thought nothing of the nature of his inquiry throughout the service, nor the hymns, nor the short carriage ride home, until half past eleven, when I heard the doorknocker. Doctor Mead called once a month or so — he had been a friend of Daniel's, and was two or three years younger than him. Daniel would now have been thirty-five, though he'd only ever reached twenty-eight. I would not see him grow gray hairs, or lines at his eyes, or a rounded belly from decades of port and cheese. I showed Doctor Mead upstairs to the withdrawing room, then went to the kitchen. Agnes set about warming the kettle and collecting saucers, and I asked Maria what time the lamb would be ready. She pursed her lips and said half an hour, after it had rested, but would not look at me. I wondered what had displeased her, then remembered the weight of the key at my thigh. I drew it out and set it between us on the table.

"Doctor Mead so enjoys your roasted potatoes." I looked at her until she met my eye, which she did with a resigned wariness. Then, seeing my expression, her frown melted and she drew the key toward her.

"I shall give him extra, then," she said, and I knew I was forgiven.

I thanked her, and went back upstairs to where Doctor Mead was sitting in my chair, but I did not mind.

"Is your sister well?" he asked as I took the seat opposite and settled my skirts around me.

"As well as ever. She has gone to the north with her family."

"Very sensible. London in winter is dreadful."

I wondered if he had heard of George's indiscretion with the viscount's daughter, and decided not. Doctor Mead did not open his ears to salon gossip, and would not know half the people discussed if he did. As far as I knew he did not attend salons at all, much to the frustration of preying mothers with eligible young daughters, who they wished to present to him as neatly and deliciously as a box of macarons. Doctor Mead had never married or even been betrothed. With his charming looks, respectable occupation, vast Bloomsbury townhouse and family connections, his bachelorhood was regarded in some drawing rooms as the biggest misfortune since the South Sea Bubble.

He had been a very great friend over the years, and accepted my way of living without comment or interference. Once or twice he had suggested Charlotte take exercise, but had dropped the matter when I refused. At Daniel's funeral, on a warm day in the middle of April, I had told him in the church that I would not be leaving the house again, and I kept my word.

I felt no grief traveling back to Devonshire Street that day, knowing I would no longer feel the sun on my face or a chill wind down my neck. I had been wiped clean by loss, and felt only a sense of relief when I closed the front door behind me, as one does climbing into bed after a long day.

Charlotte came soon after, and three years of solitude passed comfortably. I raised her in peace and safety, until one summer when she was three years old, and the house hot and stuffy, and she cried for three days in a row, driving me half-mad and close to despair. I'd sent a tearful letter to Ambrosia, who came at once and took her on a walk around Queen's Square at the end of the street, and twenty minutes later she returned a different child. Their excursion persuaded me that a change of scenery was necessary once a week for the child's well-being, if not my sanity, and Ambrosia suggested the new chapel at the Foundling Hospital, not three streets away. Daniel had been buried next door at St. George's, so I knew it, and agreed more quickly than she expected.

On a bright Sunday morning in April she collected me in her carriage, and I put on an outdoor coat and hat and stepped outside for the first time in three years. I had been so dizzy with anxiety I remember only clutching Charlotte's hand as if she was *my* mother, and her clutching mine, and the odd sensation of being close to other people again, and the quick and unpredictable way they moved. I would have preferred a quiet, modest place of worship, but this chapel was so new one could almost smell the paint. The pews were cleanly varnished, the prayer books crisp. The ceilings were high and the windows sparkled. Its youth was a balm — it had seen nothing of sorrow: mine or anyone else's. The day was a dream to me, but that evening I went to bed feeling as though I had crossed an ocean and was standing with shaking legs on a foreign shore.

Doctor Mead had been almost as delighted as Ambrosia to see me out of the house, and remarked that he would get me to the theater yet. I teased that it had taken me three years to come to church, so a play would take fifteen, and he laughed. We both knew I would never go, and had not even been with Daniel, who went everywhere and did everything without me. If people felt pity for me, it was because they did not know it was at my design.

I was grateful to hear Agnes at the door with the tea tray. She put everything out, as well as a little plate of sponge biscuits, then bowed and left the room. Doctor Mead reached for one.

"Make sure you save room for Maria's lamb," I told him, and he paused with the biscuit halfway to his lips, looking so much like a chastisted boy I could not help but smile. "Sponge biscuits were Mother's favorite," I went on. "She kept them in a little walnut box on her dressing table. I was allowed to take one each Sunday before bed, when she would comb my hair. Sometimes, when she and Father were out, I would creep into her bedroom and steal one. They were delicious. Maria makes very fine ones, almost the same."

I realized I had quite forgotten myself, and was staring at Mother's picture. It was easy to imagine she was listening, for she looked as though she was enraptured by the most engaging tale, with her eyes bright and her lips gently parted in wonder. Doctor Mead cleared his throat and ate the biscuit politely, dabbing at his lips with a napkin.

"Before we eat," he said, "I wish to speak to you about a matter quite . . . ah . . . delicate."

"Oh?" I sat up straighter.

"It regards your daughter."

"Charlotte?"

He smiled, and I noticed the tiniest crumb at the edge of his lips, and resisted the urge to brush it away. "Have you another?"

I blushed and set my cup on its saucer.

"Have you considered a nursemaid for her?"

I took a sip of tea. "I have not, in truth."

"It might be rather beneficial for her. Many households like yours have them now."

"But Charlotte is not an infant. She can dress herself and read to herself and she takes her meals and lessons with me."

"They are not just for babies. My sister

157

has one for her three children, the oldest of whom is fifteen. Their nursemaid looks after them, takes them on walks, that kind of thing." His expression changed, and his cup slipped from its ring, spilling ever so slightly. "Of course, walks are not compulsory. She can prepare Charlotte for becoming a young woman. They can read together, sew . . . Whatever it is you fair creatures do to make a home lovely."

I imagined a strange woman coming into my house and eating my food, sleeping under my roof. Occupying my daughter. For so long it had been Charlotte, Maria, Agnes and me. Another person would change the dynamic irrevocably.

"Did you not have a nursemaid as a child?" Doctor Mead asked.

"No, I did not need one."

"You must have been quite lonely."

"Not at all. I had my parents, just as Charlotte has me."

Doctor Mead set his cup gently back on the table. I waited.

"There is a woman whom I met recently in my work," he said. "She has not been fortunate in life, and I wish to help her. Unfortunately there is no position in my household for her — as you know, I get on perfectly well with a cook and maid."

"And you wish for this woman to become Charlotte's nursemaid?"

He cast about for his next words. "If you were able to find room for her in your household, yes. She has suffered the most unlikely misfortune. I hope it would not offend you if I offered to pay her wage."

"That would not be necessary," I said, sitting a little straighter, smarting slightly at his implication I could not afford a third servant. The clock ticked, and from the street below came the sound of a cart unloading boxes or barrels. "Has she experience of being a nursemaid?"

"She has. She worked for a family in London, caring for their two sons."

"What part of London?"

"Spitalfields, she said, so silk weavers, perhaps."

"So she has no experience of girls." I stared at the dark windows of the house opposite, and saw the delft jug. "We don't have the room."

Doctor Mead blinked in surprise. "In this house?"

"Agnes and Maria have a room each, and I could not ask them to begin sharing."

"My sister's nursemaid sleeps with the children."

I rearranged my feet on the carpet and

159

pressed my shoulder blades into the chair. If Charlotte had a nursemaid sleeping in her room, she would be a guard — a protector. The slightest cough, a feverish forehead, all her ailments could be relayed to me. And if there were an intruder . . . well, Charlotte would have somebody with her, to alert the household and take her to safety. With no men in the house, many times at night I'd imagined the tread of footsteps on the stairs, though of course our rooms were all locked. A fifth person would be another mouth to feed, another outgoing in the accounts book, but another pair of ears to listen, and eyes to see.

"Her name is Eliza Smith," Doctor Mead said.

"And how old is she?"

"She is in her midtwenties."

I raised an eyebrow. "How did you meet her?"

Doctor Mead shifted in his seat and I poured us more tea. "This is the delicate part. She is, shall we say, a patient," he said.

I looked at him. "An unmarried nursemaid can afford the fees of a Bloomsbury doctor?"

"Her circumstances are extraordinary."

"Ah." I understood. He would not, of course, say that she was one of the unmarried mothers he had met at the Foundling Hospital, with an illegitimate child. Asking him would require him either to lie or else make known a shameful truth. I had long known that it was in his nature to help people, as if they were birds fallen from their nests, cared for in boxes by the stove. I looked to my parents. Mother's face was encouraging; Father's inquisitive.

There was a knock at the door, and I heard Agnes on the landing: "Luncheon is served, madam."

"All I ask is that you meet her," said Doctor Mead.

I rose from my seat and he did the same, but instead of going to the door, I went to stand at the window. There was nobody much about, and the weak light looked as though it was ready to retire. A crossing sweeper completed one length of the street and disappeared, and two well-dressed gentlemen in frock coats let themselves in at no. 40. The drapes had been closed at no. 28, directly opposite, likely to keep out the chill.

"Then I will meet her," I said, turning my head a quarter of the way. "You may bring her here this week, on a day that suits me. Have you told her about me?"

"About you, Mrs. Callard?"

"You know what I mean. Not many young women would wish to be confined to such a modest house, day and night."

I felt him move closer to me, but kept my eyes on the bricks opposite. The space between us grew smaller.

"Perhaps . . ." he said, and then, more quietly, "perhaps she might take Charlotte out to the squares and parks. Many nurse-maids and their charges —"

"Charlotte does not leave this house, therefore neither will she. She may have a half day off per month. If those terms suit her, by all means I will meet her to judge her suitability for the position. If not, there is no position. Now, let's not keep Maria's lamb waiting."

CHAPTER 9

On a cold, foggy morning three days later, Doctor Mead's black carriage glided up Devonshire Street and slowed to a stop outside the house. I was watching from the window, half-concealed by the drapes. I saw the doctor's hat appear from the cab, and his slim, dark coat, then he held out his hand, and a smaller, ungloved one slotted into it, followed by a white bonnet, and beneath that a pale heart-shaped face that turned upward to look at the house. I drew backward into the shadows.

The room was quiet, the oil lamps lit. I wondered how I should receive them: standing at the window or the fireplace, or seated, perhaps with a book in my lap, or a newspaper? The rap of the doorknocker came from the floor below, followed by voices in the hall. Agnes would meet her before me. The two servants had seemed pleased by the idea of me hiring a nursemaid, and said it was a splendid suggestion. I did not know what they said when the kitchen door was closed.

I'd spent the days since Doctor Mead's proposal in a state of pensiveness, forgetting to eat my toast and lying awake when the house was asleep. The notion of a fifth member of the household was both frightening and intriguing, and a young woman, too — a creature as exotic as Charlotte's turtle at our house. I wished Ambrosia was here with me, but then she did draw all the light and energy from the room, and from me, reflecting it back like a chandelier. It would not do; this I had to do alone. I could not recall the last time a stranger had visited. There were knife men and butchers' boys and milkmaids always calling at the basement door, but Agnes and Maria knew to admit only those on the list pinned by the back door.

I heard Agnes's polite knock of announcement at the withdrawing room door, and realized I was halfway between the window and my chair, and it was too late to settle on either. The door opened and Agnes held it for Doctor Mead, who came first, tipping his hat and smiling, and after him the young woman.

"Mrs. Callard," he said pleasantly. "This

164

is Miss Smith."

She was tall, with dark hair and eyes, and a scattering of freckles across her face. Her hands were clasped nervously, and she moved one toward her neck, where her cloak had been fastened.

"I know you," I said.

Her dark eyes were very wide, and she stopped on the threshold, frozen like a porcelain maid, or a shepherdess, neat and plump with her large bosom and slim wrists. Her hair was deep brown and curled at her neck, and there was a pleasant rosiness to her cheeks. She was a few inches shorter than me, but most women were.

Doctor Mead spoke first. "You are already acquainted?"

"You were at the chapel last week."

"Oh," she said, and her voice was soft. "Yes, I was."

She was dressed smartly, in a cream printed frock and black jacket trimmed with velvet. The way she pulled at her cuffs suggested it was new, though no doubt second-hand. She was looking at me in a peculiar way, and I wondered what Doctor Mead had told her about me. Certainly that I was a widow; perhaps she had expected me to be older, or infirm, or unfashionable.

Ambrosia once said it was a shame I did

not go out, because half the men in London would be in love with me. "The half that aren't in love with you?" I had teased, and she'd replied that *all* of them were in love with her, but many were not loyal in their affections.

After a moment Miss Smith must have realized she was staring, because she colored slightly, though her cheeks and nose were already pink from the cold. She looked at her feet, and then at Doctor Mead, who gave her an encouraging smile.

"Miss Smith, this is my dear friend, Mrs. Callard."

"Eliza, please," she said.

Then she began glancing furtively about the room, at the portraits of my parents, and the oil lamps, and the ornaments, as though assessing their value. I watched her, and she saw me looking, and quickly moved her gaze back to her feet.

"Eliza?" I prompted, half-amused at her boldness.

"I just thought, madam," she said, almost in a whisper, "that the little girl might be here." Her accent was strong, and she pronounced it "gell."

"It is not necessary for you to meet my daughter until I have decided you are fit for the role."

Fleeting disappointment crossed her face. Then she nodded, and gave a small smile. Conscious, no doubt, to avoid unpleasant beginnings, Doctor Mead directed her farther into the room, and I went to the little table and took a seat in a high-backed chair. Doctor Mead did the same, and held out another for Eliza, who hesitated above it, and then sat. The room was very quiet, the only sounds skirts rustling and chairs creaking into submission, and then I remembered I was to direct the conversation, and sat a little straighter, and so did she. Now I was closer to her, I noticed a very faint smell about her, of fish, or brine, as well as cold weather and a slight, cloying mustiness from the jacket.

"Eliza," I said. "Doctor Mead informs me you are looking for gainful employment as a nursemaid."

She nodded, and I realized I did not know what to say next.

"Eliza was a nursemaid for two young boys," Doctor Mead remarked, with as much pride as if she was his own daughter. Briefly I wondered if he was in love with her, and decided it unlikely.

"And why no longer?" I asked.

She blinked, and looked blank for a moment. "They moved away," she said. "They went to live in Scotland."

"Scotland? Doctor Mead told me they lived in Spitalfields. Were they silk weavers?"

"No, madam. Mr. Gibbons was — is — a musician."

"What instrument?"

"Violin."

"A violinist from Spitalfields," I mused. "And have you a written reference?"

"Yes." She reached inside her jacket and withdrew a folded piece of paper, setting it on the table between us and pushing it slowly and hesitantly toward me. I opened it and scanned it briefly. It was still warm from her body.

"And you did not wish to move with them to Scotland?"

"My home is London," she replied. "Madam."

"Whereabouts?"

"Just off Poultry. Next to the Hog's Head. Do you know it?" Her eyes were bright, and she appeared very anxious — her shoulders were rigid, her eyes solemn.

"I do not," I said after a meaningful pause.

I knew she was lying. I decided not to examine her further, and folded the false reference that was riddled with spelling errors.

My friend had brought me a nursemaid who had almost certainly had a child with her master and been cast out without a reference, and I suspected he did not realize it. He knew, of course, that she had an illegitimate child, and would know that I understood as much. There had been an unspoken agreement that Sunday, over the sponge biscuits. I wondered if she had written the reference; the handwriting was literate, but barely. It was not Doctor Mead's. Besides, he would not be so duplicitous. It was her deceit, then, not his.

I knew I would likely never discover the truth, and thought it a shame, because I wished women could speak more freely of these things. Perhaps they did in the chophouses and taverns; I would not know. Just as I would not know if Eliza's musician master forced himself on her, or if she was in love with him. Neither would I know how it was to give birth to a child and surrender it to the Foundling Hospital, never to see it again. The woman before me had lived a life I could only vaguely imagine — she had been a mother, and was now no longer. She had loved, and lost. We had something in common, Eliza and I.

I sighed deeply, and she held her breath. Her eyes took on a resigned look: one of guardedness, and pride, and there was fear there, too, though she did not wish to show it.

"I would not move to Scotland, either," I said.

She paused for a moment, and then broke into a wide smile. Her teeth were small and neat. One at the front had chipped slightly, and was shorter than the other.

"Are you employed now?"

"Yes, madam."

"Where?"

"Rag Fair, by the Tower."

"You sell clothes?"

"Yes, madam. Helping a friend. But I'd like my old work back."

"And why is that? You have freedom, I presume, as a trader? A family to go back to? Friends to see?"

"I like living in, madam. And it don't pay well."

I sat back and regarded her. "I presume Doctor Mead has told you of the nature of the job?"

The girl nodded. "Yes, madam."

"And the nature of the . . . lifestyle I have?"

She looked blank. "Lifestyle?"

"In relation to the proximities in which Charlotte and I exist."

Eliza blinked and looked first at Doctor Mead, then at me. "I don't understand."

"I do not leave the house."

Comprehension swept her face. "Oh, yes. I know that."

"And neither does my daughter."

She nodded, though her dark eyes were troubled. "Not anywhere?"

"Only to church on Sundays. That is the limit of our world. And that, therefore, will be the limit of your world, too."

I waited for her reaction, and she seemed to consider it, and licked her lips, looking as though she was burning to say something, but contained it, and extinguished it. Her face went smooth and blank.

"I understand," she said. "And I'd be happy with living that way. You've a lovely house and you've no need to leave it. Why would you, when you have all you need? Food, and a cook, and lovely fires. And no man about the place. That sounds rum to me." She allowed herself a small, private smile, which I could not help but return.

"You have no intention of marriage at this time?"

"No," she said, with conviction, and then again, as an afterthought: "No."

I took the measure of her, and she me, and in that moment I made two decisions:

171

one of which I could act on immediately, the other later. I rose from my seat and Doctor Mead sprang up beside me.

"If you'll excuse me," I said, and left them in the withdrawing room, closing the door quietly behind me and going upstairs.

Charlotte was not in her bedroom. I sighed and called her name, and heard a scuffling above, where Agnes and Maria slept. A moment later her round face appeared at the top of the staircase, looking thoroughly guilty.

"Charlotte, come down from there at once! You know you aren't allowed up there."

Silently, she slid down the staircase and streaked past me like a cat, darting toward her nursery. "There is someone I want you to meet, but if you are misbehaving I shall have to tell them you are too insolent today."

"Who is it?" she asked, pausing on the turn and fixing me with a curious stare.

"Are you misbehaving?"

She shook her head.

"Where is your indoor cap?"

Her shoulders lifted to her ears.

"Find your cap and put it on, then come to the withdrawing room."

She brightened visibly and threw herself into her bedroom. In the withdrawing room,

I found Doctor Mead and Eliza in furtive conversation. Charlotte appeared behind me and stayed behind my skirts. Her cap had been stuffed hastily on, and I arranged it more neatly and pushed her forward.

"Charlotte," I said. "You know Doctor Mead, of course, and this is his friend, Eliza Smith."

At once, the strangest thing happened: Charlotte, who was wary of strangers, not having met many in her short life, moved toward the young woman. Eliza in turn got down from her chair to kneel on the carpet. A smile — that easy smile — split her face, and she reached to take Charlotte's hand. The gesture was so instinctive, so unrehearsed, and I watched with mild surprise as Charlotte shyly gave it to her. Doctor Mead and I looked at one another, and he was delighted.

"Hello, Charlotte," Eliza whispered. Her eyes shone. "It's a pleasure to meet you."

Charlotte's dark hair spilled down her back, and dust streaked her skirt. I hoped she had not been rummaging around upstairs again. A year or so ago, Agnes had found under Charlotte's bed a box of trinkets she'd stolen from all of us — thimbles, bits of paper and even a hairbrush Maria had missed for months. From my room she had taken a miniature looking glass, a dried pressed flower and a love token Daniel had given me years before: a heart made of whalebone, cut in half. As punishment, I had taken all her toys, games and books and locked them in my bedroom, and she had to do without them for a week. She had been so bored and vexed it had been punishment for me, too, and I was as glad as she when the week was over.

"Your mother has told me all about you," Eliza was saying. "What a nice home you have. Do you have lots of toys?"

Charlotte gave a small nod, her cap bobbing up and down. Eliza was still holding her hand. I signaled to Doctor Mead that I wished to speak privately with him, and he rose again and followed me to the fireplace.

"She has great affection for children," I said in a low voice. "But I worry she may spoil the child, or make her soft."

"She has a natural, feminine touch," Doctor Mead said, looking at her. "She will set a good example for Charlotte."

"She does seem very easy with her."

"Better than difficult, is it not?"

"Perhaps. Though Charlotte is not a kitten to be petted."

"Of course."

We stood for a moment, watching them.

Charlotte was telling her something, swinging her arms in a carefree way, and Eliza was listening, enraptured, as if it was the most fascinating story in the world. I decided to share with Doctor Mead the decision I'd made earlier.

"Eliza has a position here, should she want it," I said. "I am willing to grant you this favor, as your friend, if it benefits both of you as much as you say it will. But I will not hear another word of you paying her wage, and will find it insulting if you offer again."

Doctor Mead gave a winning smile, and put a hand on my sleeve and squeezed. I flinched, and brushed at where he had touched me, as though it had been dirtied, but he did not look offended.

"Mrs. Callard, I am so glad," he said. "Thank you. You will not regret it." He grew confidential, and his clear eyes clouded. "I wish I could tell you what hardship she has been through."

"Say nothing of it."

My arm felt hot. I had not been touched since Daniel died, by anybody save for Charlotte, and that was seldom. Even with her I was uneasy; I did not have Eliza's maternal instinct, or Doctor Mead's merry generosity. Intimacy was something I endured, rather than indulged in, and so it was one of the things Daniel had sought elsewhere. I knew that his urges were fulfilled, and was glad of it. Besides, Ambrosia told me it was as natural for men as visiting the chamber pot.

That I could not provide that side of things did not concern me, but what did was the other type of intimacy I could not provide either, that came naturally to wives: removing their husbands' hats after a day's work, and tidying their hair, and knowing when they wanted a bath or a glass of brandy. I suppose you would call it affection. I would watch couples walking down Devonshire Street arm in arm, twisting this way and that, pointing, laughing, kissing and stroking, feeling as stiff and inanimate as one of Charlotte's dolls. To those women, women like Eliza, brushing a little girl's hair and making a seat of their knee came without effort, without thought.

I stood watching them, and felt, very faintly, the tiniest splinter opening inside me. Whether it was envy, or grief, or guilt, I could not name it, and did not care to examine it.

I stood up straighter. "Charlotte, go upstairs," I said.

The tender little scene disbanded and

Charlotte, with her fingers on the doorknob and a last, lingering look at Eliza, like a lover off to sea, left the room. Eliza got to her feet, and brought her eyes to me. They burned with want, and I saw for the first time how badly she needed the work. We stood looking at one another, as hooves clattered on the street below, and carriage wheels trundled. I wondered if Agnes had properly bolted the door after admitting them, and tried to resist the urge to go down and check.

"When are you able to begin?" I asked.

She had been holding her body very tensely; now her shoulders sank, and her face cleared. She clasped her hands in front of her, as if she did not know what to do with them. "As soon as you would like, madam."

"I shall need to order a bed for Charlotte's chamber — we've no room with the servants, so that's where you will sleep. Your wage will be two shillings and sixpence a week. Would a week today suit you?"

"Yes, madam. Very well. Very well, thank you."

Once they had left and I'd locked and bolted the door myself and checked the others, I went to find Charlotte. She was sitting at the window in her bedroom, looking down at Devonshire Street. Her turtle was on her lap, moving its ancient head toward a sprig of parsley she was holding. Her room was square, and smaller than mine, with striped wallpaper and a narrow rosewood bed pushed against the wall. A dresser sat beneath one window and a stuffed footstool beneath the other, which Charlotte knelt on to look outside. Toys and games covered almost every surface: wooden horses, baby dolls, spinning tops. I ought to stop buying them for her, as she would soon grow out of playing. But what then: What did a girl of ten, twelve, fourteen do, if not gallop horses in a carpet race? She could speak French, though she would not go to France. Her pretty gowns would be seen by no one; her curls admired only by Agnes and Maria.

"Do you like Eliza?" I spoke from the doorway.

She had not heard me come in and jumped, whipping around as though caught in some private act. Her cap had skewed again, and her white dress was creased as well as dusty. She appeared not to have heard me, so I asked her again, and her face lit from within, and she smiled and nodded with great enthusiasm. Her teeth were her first still, like a row of little pearls.

"Would you like it if she was your nurse-maid?"

"What's a nursemaid?"

"Somebody who cares for children. She will live in the house with us, and sleep here in your bedroom."

"Where will I sleep?"

"In here with her. We will get her a bed and put it here. You must tidy away your toys, though, or there won't be room for her things."

She looked pleased, and gazed happily at the space Eliza's bed would occupy opposite hers. What she said next surprised me.

"I know her."

"Pardon me?"

"I know her. Eliza."

"Yes, you saw her at church."

"I met her."

I stared at her. "At church?"

She looked down and began picking at the hem of her dress. "I like her," she said.

From the floor below came the jingling sound of Agnes on the stairs, and with a jolting clarity I realized it was three o'clock, and I would be late for tea with my parents. I had not read the newspaper; I had not even looked at my map book to follow Ambrosia's journey north. Immediately I fell into a panic. Organization was needed;

179

routine. But the way of things would last only another week, and then a new structure would begin. If I thought about it at length I would change my mind altogether, so I left Charlotte's room and closed the door gently behind me, and a moment later her soft voice came from within, interrupting my thoughts. Pressing my hands to the panels, I rested an ear to the wood and listened.

"Hello, Charlotte, I am pleased to meet you," came her little voice. I frowned, and listened harder. "My name is Eliza, and I am here to take care of you. I will love you, and cherish you, and play with you all day long, and at nighttime, too."

I closed my eyes and thought of Ambrosia. For seven years I'd been my parents' only child, and if I tried hard enough I could still conjure the memory of being the singular object of their affections. I had basked in their love like a cat in a sun spot, and wanted for nothing. A brother came in between us, departing as swiftly and noiselessly as he had arrived, and leaving Mother tearful for some time. But then Ambrosia came and stayed, scowling and mewling in my mother's arms. I had been alarmed, and for a time felt woefully discarded. But then she grew and began to look like a person, and became a warm body in my bed. She prodded me with chubby fingers, fascinated by my hair and nose and teeth, and followed me around like a little lapdog. She began to speak, and said my name as "Assander," with a little lisp. I was precious to her, and she me, and to our parents' delight we adored each other. I felt pity when I thought of how Charlotte would never know what it was to have a plaything, a companion.

Her chatter came again: "Eliza, do you take sugar in your tea?"

I kept my forehead on the door, and two floors below the long-case clock in the hallway chimed once, twice, three times. We had only just met Eliza, and already the cogs of the household were shifting. The day was off its axis, and I was late for tea.

CHAPTER 10

"Is that all you have?" I asked, and of course it was. Eliza had arrived with only a canvas bag, and even that was only half-filled, giving it the appearance of a bagged cat ready for drowning. She had already made one mistake, calling at the front door and not the cellar steps, and Agnes had dithered on the doorstep before hurrying her inside. I watched from the staircase, and Agnes near jumped out of her skin when I spoke from the gloom. I had been on my way up from the kitchen, where I'd exchanged cross words with Maria over the new butcher's order. The slow-witted cook had uttered the same sentence repeatedly, asking if we needed more tripe, liver, gammon, and eventually I lost my patience altogether.

The hallway was dark, and I could not see Eliza's face as Agnes shuffled back down the hallway. Eliza clutched her bag to her stomach, and I saw only the pale glow of her bonnet, and the outline of her drab cloak.

"Do not call at that door again," was all I said, before going on up the stairs.

Agnes had been instructed to show her where she would sleep and put her things, but I was not halfway up the stairs before Charlotte came bounding down. I blocked her way with my skirts.

"That is *not* how ladies descend a staircase. That is not even how children descend. That is how dogs descend. Are you a dog?"

She froze, her indoor cap askance. I sighed and straightened her, and she submitted placidly. There was a smudge of dirt on her cheek, and her fingertips were black.

"Have you been feeding your toys coal again? Oh, you are willfully disobedient! Coals belong in the scuttle — how many times must I tell you? Eliza's first task shall be washing you properly. She has not even set her things down and you are already creating work for her."

Charlotte's large brown eyes were solemn. She was wearing her best dress — a stiff little gown of rose pink and white, with delicate ivory tassels down the stomacher and on the sleeves. She had fixed a silk ribbon at her neck and put on her best gold slippers. She saw me notice this, and her eyebrows drew closer together in defiance. Her breath came hot through her angry little nose, and her nostrils flared. I lifted a finger as though to touch the white ribbon around her neck, but let it fall. I should have said: "What a pretty effort you have made for Eliza." I should have said: "You look beautiful." But what I said was: "Blue would look better next time."

As the words fell from my lips I heard them thud dully at Charlotte's feet, cruel and misguided. Eliza stood silently behind us. I knew that I did not know how to speak to my daughter, and now so did she. I knew that I did not know how to love my daughter, and so would she. *You know why that is,* came that spiteful voice in my mind, the one that sometimes used my lips as an instrument.

Charlotte was staring unhappily at the floor, smarting from my words, and Eliza was standing damp and timid in the hall, as Agnes awaited instruction. Suddenly I could not face them, any of them, and I picked up my skirts and continued my climb, bypassing the parlor altogether and going to my room.

On the dresser between the windows the crystal decanter glowed dimly. It had been filled, and I let out a sigh of relief. I locked the door and removed first my slippers, then my jacket and stays, setting them on the chair and standing upright with my hands on my hips. I leaned left and right, and stretched upward and forward, and breathed in and out. I scratched an itch on my back, and unpinned my hair. The drapes I drew halfway so that the room was soft and darkened.

From the bureau in the alcove next to the fireplace I took out my special box, brushing off imagined dust with my palm. It was ebony wood, with little oriental figures inlaid with mother-of-pearl and gold-leaf bamboo. I traced the lid with one hand and poured from the crystal decanter with the other, taking the box and glass, and going to sit on the floor at the foot of my bed, putting them both on the carpet in front of me. I crossed my legs and tucked my skirts beneath them, put my hands over my eyes, and breathed.

One by one, like picking grapes from a stalk, I took out the contents and arranged them on the floor. The order I had perfected over time. First came Mother's ring, and the pearl drop earrings she'd worn on her wedding day. Next came Father's military badges, three of them, which I breathed on and polished with my thumb and placed in a proud triangle. They were followed by Daniel's miniature, which I'd wrapped in a handkerchief. I peeled back the silk as a lover might to reveal his face.

In the likeness, painted on smooth ivory, Daniel was captured sideways, looking as though someone to his left had called his name. He wore a gray wig and a red jacket, and his gaze was winsome, and playful, and proud, just as it had been when I'd met him in the empty kitchen of my aunt's house at nighttime, hiding from a party. I found myself smiling, and remembering.

"I did not see you," he had said, finding me heating milk at the fire. "You are quiet as a mouse."

The servants were all at the party, too, and I had gone downstairs in my stockings, hoping not to be seen. I ignored him, and wrapped my shawl more tightly around me, watching the pan grow warm.

"Are you a guest?" he had tried again. "I have not noticed you."

"No, I am a niece," I'd said, without turning around.

"Ah, the *niece.* I have heard about you." His voice was much closer, and I did not like the knowledge in it. "Your aunt Cassandra says you do not attend her parties, and sit in the attic rooms sewing a cloth of dreams. Is that true?"

Was he teasing me? I looked at him for the first time, and saw that he was handsome, in a dandyish sort of way. He was younger than me, by a few years, and shone with boastful youth. I turned away again. He asked me for a tinderbox to light his tobacco pipe, and dryly I told him there was a fire before us, and he might save himself the effort of lighting a box, and he laughed, and found a splint in a jar on the mantelpiece. He lit his pipe and breathed deeply in, as though he had been waiting for the moment all night. I stood stiffly watching my pan as he smoked beside me and asked me my name.

"Alexandra."

"Ah yes, your aunt said. I met your sister, Ambrosia; isn't she a Catherine wheel? Who is your father?"

I was silent, and after a moment said: "Patrick Weston-Hallett."

"Why do I know that name, Weston-Hallett?" he said thoughtfully. Then, a moment later, with a change in tone and the flat note of recognition: "Oh. My apologies."

His sympathy seemed genuine, and it disarmed me. I looked at him again, and his light eyes saw me, and who I was. He told me his name was Daniel Callard, and asked

187

me to sit with him in the empty kitchen while he finished his pipe, saying he hated parties, but I knew it was untrue. He was twenty-four years old, and had recently finished an apprenticeship with a porcelain merchant in London. He was in the early stages of setting up his own business buying and selling whalebone, but he needed an investor. A benefactor, he said, making the word sound exotic and foreign. He told me how they caught the whales and brought them to London and gutted them at a dock at Rotherhithe, where the merchants would pick over the carcasses, lighting on a rib here, a bit of skull there. How their blubber was used to make oil for lamps, their bone for women's stays.

"You women are more familiar with it than men," he told me. "You touch whalebone every time you dress."

I had blushed then. That night I had left my bedroom for a cup of milk, and gone back to it in love. But I was twenty-nine years old. I had lived with my aunt all my adult life, and never been to school, or Europe, or even Cheltenham, which was the nearest town. My world had shrunk to the size of a nut. And then Daniel came to one of Aunt Cassandra's parties, and cracked it open.

I'd gone to sleep that night with a head full of whales, and ships, and crashing waves, and Daniel, Daniel, Daniel.

The next day he came again to see me at Aunt Cassandra's damp, drafty house ahead of his return to London, and I told him he could have my money for his business if he married me. As a girl, I'd watched how Father dealt with his contemporaries when they came to our house, and made Daniel a proposal: we could live in the Bloomsbury house, and I would set him up in trade. He had listened in disbelief, and by the time the teapot grew cold he had kissed me on the mouth.

Aunt Cassandra almost expired with shock when I told her I was to marry a man I'd met in her kitchen the night before. I knew she had resigned herself to never being rid of me, especially as Ambrosia had married George the year before, well and truly sealing the dust that coated my prospects. Cassandra had tried, bringing a parade of bachelors through the doors at Knowesley Park, and to her frustration I'd turned down them all. I had my parents' money and did not want a husband. I had not thought to marry or change my circumstances at all, and was too old, besides. That was until Daniel Callard walked into the kitchen looking for a light, and it turned out I was it.

We married on a freezing day in January a month after meeting, and turned out the tenants at Devonshire Street. The wedding had been the first time I'd left the house in five years, and the curate had placed a chair before the pulpit, thinking me a cripple. I'd dreaded getting in the carriage, and shook the whole way to London, but Daniel had locked his fingers tightly in mine. I'd looked at our bright gold wedding rings, and felt as though I was looking at someone else's hand.

I took out his ring now and slipped it onto my widest finger. Somehow, even now, it was never cold, as though he had just removed it.

There were a few more things in the ebony box: the first tooth Ambrosia lost, and a bouquet of our hair — mine, Ambrosia's, Mother's and Father's — tied in a ribbon.

There was the mourning brooch I commissioned after Daniel's death, studded with seed pearls, of a woman strewn against a plinth as willows wept above her.

And last of all there was the tag, with the number 627, and two pieces of scrimshaw, carved with initials, which put together made a heart.

Later that afternoon, I went to the kitchen to ask Agnes and Maria if Eliza should eat with me in the dining room or with them in the kitchen. The pair of them stared blankly at me and I sighed.

"What's usual for our type of household?" I asked.

"Nowhere I worked ever had a nurse-maid," was Agnes's reply. Somewhere in her late forties, she had worked in service since the age of ten.

"Mine neither," said Maria. "Mr. and Mrs. Nesbitt was old when I began working for them, and their children had grown up and left."

"If she sleeps with Charlotte, would they eat together as well? If only I'd asked Doctor Mead."

Maria stood at the blackened range, stirring a pot of applesauce. "I think that would be proper, if she ate with you," she said decidedly. Probably the two of them had already discussed it. I understood: they, too, had their own way of life here, and after several years did not wish to change the order of things. They were wary. Well, so was I. The air thickened while they waited.

191

I did not wish to displease them and lose them to another household. One new servant was tolerable; three would be unbearable.

"She will dine with us, then," I said, more convincingly than I felt. I checked the door out of habit and went upstairs to Charlotte's bedroom.

Eliza and Charlotte were sitting on the floor with their legs tucked under them and Charlotte's dolls spread before them. A second bed had been placed against the left-hand wall, made up with fresh white linen. It must have taken Eliza all of a minute to unpack her bag, which was nowhere in sight. I suddenly had the thought that the one person in the house who knew where she should dine was Eliza herself, but I would not ask her. She peered up at me, expectant, almost childlike herself. I knew almost nothing about her yet she would come to know plenty about me. It was a common enough exchange, but a queer one — people understood very little about their servants, yet servants knew their masters intimately, in almost every way. Mine observed many things about me, but not everything. Like sunlight on a yard, there were some parts always in shadow.

"Eliza," I said. "You will dine with Charlotte and me every evening at five o'clock."

She nodded. "Thank you, madam."

I wondered if there was anything else I should say: that I hoped she liked the room, that laundry day was Monday. Impatience was simmering off Charlotte like steam from a pan — I had interrupted them. I let myself out, closing the door behind me. I was not wanted in the kitchen, and now I had no place here.

Then I realized something: that for a long time we had been two pairs — Agnes and Maria, and Charlotte and me. Now there were two new pairs, and I was alone. The child and her nursemaid, the maid and the cook, and me. The mother. The widow. The mistress. For one person I had many hats, yet rarely felt like wearing any of them. Why had I suddenly no notion of how to be at peace in my own home? I remembered Ambrosia and my map book, and set upon examining her route in the parlor.

When dinnertime arrived I took my usual seat at the table, in between the soup tureen and a dish of boiled ham. The shutters and drapes were closed to keep out the cold. Eliza and Charlotte came in, and I sat a little straighter and smoothed my napkin. I had not dined with a relative stranger in a long time. I noticed Eliza had changed into a plain green dress that showed her fore-arms, and she saw me looking, and I turned my gaze to the dish of ham. Neither of us spoke, and Charlotte took her usual seat opposite mine, but Eliza did not move from the end of the table.

"Are other people coming?" She sounded confused.

"I beg your pardon?"

"All this food . . . Is this for us?"

"Yes, it is for us," I said. "And I would like to eat it while it's warm, if you would be so kind as to take a seat." I felt myself color. The insolence of her, suggesting I ran a wasteful house! This was a modest spread, far less than the groaning tables I'd seen framed in windows on the same street. Hot with irritation, I ladled soup into each of our bowls. Charlotte kept her gaze on her plate, and I noticed her ears were red. Eliza's dark eyes continued to travel over the table.

"Tell me, Eliza," I said, "how does your father earn a living?"

She watched me select the soupspoon and found hers at her elbow. "He's a lighter-man, madam."

"A man of the Thames. Which dock?"

"The Pool of London."

"What cargo?"

"Anything he can get. But mainly to-bacco."

I took a sip of celery soup. "So the ship-ments come from the Americas?"

Eliza stared at me. "You know about trade, madam?"

"My late husband was in seafaring."

She looked down at her soup. "Which trade?"

"Whalebone. He was a merchant."

The silence was broken by the gentle clink of soupspoons against porcelain.

"When did he die?"

I glanced at Charlotte. The topic was not appropriate, but she did not upset herself over him, because she did not know him.

"He passed before Charlotte was born."

"How?" It came so softly, like a little gasp. But her dark eyes were burning at me across the table with such fervor I was disarmed. I wiped my mouth with my napkin.

"I'm sorry," she said. "You must think I'm rude."

"I don't," I thought aloud. "It is a reason-able question, is it not? Death befalls every one of us, after all. It's just nobody has asked me about Mr. Callard in a long time." His name felt odd in my mouth, and in the room, in which he had sat countless times, in the seat Charlotte now used. It was no

195

different — the same eggshell-blue walls, the same walnut table and chairs — yet somehow it was utterly changed.

It had been a Saturday morning in April, and at breakfast he'd closed his eyes and put his head in his hands. I expected he'd drunk too much the night before, and poured him more coffee, and spread marmalade on his toast. It was not an unfamiliar sight, and I was not worried, so once I'd finished eating I took my newspaper to the parlor. I remember the advertisement I'd been reading — for gingerbread, at a bakery in Cornhill — when I heard Agnes's shriek, and her calling me. I had thought she'd seen a mouse.

Daniel was collapsed, half on the floor, half on his chair, with his head in his hands, moaning in agony. Agnes, Maria and I lifted him and carried him with difficulty to the stairs, where he vomited on the first landing. By the third floor he was slick with sweat, and we pulled off his jacket to find his shirt beneath soaking with it. Outside our room, his eyes rolled into his head, and his limbs jerked noiselessly in little shivering movements. By the time we heaved him onto the bed, it was clear he was going to die.

There were hours I do not remember, but

the day turned to night, and my legs were numb from kneeling. Doctor Mead was away studying abroad, so a different doctor was brought — one Daniel and I did not know, and who did not treat him with the familiar care we'd come to know from our friend. He asked me if Daniel had been suffering from headaches. I thought of the three or four times that year when the pains in his head had been so terrible they'd kept him in bed all day, but usually by evening he was recovered, sitting upright and eating supper from a tray. Perhaps a small part of me wondered if something was wrong, but I did not allow it to take shape in my mind, closing the door on it and retreating with my newspaper, telling myself it was all the liquor he drank. I had not — could not — allow myself to imagine losing somebody again, and wrongly thought that by taking a younger husband I would be spared from it for years, decades, even. I should have remembered that death as well as life was attracted to youth and beauty.

"The doctor said it was his brain," I told Eliza. "He complained of a headache at breakfast and died the same night."

She and Charlotte were both staring at me, grave and attentive. I picked up my spoon and began to eat, but I'd brought death into the room, and now it lingered like cigar smoke. Its presence remained in our house for a long time after Daniel, and sometimes I still went to Charlotte at night to check she was breathing. It had been twice an hour when she was a baby, even with the wet nurse slumped and snoring in the corner. I sought out the soft snuffle from her tiny nose, and touched her silky skin to check she was warm. She was not wary of me in her sleep, and her peace soothed me and made me feel all was safe, for now. Then she began to move herself, crawling and walking and rolling. There were stairs to fall down, fires to burn, small objects to swallow: coal, thimbles, candle stubs. I had them all guarded or set up high, out of reach of plump, sticky fingers. If I could have tied cushions to every surface and sanded every corner, I would.

"Tell me, Eliza," I said, "were your previous charges frequently struck down by illness?"

"No," was her reply. "They were solid little boys. I suppose they had the sniffles now and again, but they never had the pox or nothing."

Solid. Did Charlotte seem solid, with her paper-white skin and tiny frame? She did not have a large appetite, or the pink cheeks and fat legs of the children I saw in the street.

"Did you take them outside often?"

"They were always outside, madam. I could never get them in."

"And they caught no diseases?"

"No, madam."

"Not whooping cough, or chilblains?"

"Not one."

"Two young children out on the streets of London with the cesspits and rats and animal carcasses heaped in the street. You were not concerned for their health?"

"No, madam." Her voice was small.

I sighed and heaped applesauce onto my plate, though I'd lost my appetite. "That seems rather careless to me."

We ate in silence, and I had thought the conversation finished, but it seemed Eliza had only been thinking of her response.

"Many people *have* to go outside, madam," she said through a mouthful of potato, swallowing with relish. "Children don't always, that much is true, unless they work. But plenty of people live long lives who are outside all day. My brother's a crossing sweeper." She took another great mouthful and chewed gustily. "If anyone was going to drop down dead from disease, it'd be him, and he's never had so much as a measle in his life."

A crossing sweeper! And a father who rowed tobacco for a living. I regretted not asking Doctor Mead more about Eliza's family, having mindlessly assumed nurse-maids were the comfortable daughters of shopkeepers and counting house clerks. I should have known from her city accent that chimed of narrow tenements and five to a bed, and there had been that odd smell about her. I'd have Agnes clean her clothes tomorrow, though it was not Monday, and I'd speak to Doctor Mead, and tell him — what, exactly? That I was disappointed with Eliza's family? That he had brought me a common Cockney girl, and no matter how fond Charlotte was of her, she would learn nothing of value, of manners or refinement? I could imagine his expression, alert and helpful, and how I would sound: like a dreadful snob. I finished eating, dabbed my mouth, pushed my chair from the table, then left without saying a word.

Agnes was lighting the lamps in my parlor, so I went to the withdrawing room to look out. The street was dark, and a linkboy was directing a sedan chair to one of the houses opposite. Its occupant crawled out and paid the men. The linkboy pocketed the coin and put out his torch, and the three of them were swallowed by the night. I shivered and drew the drapes, and went to sit in my chair.

"I wonder if I have made a mistake," I told my parents after a long silence. I could not see their faces. It was cold, with no fires lit, and the idea of moving to the warmth and light of the parlor was inviting but felt like a great effort, and I was full from the food, and tired, so I allowed my eyes to close for a moment.

There was a small noise at the door, and very slowly I heard it open against the carpet. A lit candle appeared, throwing its warm glow over its beholder: a round face, with plump cheeks and dark eyes. It was Eliza. I sat very still in the shadows, and waited. She closed the door quietly behind her, and I watched the flame travel to the end of the room farthest from the door.

Her steps were tentative, her tread on the carpet silent. I moved my head very slightly and watched as she held the light up to the walls, as though searching for something. She walked the length of the room, behind my chair and all the way around, coming to a halt in front of me before the fireplace. As though at a fork in the road, she looked left at my father's picture, and right at my mother's, and decided to visit my father first, taking small, timid steps with the candle held aloft, and stopping a foot or two in front of him. Examining him with her head on one side, the lines of her shoulders dropped, as if she was disappointed. She stayed there for a moment or two, and both of us stared at him in the flickering light: his solemn brow, and kind eyes. Then she moved to my mother, illuminating parts of her — rosebud lips, golden curls — then letting them fall into shadow. She sighed, and the flame lowered, sending the weak light over the bureau positioned beneath mother's picture, and coming to rest at her waist. That was when I decided to speak.

"The artist got everything right except for the color of her eyes, which were more hazel than blue."

Eliza jumped out of her skin, letting out a girlish squeal that pierced the velvety peace of the room. She dropped the candle and it thudded dully to the floor and went out. I leaned over to retrieve it from where it had rolled toward my skirts just as the door flung open, revealing Agnes's frame silhouetted against the landing.

"Madam? Is that you?" she asked.

"Agnes, we will be needing a candle or two," I said. "Eliza's sadly went out. And the wax will have dried into the carpet; I'm not sure what you use for that but I do hope it will come out."

She looked blindly into the darkness, then nodded and descended the stairs. I heard Eliza's breathing — shallow and gasping — and could almost hear her heart thumping against her chest.

"Madam," she said. "I didn't know you was there."

"I go wherever I choose to in my house. You, however, may not. Before you leave, which you will imminently, and without a reference, do you wish to tell me why you were skulking around my withdrawing room in the dark?"

She was silent. Agnes reappeared with two lit candles, and her pupils were large and curious, roving from Eliza to me.

"Thank you, Agnes. I shall take them."

She put them both into my hands and closed the door. I stood and handed one to Eliza, holding the other up toward my mother's picture.

"This is my mother, Marianne. She was twenty-four when this was painted — my father commissioned it as a wedding present. She believed the background too dark and miserable; she would have liked clouds and blue skies, but instead got storm clouds and shadowy trees. Quite prophetic, as it transpired. It was as though the artist knew what was to come."

Eliza was staring at me, openmouthed, her black eyes shining.

"And my father, Patrick." I moved toward his picture in the left alcove, and she followed, dumb as a lamb. "Handsome, is he not? He was born in Barbados. Can you imagine such a place? He would tell me of it when I was a girl: the palm trees, and the warm winds, and the sun that blistered your skin if you stayed too long in it. He said the sea was bluer than anything you could imagine: bluer even than the sky, or a sapphire. He never could get warm in England. He wore a bed jacket under all his clothes."

I moved back toward my chair, taking my pool of light with me. "Now," I said. "You may tell me what you were doing tiptoeing about, or Doctor Mead, for I will send a note to have him attend in the first instance. If you shan't tell either of us, the night watchman will be passing soon, on his rounds. Whatever, it is your choice, but I will know."

The girl was quite rigid with fear; even her flame jerked anxiously, as though held too tight. "Madam," she said, ever so quietly. "I was doing no harm, I promise you that.

Only what you said at the dinner table earlier, about your husband dying . . . I wondered if there was a portrait of him somewhere in the house."

"And why," I asked, "might you want to see a portrait of my husband?"

"Only because he sounded so tragic, madam, if you don't mind my saying so. I wished to see him more clearly, in my mind. I am sorry if that was wrong of me."

I considered. "Impertinent, perhaps. Bold, certainly. Do I wish to have a bold nursemaid in my house, Eliza? Would you?"

She opened and closed her mouth.

"I do not," I said. "Nor do I wish to inspire such qualities in my daughter. Curiosity is a different matter, but not when it is improper."

"Oh, she is very curious," said Eliza, and there was a change in her voice. "She's asked me all sorts already, about myself and London and . . . everything, really."

I watched her steadily. Her face was lit from within as well as without, by something other than the naked flame.

"Is she?" I asked. "And what do you tell her?"

She lifted a shoulder. "This and that. Earlier I told her about the menageries on the Strand. Have you been? No, of course not. Sorry. There's a house with an elephant in it. And at one of the inns there's two camels in the stable."

"Camels at an inn? Are we in London or Bethlehem?"

She laughed, and immediately covered her mouth. "Wallis and Winifred, I think they are called. They stink to high heaven. And they spit. You don't want to go in twenty yards of 'em."

"What else is there?" I asked.

"There's a very odd creature. I forget its name. It looks like an elephant, but with short legs. And it has a big horn on its face, made of bone."

"You are teasing now."

"I ain't, I swear it! I saw it myself. Me and my friend went. They said it was from Africa so she wanted to go."

"Africa, here in London," I said. Even the word sounded rich and exotic. "I suppose they have different creatures there."

"You can pay sixpence and go and see the elephant. It's up a narrow flight of stairs, in a room overlooking the street, and it barely fits, the poor devil. Its feet are in chains, and its neck, but it's only the floorboards and the ceiling keeping it there, and I don't fancy their chances. They'll splinter like coals, I said. It looks like it could crush three men and their barrows with one swipe of its trunk. I didn't go too near myself. My friend, she knew the man on the door so we got in for thruppence each. He said we could go up again if it was quiet, but we didn't want to. Once I'd seen its eyes, I didn't want to see no more. I felt like I could see its soul. I didn't like looking at it."

"Why not?"

"It was . . . sad. I know it's an animal and it can't have feelings, but as I know my own name I know that creature was lonely. It weren't where it was meant to be."

We stood in silence for a moment as I tried to picture the leathery beast I'd seen only in engravings.

"Charlotte loves animals, don't she?" Eliza said.

"Yes," I sighed. "She has spoiled the kitchen cat, and made it fat, so now it's good for nothing but lying by the stove. She has a budgerigar, and a turtle. I won't get her a dog — I cannot bear the noise, or the hair, and the mess they make . . . no." Forgetting myself, I shook my head and stood. "I will write to Doctor Mead, and you will go and pack your things. You may tell Charlotte in the morning. Is she readying herself for bed?"

Eliza had the grace to look contrite. "Yes, madam," she said, without moving. We stood looking at one another, and I felt that she had several things to say but could not say them. I felt relief that I had a reason to release her, one that was not simply my own prejudice.

"Stay tonight, as it's dark now," I said. "But you will leave before breakfast." I opened the door for her, and followed her into the quiet house.

CHAPTER 11

An hour later, I was sitting in the fiery warmth of my parlor when Agnes announced Doctor Mead and admitted him, and the sight of my friend made me sit up with astonishment. His face was ghastly, his eyes dark, with violet smears beneath them.

"Doctor Mead," I said, going to him at once. "Whatever's the matter?"

He said thickly: "My grandfather has died."

We stood facing one another in the little room. I had a fleeting impulse to embrace him, quick and crackling as an ember sparking, and then it disappeared. I settled with placing a hand on his coat sleeve, which was damp.

"Agnes has not taken your coat," I said. "Here, let me do it for you. I will send for some brandy. Or would you prefer port? Or claret?"

He was at a loss for words, and clearly

heart-struck. I helped him off with his coat and went down to the study, where the best liquor was kept in a locked cabinet, deciding on impulse to dust off one of the nicer brandy bottles sent by my brother-in-law one Christmas. I had been waiting for the right moment to open it. In less than a minute I was back with Doctor Mead in the warm, low light of the parlor with two crystal glasses, unplugging the bottle and pouring with haste.

I could not look at him, because his grief was raw and exposing. He did not know how to sit with it yet, or what to do with it. I knew that feeling well.

"I am dreadfully sorry for your loss," I said. "To your grandfather." We clinked glasses and drank deeply, and he sat back in the stuffed chair as though something other than his coat had finally been removed.

"When did it happen?" I asked.

"This morning." He ran a hand over his face and rescued the strands of hair fallen from beneath his hat. Then he removed the hat altogether and set it on the floor by his feet. "He was eighty. A remarkable age, as they say. Still, it only meant we had longer with him, and loved him all the more."

"Should you be at home? I am sorry to have called you here. Had I known . . ."

"Home," he said hollowly. "With my servants?"

"No, with your family."

"Grief falls to the women to manage," Doctor Mead said. "My mother is very busy at his house, and I would only get in her way."

I knew Doctor Mead had a flock of sisters, and a shepherdess of a mother who tended them, and was so consumed by them and their families that her only son was quite neglected. His father had died years before, and his mother still inhabited their Berkeley Square mansion and kept a busy calendar of appointments, though she must have been sixty. With so many women to provide for, and so many babies to care for at the Foundling, it was a wonder Doctor Mead found the time to shave.

"I am sorry," I said. "At least London is still left with one Doctor Mead."

He gave an effort at a smile, and with nothing more to say, we drank again.

"What was it you wanted of me?" he asked after a short silence.

"Me?" For a moment I was lost, and then I remembered. Eliza. That encounter across the landing an hour ago. It all seemed quite insignificant now. I did not trust her, but then I did not trust anyone.

I looked into Doctor Mead's face, helpful and giving, and decided I could not disappoint him unnecessarily. The man had had enough unhappiness for one day. "Oh," I said. "Charlotte had a slight cough, but I think she shall live." *Live!* How callous. "What I mean to say is she is already recovered a great deal. A childish fever, gone as quickly as it arrived."

"I am glad to hear it. Would you like me to look at her?"

"No, no. There is no need. You are not working tonight."

A trace of a smile passed his mouth. "That is most unlike you, Mrs. Callard. Usually you have me check her at the slightest sniff."

"Perhaps I am growing negligent in my old age."

He smiled. "How many years have we known one another now?"

"We moved here eleven years last month. You were still a scholar then, I think."

"I was. I remember thinking how grown-up Cal seemed, marrying you and starting his business, and I still at Cambridge."

"I forgot you called him that."

"I have called him worse still."

I was glad to see him diverted; that I had diverted him.

We watched the fire crack and pop. The drapes were closed against the cold, and in my little ship's cabin, with my eyes half-closed and the other chair filled, I could almost pretend Daniel was with me. The singular thing I missed about having a husband was masculine company. When women talked to one another it was of domestic things, like servants and drapers. Men spoke of ships and business and foreign shores. I could not contribute, but when Daniel brought acquaintances to the house I would listen in rapture.

We were only married four years, and though it was the shortest era of my life, I learned more in it than in all the years before and since. Four winters, four summers. Had I known that would be all, would I have tried to go out with him? Strolled around the square on a warm spring evening? Taken the carriage to the theater? Should I have climbed the narrow stairs on the Strand to show him the elephant wreathed in chains?

"Alexandra?"

I started. Doctor Mead had narrowed the space between us, one side of his face warm in the firelight. He held it there and did not move, and before I turned away something passed between us.

213

"Your glass is empty. How negligent of me." I filled it halfway again. "Tell me, will your grandfather's funeral be held at the Foundling chapel? He was very fond of the hospital."

"Yes, that I know. But Temple Church is the place, according to his wishes. Will you come?"

With great difficulty I shook my head.

"Of course. Forgive me. It would cause you distress."

I imagined him climbing the stairs to his bedroom tonight, and blowing out his candle, and pulling the sheets over himself; the hollow space next to him. He said in jest he was married to his work, but his work could not place a comforting hand on his arm, or bring him a cup of chocolate, or hold him close when the grief came in the darkest part of the night. As well as his work at the Foundling, he attended the poorest neighborhoods, going to the coffeehouses at Holborn and St. Giles, and administering to those who could pay a penny's entrance. Sometimes he went with them to their homes, their dank rooms and hovels, if a baby or a wife was ailing. He would not charge them, but they would pay him: with flour, with candles — trifles that he could not refuse because to do so would be to offend them. His grandfather had done the same, even in old age, and was deeply respected for it.

"You are tired," he said. "Thank you for the brandy."

"No, I am not. Stay. Tell me about your grandfather. Tell me about the other Doctor Mead."

He moved his glass from one hand to the other. The liquid glowed through the chasms of crystal. "What would you like to know?"

"We may as well start at the beginning, so I would like to know where he was born, first of all."

"Stepney, of all places."

"Then he has come a long way to Bloomsbury."

He smiled. "That he has. Do you know he lived in Italy? He has a degree from the University of Padua. That is the reason I studied there, too. And," he went on, warming to his instruction, "he attended Queen Anne on her deathbed."

"He did no such thing."

"That he did! She had a very great thirst toward the end, and no drink would quench it. He advised grapes, and the next time he went to her there were platters of them all around the room; thousands of them."

"And he was the king's physician, was he not?"

"He was. Though, if I may be frank, I found his work at the coffeehouses more impressive than the court. That was where he did his best work. That is the man I wish to become."

"That is the man you are," I said.

A thoughtful silence. "One of his friends called at Great Ormond Street to pay his respects today. A writer. What did he say? Let me remember it . . ." He narrowed his eyes and the tip of his tongue appeared thoughtfully at his lips. " 'Your grandfather lived more in the broad sunshine of life than almost any man,' he said to me. I'll never forget that, as long as I live."

We sat in contemplation, and I realized I had not once thought about anything other than where I was, and what was being said. It was an unfamiliar sensation. Maria would be preparing supper in the kitchen; Agnes would be warming the sheets; Charlotte would be put to bed on the floor above.

And then, as though my remembering her conjured her into the room, Doctor Mead said: "How is Eliza faring?"

I thought of her quiet tread on the carpet, her curious flame. Her mouth filled with potatoes, and her tales of camels and elephants. She had been here a day yet it felt like a month, as though she fit into some vacant space that none of us had known existed. I decided I would keep her in employment for now. For my friend.

"She is tolerable," I said.

He raised his brow. "Tolerable?"

"It has not yet been a day."

"I hope she has not displeased you?"

I could tell him. I could disappoint him, and splinter his spirit further. I set my glass down on the table and licked my lips. "You are well acquainted with me by now, Doctor Mead. I would find fault with *you* if you began working for me, at first."

He smiled, and seemed pleased. "I confess I'm not certain I'd make a splendid nursemaid." What he said next surprised me. "What do you think Daniel would make of it?"

"I have not given it much thought. He may have commented on the imbalance of females in the house, but then he might have found it quite entertaining, too."

"I am inclined to think it would be the latter."

"He had no siblings, after all. Though with no inheritance to speak of, he did not care for children."

"But you had Charlotte," he said kindly.

"He did not leave you quite alone. What a shame it is that he never met her. What a shame it is that I was not here."

"You were in Padua. I had my sister. Ambrosia was all I needed, and often too much." After a moment, I said: "I am sorry not to come to the funeral."

"Think not on it."

We sat in pleasant quiet. I had never asked Doctor Mead what opinion he had of me when we met, a week or two after the wedding. That I was twenty-nine and not a widow was deeply shocking; the only unmarried women of that age were either creatures of mourning or creatures of the night. I had no wish to be a society wife, with the doorknocker always going, serving custard tarts and punch from dainty cups, and at such an age I did not know if I could be a mother. Thankfully, Daniel did not give much thought to what he wanted, and took me for what I was. Most brides felt love and happiness on their wedding day, having pursued them for many years. I felt relief. I had searched for safety all my life and found it at last.

Eliza settled into life at Devonshire Street, and her routine went like this: at six o'clock she rose, made the fire, brought the water and ate breakfast. At seven she woke Charlotte and washed her with a sponge, after which she rubbed her quite dry and dressed her. Charlotte had previously cleaned herself, but now Eliza could do it for her, and examine her for signs of approaching disease. When she was ready, Eliza delivered her to me for breakfast and returned to the nursery to open the windows, shake the beds and clear the slops. Charlotte read to me for an hour and we did our lessons as usual: arithmetic, French and the pianoforte, plus Italian one morning a week. Eliza mended Charlotte's things while she was occupied, then Charlotte joined her for needlework, which I had never taught her. The two of them would play chess and cards in the afternoon, then Eliza would wash Charlotte's hands and prepare her for dinner, to be served promptly at five o'clock. Within three days Eliza had fashioned two cotton handkerchiefs with plain borders from Charlotte's outgrown nightdresses. On the fifth day we went to church together in the carriage, and sat in our usual pew, attracting several curious glances at our expanded party. Eliza kept her eyes down modestly, and was altogether meeker and more subservient than I had ever seen her. Doctor Mead was absent, and I said a prayer for his health, and for his grand-father.

One morning, a week after Eliza arrived, a letter from Ambrosia lay propped against the salt and pepper pots at breakfast like a fourth guest. I was overjoyed, and took it to my parlor to enjoy later, where it winked at me from the mantelpiece. It was a bright, cold day with a crisp white sky sitting atop the houses, and I was halfway through the *General Advertiser* when I was roused from my reading by an almighty noise above my head, like furniture being thrown about. I hurried upstairs to find Charlotte's bedroom door thrown wide open, and a flurry of skirts through the doorframe. She and Eliza were hand in hand, flushed and smiling, with their hair come loose from their caps, leaping from one foot to the other and laughing.

"What is this racket?" I demanded.

Eliza straightened at once, but Charlotte did not let go of her hands. "We were danc-ing, Mama! Eliza is teaching me a jig."

I was quite speechless.

"We will stop, if we are making too much noise, madam," the nursemaid said.

"You are making *far* too much noise. I thought the wardrobe was being chopped for firewood."

She put a hand to her mouth to cover her laugh, and Charlotte cackled with glee. It was an unfamiliar sound, bursting from her quite naturally.

"If you please, madam, we could practice in the yard."

"Outside? No, that will not do."

"*Please*, Mama. Look, I have almost learned it." Charlotte began prancing about in a lively way, her cap skewed and her hair flying all over.

"I cannot imagine a time nor ocassion for which you should need to know that dance. Now stop crashing about, you are disturbing me."

"If you let us go outside we will stay where you can see us, madam. We'd be less noisy out there."

"Yes, the yard, the yard, the yard!" Charlotte began shouting.

"That's enough!" I sighed. "Go now, before you give me a headache."

They ran out before I could change my mind, tumbling over one another to get to the stairs, and I called after them to lock the back gate.

Charlotte's bedroom was a riot of toys and games, with spinning tops tipped on their sides, dominoes scattered like leaves and dolls flung on their backs. This would not do; I would tell Eliza later. But almost immediately a different thought arrived: this is what my own nursery had looked like when I was a child, when I'd involve Ambrosia in my elaborate games. Charlotte now had her plaything, her companion, who I had never been able to give her. I sighed, and closed the door.

The walled area at the back of the house was no larger than seven or eight yards by three, as were all the others on Devonshire Street and the terrace beyond. Eliza and Charlotte were bundled against the cold — Eliza in her plain wool cloak, though her hands were bare, and Charlotte in the thick serge one she wore for church. Her own hands were plugged into a muff, and peering from her cloak were kid leather boots that were so rarely worn outside they hardly needed cleaning. I watched the pair jig about, hemmed in by three brick walls like pigs in a pen, their breath steaming from them in little clouds. A large tabby cat appeared on the wall overlooking the alley, and Charlotte pointed in delight. The cat regarded them with indifference as they went to look at it, and the next thing I knew, Eliza was lifting Charlotte up and Charlotte was pulling a hand from her muff and reaching out to touch it. I felt my mouth fall open to shout at her to stop, but a pane of glass separated us. I could only watch as she stroked the fat creature once, twice, before it had enough and toppled from the wall and out of sight. As though sensing my attention, Eliza glanced over her shoulder at the house and saw me watching, giving me a half smile before crouching down to speak to Charlotte. She pointed up and Charlotte followed her finger, and they both waved. After a moment I raised a hesitant hand in return, noticing how similar they looked from a distance, with their pale round faces and dark hair and straight brows that huddled on their foreheads. I felt curiously detached, as though they were perfect strangers. Then they dropped their hands and turned again to each other, and I retreated self-consciously from sight, feeling as though I had waved them off on a ship bound for some faraway port, while I was left ashore.

Searching for distraction, I reached for Ambrosia's letter, and went to fetch the letter opener from the bureau beneath the window, glancing as I did through the panes again, and seeing not two shapes but three.

A man was standing on the other side of the wall, peering over, and Eliza held a protective arm around Charlotte's shoulder.

Terror struck me at once, but before I could rush downstairs I was struck by the man's expression. It was not fierce or leering, but pleading. He had red hair curling beneath a black cap, and paper-pale skin, and his coat was far too thin for February — a beggar, surely, for Eliza was shaking her head, telling him no, and I felt light-headed with panic as I imagined him taking out a sheath or a pistol. I hurried downstairs with all manner of scenarios racing through my mind: him blowing holes in their heads, or slicing them into ribbons and leaving them to leak their life into the mud. I reached the kitchen stairs and bolted down them, barging past Maria, who was kneading dough at the scrubbed table.

"M-madam?" she stuttered as I flung open the door.

Three faces looked upon me, startled by the noise.

"Charlotte," I said slowly, clearly, as one might address a spooked horse. "Come to me at once." My breath clouded before me. She looked up at her nursemaid, who nodded, and came obediently toward me, standing at my side. Maria watched from the doorway, her rolling pin brandished like a weapon.

"Eliza, who is this man?"

Her voice was weak and frightened. "It's my brother, madam."

"Your *brother*?"

My eyes traveled over what little of him I could see upward of his dirty neck. He did not have his sister's dark coloring, though they had the same wide mouth and prominent cheeks. Come to think of it, Eliza did have a glint of red about her hair, like firelight shining on a chestnut shell. I took the measure of him, and he me from half a dozen yards away, while Eliza stood mute between us.

"Brush off, Ned," she said eventually. "Go on."

He nodded and scratched his head, and with a final glance at me he disappeared downward, as though a trapdoor had opened beneath him. He must have been standing on something to look over the wall, which had been built at a height for privacy and security, so that people wandering down the path behind could not help themselves to whatever was drying in the yard or look in, yet here was Eliza's brother, doing precisely that, no doubt during a break from shoveling manure in the streets.

"We do not have visitors at this house," I said when we were all back in the kitchen, and the door locked. I was white with fury.

"I didn't invite him, madam," the girl said.

"Then what was the purpose of his visit?"

"Whose visit?" Agnes came in with a pail of used tea leaves for cleaning the carpets, and set it on the table. The rolling pin clattered to the floor, and Maria bent her wide frame to retrieve it.

"I dunno, madam," Eliza said. "He knows I live here now, so I expected he wanted to see how I was coming along."

"He is not welcome at Devonshire Street again."

Eliza nodded, but looked troubled for the rest of the day. Each time I looked at her I wondered if the man really was her brother, inquiring of his sister's welfare, or if his visit had a different purpose altogether.

Eliza Smith was a puzzle to me, and I had never been one for games.

That night I lay awake with the bedcurtains and drapes open, looking at the moon. Its misty face hung above the backs of the houses in Gloucester Street opposite, shining through powdery clouds. I had sat up late writing to Ambrosia, who had reached the northeast safely and found a house to rent on the outskirts of Durham, belonging to a duke who wintered on the continent. There were several acres, she wrote, and a stable block full of horses, and they went riding together, when the children were not running about like puppy dogs getting perfectly filthy. Knowing she had arrived safely, I felt a loosening — my jaw, I realized, had been clenched for a fortnight, and I pushed my fingers into it, kneading the tension, and poured myself a glass of brandy from the decanter beneath the window to celebrate her safe arrival.

The clock in the hallway distantly chimed midnight. My stomach burned from the drink, and my stomach was empty. I wanted some bread and cheese, and decided to make my way downstairs, my stockinged feet soundless on the carpets. In the basement there was a chink of light around the kitchen door, and low voices, and I pushed it open to find Eliza and Agnes at the kitchen table. Eliza had her back to the range, and Agnes sat facing the door. They had the solemn, furtive look of men at a card game, and if they were startled to see me they did not show it, nor I them. I pulled my bed jacket tighter around me, though the kitchen was still warm, with dying embers in the range.

"Madam," said Agnes. "We thought you was a spook."

"I thought there might be some bread and

cheese left over from supper."

Agnes got up, busying herself in the larder. Eliza would not look at me, examining her nails and then rubbing at knife marks on the table.

"I hope you shall not be tired in the morning," I said.

"No, madam," she said softly.

I had interrupted some private exchange, most likely about myself.

Agnes set a small glass of milk in front of me and unwrapped the cheese from its cloth. I stood waiting for Eliza to leave, but she did not.

"I heard Charlotte stirring on my way down," I said.

Without looking at me, she peeled herself from the table and padded quietly from the room.

"What were you and Eliza discussing?" I asked Agnes.

She arranged a heel of bread and some cheese on a plate. In the light from the single flame, the lines on her face looked deeper. "This and that. Time ran away with us." She yawned. "I should be going up."

I checked the back door, and Agnes closed the shutters and took the candle, and we made our wordless pilgrimage to bed.

CHAPTER 12

"Agnes, there is a Negro outside my house."

A young woman in a sable-colored skirt and black jacket was standing outside the dining room window, looking up and down the street as though waiting for somebody. Her hair was tucked into a mobcap and she was quite composed. I wondered if she belonged to one of the larger houses on the square, but there was something about her air and the way she dressed that made her seem like her own woman, belonging to no one. I had read about the blackamoor population of London, who lived mainly in the east around the rookeries of Moorgate and Cripplegate, and who had never been slaves at all. The children of freed men and women, they kept their own trades and lived in lodging houses like the rest of working London. My father had been raised on a sugar plantation in Barbados, and I wondered what he would make of this woman, who appeared as ordinary and unremarkable as any English person.

Agnes, who had been clearing the breakfast things, stopped piling porcelain onto her tray and joined me at the window. "Well, I never," she said. "She looks as though she hasn't a care in the world."

"Where do you think she is from?" I asked.

"I'll be off, Agnes," came Eliza's voice at the doorway. It was Sunday, and Eliza's first half day since she'd joined the household. She had said she would not join us at chapel, if it was agreeable to me, so that she might visit her family. Charlotte's face had fallen dramatically, as though she could not bear to be left with me, and it had put me in a sour mood.

I imagined Eliza stepping out into the clear morning with her basket on her arm, weaving through Bloomsbury, where the handsome houses and green squares would eventually give way to crumbling tenements and alleys so narrow you could stand at a window and shake the hand of the person in the one opposite. I tried to imagine her home, one or two rooms, simply furnished, with her father and red-headed brother sitting at a table eating a roasted bird with their fingers. I wondered if she should bake her clothes when she returned: the city was where the plague had spread, among other diseases.

She noticed me with Agnes and came over. "What you looking at?"

"She is quite well dressed," I observed.

"I'll tell her to move on," Eliza said quickly. "I'm leaving now, anyway."

Charlotte was waiting for her in the hall, and when her nursemaid embraced her, she clung to her skirts like a barnacle made of brocade. I watched as she pulled at Eliza's sleeve, and Eliza leaned down to listen as the child put her lips to her ear.

"Yes, of course I'm coming back," she said. "I'll be here before dinner to wash your hands. All right?"

But the child's frown did not smooth, and her mouth was set in a worried line. Eliza had shown her how to sleep with her hair in rags so it tumbled into curls, and this morning she had decorated them with ribbons.

"Charlotte, leave your nursemaid at once and fetch your hat for church. The carriage will be here any moment."

Agnes rattled off with the tray, and when she had gone I heard Eliza's and Charlotte's hushed voices in the hall.

"Don't be sad," Eliza was saying. "You're going to church with Mama, and you'll come back and feed your budgie and your

231

turtle, and tidy your things away, and then I'll be back before it's dark."

"What time?"

"Three o'clock."

"Where are you going?" Charlotte whimpered, sounding as though she'd buried her face in Eliza's front.

"I'm meeting my friend, and we're going to walk about for a bit, and when we're so cold we can't feel our hands, we're going to find a nice, warm chophouse for something to eat. And then I'll go to my brother's house and see my niece and nephew, then I'll call on my old man and then I'll come back!"

"You won't get lost?"

She laughed. "No, I won't get lost. I best go."

But Charlotte began weeping. Her quiet little sobs floated into the dining room, where I stood clutching the hard-backed chair. "Please don't," she said.

I went to the door. "Stop weeping at once," I commanded. "Eliza is entitled to her half day, and you have managed without her these six years."

Charlotte pulled away from Eliza's stomach and regarded me with pure contempt. Her hot, dark eyes burned, and her face was scrunched into a scowl. "I want to go with her."

"You will do no such thing."

"I *want* to!" She stamped her foot on the floor, making me exclaim.

I gripped her wrist and shook her. "Oh, you insolent child. Go to your room at once. You will not come to church with me, nor will you play in the yard this week. Go!"

She fixed me with a most vicious stare, then turned on her heel and fled, leaving me with Eliza. The nursemaid glanced at the stairs where Charlotte had disappeared and, after a moment, said: "Shall I stay, madam?"

"No."

She swallowed. "Will you still go to church?"

"My attendance is expected."

"You'll leave her here alone?"

"She will not be *alone,* with the cook and the maid. You may lock her in her bedroom, and then you may go. The key is kept on the mantelpiece in my bedroom, in the pink vase. I shall let you explain to the child why she is being punished, if she does not understand already. When I return from church I will expect her bedroom to be locked, and the key returned to its rightful place. Is that understood?"

She nodded, looking at her feet. I returned to the dining room to watch for the carriage, and saw the Negro woman still standing there, looking patiently up and down. A few minutes later I heard the street door close beneath the dining room window, and Eliza came up the steps and opened the black gate.

I could not see her face. She spoke briefly to the woman, who smiled pleasantly when she saw Eliza, but the smile faded when Eliza spoke, and she nodded, and moved on up the road. Eliza watched her go, and pulled her cloak tighter around her. She glanced back at the house, catching my eye and looking instantly away, then walked south, toward the city. She had only just disappeared from view when the black carriage rolled up, the horses' breath pluming in misty fronds in the cold morning.

I was always anxious about venturing outside, and now I stood for a full minute at the front door, my nerves jangling like marbles in a bag. They were set off so easily; perhaps it was Charlotte's retaliation; perhaps that Eliza was leaving Charlotte and me alone for the first time in almost a month. Perhaps it was the effortless way she left the house, walking purposefully off into the great, teeming city. Or perhaps it was the way my child loved her nursemaid more than me.

"Madam," came Agnes's voice. "Henry is arrived with the coach."

She saw me off at the door with a gentle push, and rubbed the tops of my arms as the chill flowed in. Henry helped me into the coach, and we trundled through the streets, turning right into Great Ormond Street, where the late Doctor Mead had lived, directing my thoughts once again to his grandson. The funeral had been and gone, and I had not been there to support my friend, but I thought of him all day, and imagined how it would be to smile up at him from a pew, and have him find strength in my presence.

"No pretty daughter today, Mrs. Callard?" said an older woman at the church as we were handed our hymn books by a well-dressed Foundling boy. I recognized her as Mrs. Cox, the wife of a Whig Party member. She was wearing cornflower blue and maize-gold silk, and her gray wig sat higher than most. I shook my head and tried to move on.

"Might you be visiting Richard Mead's house after the service? The auction begins today."

"Auction?"

"Of the late doctor's estate. There are thousands of items for sale: paintings, artifacts, books. Some of them quite rare. Did you not read about it in the newssheets? It has been widely reported in our circles." She placed an emphasis on *our,* which served to exclude me, a mere merchant's widow.

I was at a loss for words. An auction meant the old man had died in debt, but Doctor Mead had given no indication. "I must go home after the service," I said.

"All of London will be clamoring to get its hands on his Rembrandts and Hogarths. I heard there are even first editions of Shakespeare."

"Good day, Mrs. Cox."

After the service I went directly to Doctor Mead, who was beside his usual pew, flanked by hangers-on, whom I longed to scatter like a cloud of flies. A full five minutes passed before the final well-wishers bade him farewell with a lift of their hats.

"Alexandra," he said with a smile, taking my gloved hands in his.

"How was the funeral?"

"Magnificent."

"Only you could say such a thing. Befitting of Richard, then."

"Thank you, it was. No Charlotte today?"

"She is tired this morning. I let her rest. What is this talk of an auction?"

His expression changed at once. He shook his head. "Grandfather left the world with little more than he arrived with."

I frowned. "How little?"

"He left a large amount of bills unpaid. A large amount of *large* bills. And as you know, he departed this life with no time to set his affairs in order, so you can imagine there was quite a swarm."

"A shock, I'm sure, but I hope not a disastrous one?"

"Disaster can be avoided if we sell everything."

"Everything?"

"I must go. I'm sorry. The exhibition at his house starts now. I won't ask if you can come." He spoke kindly, but his words stung all the same. "I shall call at Devonshire Street when I can."

A short woman in a blue bonnet passed and placed a hand on his arm, wishing him good day.

"I wish to buy something," I said abruptly. "In the auction."

He blinked in surprise. "You do?"

"Yes. Your favorite item of his. Buy it for yourself, from me. As a gift. Whatever the price."

He opened and closed his mouth. "That is very generous. But I assure you not necessary."

"It is quite necessary to me. Your grandfather was a generous man, and we must do the same by him."

"Doctor Mead!" came a voice. We were interrupted yet again by two men in elaborate wigs, who passed their hands for the doctor to shake. "Let us accompany you to Great Ormond Street."

"We shouldn't want to miss a thing," the other said, and before I could say goodbye they were carrying him off, clutching one sleeve apiece. He made a helpless face and waved goodbye, and I waved back, and felt my joy draining.

In the carriage on the way home I lifted the curtain at the corner of Great Ormond Street to see it thronged with revelers, as though some country fair was taking place. The door to Richard Mead's house stood open to the street and a queue of bonnets and tricorn hats trailed in a ribbon down the road, with passersby stopping to inquire and broughams slowing to a standstill.

"Vermin," I muttered to no one in particular, and dropped the drape, returning to darkness.

As soon as I arrived home I went straight to the bureau in my bedroom. As instructed, Eliza had replaced the key to Charlotte's door in the pink vase on the mantelpiece, and I pocketed it, took out my private box, finding what I wanted and holding it in my palm. I went down to Charlotte's room, unfastening the lock. She was sitting quite still on her narrow bed, not looking out at the street or playing with her toys or doing any of the other things she did usually to occupy herself. She looked up hopefully, and found my face, and hers in response fell.

Oh, it said. *You are not Eliza.*

"Do you now regret your earlier behavior?" I asked.

"Yes, Mama," she said in a small voice.

"You were asked for at church today, by Doctor Mead and Mrs. Cox. I had to tell them you had misbehaved."

She looked glumly at her lap, and I felt a twinge of remorse. How was it that the love for a child was the most complex of all? How could one feel envy, grief and rejection at the same time as simple, uncluttered affection? How was it that I could barely touch her, yet would know her smell blind-folded, and could draw every freckle on her face?

I went to stand before her, and she raised her head expectantly, her little chin jutting out in defiance. Her hair was loose over her shoulders, and she was still wearing her outdoor boots. If I knelt to take them off, would she think me soft, and changed? I decided instead to sit next to her, and felt the little bed creak beneath me.

"Look at this," I said, taking out Daniel's memento mori from my pocket and holding it flat on my palm.

"What is it?" She took it from me, and it filled almost her whole hand.

"I commissioned it when your father died."

She gazed at the woman collapsed against the plinth in her theatrical display of grief. "Is that you?" she breathed.

"Heavens, no. It is symbolic. This is your father's hair." I indicated the painted strands molded to the ivory, and she traced them with her fingertip.

"Do you wear it?"

"Not anymore. I keep it safe in my bed-room. You'll have it one day."

"When is Eliza back?" she asked.

Our moment was over before it had even

begun. I closed my fingers and stood. "Take off your boots and tidy your toys. Eliza will return soon."

I suppose I had entertained the notion that she might not return. I entertained it every time Agnes and Maria took their monthly leave, too. London lay outside like an open jaw, ready to swallow whomever chose to disappear, and servants who were paid far more than mine left houses far grander. The idea of it unnerved me. It was why I kept the house warm, the bedsheets clean, the larder full: to atone for my odd behaviors, my stony countenance. I'd set in my mold for too long to change, so instead I ordered wax candles for their bedrooms and bought them presents for their birthdays: boxes of sugared almonds, and bolts of calico. No servants loved their masters and mistresses; that was the stuff of sentimental ballads and children's stories. But both my servants were allowed to use their voices, had some degree of authority, and had stayed loyal these ten years. Trust was imperative, of course, and was earned, not demanded. Most other households had men at the head of them and litters of dimpled children to clean and feed and squeeze, but there was something neat about a house of women,

241

and, I hoped, safe. Providing a safe place to live was my mission, my purpose, at the center of my very existence.

But return Eliza did, with rosy cheeks and the smells of the city clinging to her: cold air, straw, manure and the tobaccoey fug of eating houses. She came through the street door, and before she could even place a hand on the gate Charlotte had come stampeding down the stairs to greet her, taking the corners like a whippet and colliding with Eliza's skirts in a heap in front of the range. The pair of them burst out laughing and embraced in such a dramatic display of affection I expected a stage curtain to close over them. I had been in the kitchen asking Agnes to place an order for a mourning brooch for Doctor Mead, to help lift his heartache. I had drawn the design myself in my parlor, and pushed it over the table to Agnes with as much dignity as I could muster, though my neck was warm.

Eliza unwound her shawl and held her frozen hands to her hot cheeks, then put them over the oven. "My pa didn't have the fire on," she said. "Neither did my brother. I've grown used to being warm all day, living here."

"How is your brother?" I asked. There was a straightforward fondness to the way she

242

spoke about him, but she did not reply immediately, and her face darkened.

"He ain't in good health," she said.

"Oh. Then I wish him a swift recovery."

She thanked me, handing Charlotte a roast chestnut she'd bought, then watching her eat it happily, but the shine in her eyes had gone. Charlotte ate her chestnut and beamed up at her, and that twinge came again — of envy, and fear — because I knew that she loved her, and one day Eliza would leave, to get married or else find work somewhere more unconventional, breaking Charlotte's heart as she went.

spoke about him, but she did not reply im-
med ...ely, and her face darkened.
"He ...ine in good spirits," she said.
"...hen I ..." ... ...
She blinked ... ... Oh.
... ...
... ...
... ...
... ...
... ...

CHAPTER 13

He arrived before noon, and I heard Agnes's feet in the hall. I stood and went to the looking glass, and tidied my hair and neatened my necklace. My heart hummed, and a year went by before I heard Agnes's knock at the withdrawing room door, during which I sat, and stood, then sat again.

"Mrs. Callard." Doctor Mead was smiling as he stepped into the room. Then I noticed shadows beneath his eyes and a dusting of stubble at his jaw.

"You are tired," I said.

"Am I? I suppose I am."

"You have not slept?"

He sighed and took the seat opposite mine. "Winter is always brutal. Four children at the Foundling have died since January. The last was buried this morning." Tiny lines had appeared at the edges of his eyes, like cracks in plaster.

"That is dreadful. I am sure you did all

you could. And winter is finally leaving us now, besides."

He nodded without conviction, and sipped his tea. I searched for a topic to divert him. "How goes the auction?"

"It limps on like a half-dead mule."

"But your grandfather passed weeks ago."

"Yes, and it shows no sign of ending. When I am not at the hospital I spend all my time at his house, helping my mother and sisters to comb through his things like a mud lark, meeting with the auctioneers and packaging things for the Exeter Exchange. Tomorrow the library will be valued. There are thousands of books — more than a man could read in ten lifetimes. It's quite the circus." He gave a great yawn.

"Oh, dear," was all I could say. "You've no aunts or uncles who can help?"

"My two aunts are both dead so it falls to my mother."

I stroked the little varnished box tucked secretly between my skirts. Was now the right time? I decided that it was.

"This is a gift from me," I said, handing it to him, and feeling my heart flutter again. He took it, looking at me in a curious, child-like way, and our fingers touched. I watched him open the lid and unwrap the silk parcel inside.

"It's a mourning brooch," I said as it fell out onto his palm. It had arrived that morning, and was just as I'd hoped: oval-shaped enamel, inlaid with an engraving of a young man in a tricorn hat setting a wreath on a marble plinth. There were tiny words the size of pinheads on the plinth that read: *Friendship in Marble, Injuries in Dust,* and propped against it was a gold-topped walking cane, for the late doctor never took a step without his, and was quite famous for it.

I watched his face as he gazed upon it. It was unreadable. He spent so long regarding it I thought he had fallen into a reverie, and was about to ask if he was quite well when he looked suddenly at me, his eyes shining with tears. He was quite speechless, and nodded his thanks, and I found tears at my own eyes. It felt, then, as though my heart left my body altogether.

I composed myself. "I know they are rather feminine articles, so do not feel obliged to wear it. It's more a keepsake. I have one that I cherish very dearly, which I take out every so often to look at."

"The cane. *His* cane." He was smiling properly now, where it reached his eyes, and I realized he had not managed this in weeks.

"It is gold leaf. I could not resist."

He tucked the box inside his green frock coat. I poured more tea and stirred in the sugar, and with the sounds of Devonshire Street drifting in from below I felt quite content.

"There is a bit of space in the hall I have meant for years to fill with a picture," I went on. "I should still like to buy one of your grandfather's pieces, if they have not all been sold."

"Not at all," he said. "What sort of thing would you like? A landscape? A Hogarth? Name your scene; I'm sure he'll have it."

I smiled. "You may surprise me. Name *your* painting, and your price."

"Very well. My mother will likely have me bid against the whole of Mayfair, but I shall win your prize, Mrs. Callard."

"What will happen to his house?"

"He left it to me. I had the idea of turning it into a medical school, so physicians might study there."

"I think that sounds marvelous, and exactly what he would have wanted?"

"Yes. I imagine he would rather have liked the idea of it becoming a place of learning."

"Would you not live in it, though, and give up your lease on Bedford Row?"

He considered the question. "His house is

large. It would be wasted on a man with no family."

I set my cup gently on my saucer. My throat felt thick. "Is that something you want?"

He sighed. "Perhaps. There is something that I want more, though."

I was very still. "And what is that?" It came out as a whisper.

He stared at the empty hearth, with its pyramid of fresh wood, and his eyes were thoughtful. "I would like nothing more than to walk, with no direction, under an open sky, with a hot pie in my hand, and be away from auctioneers, and my mother and sisters, and drawing rooms and Great Ormond Street, and sick and dying children, for one afternoon. I wish to see trees and flowers and no carriages, and not have a single person stop me and offer their condolences, or ask me about an ailment their father's brother's wife's cousin has, or tell me about their unmarried niece, who just happens to be visiting in London, and am I looking for a wife? Because I have a great many assets, and a good profession and family, and a unbetrothed man in possession of all those things is rarer than a white peacock."

I was quite silent. And then I said: "I have

read they have white peacocks at the Ranelagh Pleasure Gardens."

He stared at me, and then he began laughing: a hearty, rolling, delighted laugh that brought such great joy that I could not help but laugh, too, though I had been entirely serious. Tears ran down our faces, and after a minute or two we collected ourselves, and sat back holding our stomachs, feeling quite giddy.

"Then that settles it," he said, wiping his eyes. "There I shall go. I wish you would join me." I shifted in my seat, but before I could murmur my excuses, he went on: "But I shall not ask it of you."

"I'm sorry, Doctor Mead." I meant it.

He was watching me with an expression so tender I had to look away. What he wanted was the simplest thing in the world: to walk together, arm in arm. It was the most ordinary desire, yet I could not do it for him. If only I could, I would bid him wait while I ran upstairs for my hat, and meet him at the front door, pulling my gloves on and asking if we should take his carriage or mine, thinking nothing of it, looking forward to it, even. For most people, leaving their house was as uncomplicated as writing a letter, or eating a meal.

"You must have somebody to go with," I

told him.

"There is nobody with whom I wish to walk in companionship," he said. "And a man may not attend a pleasure garden alone without attracting attention of an undesirable kind."

"Yes, you must beware of thieves and opportunists," I warned.

He laughed again, and I knew at once what he had meant, and turned scarlet at my own unworldliness.

"Eliza will go with you," I announced suddenly. I'd said it almost before I had thought it, and when the words came from my lips they surprised us both.

"Eliza?" he said. "Your Eliza?"

"Yes. This afternoon. I can spare her an hour or two, if that is what you wish to do."

He considered it, and set his saucer carefully on the table. "That would be splendid. Are you quite sure?"

"Quite. She is a London girl, and very capable. You will be safe with her. Let me fetch her."

I found the two of them in the dining room, pretending to take tea while Charlotte read aloud. An old children's magazine was open between them on the table, and I listened outside the doorway as she read in her halting voice. " 'A woman who was just

250

by came up to her, and asked her whose little girl she was. I am, ans . . . ans . . . answered she, Miss Biddy Johnson, and I have lost my way. Oh, says the woman. You are Mister Johnson's girl, are you? My husband is looking after you, to carry you —' "

"Eliza?" They looked up, startled. Eliza had been as absorbed in *Biddy Johnson* as the child. The story was one of Charlotte's favorites, about a young girl lost in the streets of London. "Could you step into the withdrawing room a moment? Doctor Mead is here."

All the color drained from her face. She stood slowly, pushing the chair in and placing a reassuring hand on Charlotte's shoulder.

"Are you unwell?" I asked in alarm.

She shook her head, and Charlotte got down from her chair, too, as though to follow her. I decided not to protest and led them upstairs.

"Doctor Mead would like a companion to accompany him on a walk this afternoon, and I think you are just the person for it," I told her. Her face, which had been furrowed with anxiety, smoothed at once.

"Me?"

"Yes."

251

"Mrs. Callard has told me of the fabled white peacocks at the pleasure gardens in Chelsea, and I am afraid I am too curious."

"Oh," said Eliza.

"Can I go?" said Charlotte.

All of us turned to her in surprise, quite forgetting she had been there, stitched to her nursemaid's side. Her face was determined.

"I would be very happy to have the young Miss Callard's company as well," he replied. "If her mother would allow it?"

"Certainly not," I said automatically. Charlotte fixed me with a look that was quite unnerving. There was violent hatred in it, as well as fear and resignation — a rather disarming combination, and one that made me falter. "She goes only to church," I said. "She has never been to Drake Street, let alone Chelsea." I imagined my map book on its shelf in the parlor. I knew vaguely where Chelsea was, in the countryside west of the city, probably half an hour or longer in a carriage. It was unthinkable. "It is too far," I said.

"Please let me go, Mama!"

"No, and I shall hear no more about it."

She burst into sobs so luxuriant that the three of us could only watch in horror. Eliza got quickly to her knees to calm the child, and wipe her wet face.

"I do not want to be shut up here forever," she sobbed through great, tearing breaths. "I want to go outside!"

I was speechless. I should have gone to her, and comforted her, but I could only stand openmouthed as Eliza shushed and murmured, holding her and dabbing at her face with a handkerchief.

"Please!" Charlotte cried. "I want to go with you."

I had never asked her if she wished to go outside. She was six years old — in another six she would begin to grow into a young woman. I was preparing her for a life like mine, where nothing bad could happen to her. And yet she played in the yard, and peered beneath the curtain in the carriage, and always sat at the windows looking out. Was it right to keep her like a songbird, one who sang only for me?

"Please, Mama." Her sobs were hiccuping and frantic now, from where she sat on Eliza's lap on the carpet.

Everybody was looking at me, waiting, and after a very long time, I nodded: a tiny, discreet movement, but one they all saw, which changed the atmosphere immediately. Charlotte ran to me and hugged my skirts, and I gave her a brief pat on the head.

"You must take great care of her," I told them. "Neither of you are to let her out of your sight, nor let go of her hand. You will return her home by four o'clock. Do you understand?"

They both nodded, and exchanged a triumphant glance.

"You are to walk on either side of her at all times, and resist speaking to anybody. The road to Chelsea — is it quite safe?"

"Very much so," Doctor Mead said. "I'll have my carriage drop us at the gates, and collect us at three o'clock."

I could not bear the tender way he was looking at me, because it confirmed what I long suspected: he thought that I was cruel for keeping Charlotte inside, and that letting her out was right.

He came to me now, and took my own hand in his warm one. "She will be safe. You have my word in marble." At first I wondered what he meant, then remembered the memento mori: *Friendship in Marble, Injuries in Dust.*

As soon as I turned the key in the lock behind them, my stomach became a wriggling mass of serpents. I went from the dark hallway to the dining room window to look out, just in time to see Doctor Mead's carriage pull away. The horses gleamed, and the wheels began turning, and in seconds they were out of sight. I stood for the longest time at the window, trying to breathe evenly. It was a perfect March day: bright and blue, with a friendly wind that tossed hemlines and tugged at hats. I could almost taste the freshness of it, could feel the sunlight flood my eyes. I opened the window a fraction, and suddenly everything was louder and closer. Devonshire Street was no thoroughfare, but at once its proximity was overwhelming.

A strawberry seller wandered past, stopping in front of the house and proffering her basket. "Care for a dozen, my lady?"

I almost died of fright, and pulled the pane down with a crash. I had made a terrible mistake.

I called out for Agnes, and heard her feet on the stairs, then her moony face appeared in the doorway. My throat began to close, and my chest was tight, and she helped me into a chair. "Should we send someone after them?" I asked. "It might not be too late."

"They'll be halfway to St. Giles by now, madam," she said.

"Charlotte has never . . . She's never . . . ."

"I know, madam, but she'll be all right with the doctor. Heavens, if anything were

255

to happen, who better to have as company? And her nursemaid with her, too. She'll be well cared for, you know that, else you wouldn't have let her go, now, would you? Let me fetch you something to soothe your nerves."

I put my hands on my knees and tried to breathe deeply. When I felt her press a glass into my hand I drank deeply. I felt the sting in my throat and the fire in my belly.

"Try not to worry, madam. 'Tis a marvelous thing you did, letting Charlotte go and exercise out of doors. She's a lucky thing, she is, that little girl."

"Is she?"

" 'Course. She'll come back full of stories about where she's been and all she saw."

"She will?"

"Oh, that she will, madam. And she'll sleep sound tonight, mark my words."

"She has not been without me her whole life. And she wanted to go, Agnes. To hear her, you would think I am her gaoler!"

"Here, have another sip. There we are. Why don't you go and rest, and I'll have Maria send up a cup of chocolate. I've dressed your bed, all fresh and white as a snowdrift."

"Do you think Mr. Callard would want her live like this?" I stared blankly at the wall. "Do you think he would wish for her to be ordinary?"

There was a pause. "You are doing a fine job, madam. You're doing the very best you can."

They were not the same thing.

In the parlor, my map book sat open on the table. I had asked Doctor Mead's coachman to show me the exact route he would take: south to High Holborn, then through St. Giles and down Oxford Street, crawling west until the city fell away to fields. I crouched over the book and traced it with a finger. Little streets and alleys led off the route like so many thoughts. Even on a bright day like today, Doctor Mead could never know what sinister threats lurked: who watched them, flattened against a wall, or followed them at a distance. I felt my throat begin to close again, and quickly turned the book's pages at random, trying to lose myself in a map of east Surrey.

I looked at the clock: they had been gone twenty minutes. Doctor Mead had told me he expected them to arrive at half past one, and at three o'clock they would return to the carriage and travel back the way they came. So then: I had two and a half hours to fill. It had been two or three months since I'd cleaned my parents' pictures, so I sent for a mixture of vitriol, borax and water, put on an old apron and gloves, and covered the withdrawing room table in an old sheet.

I took them down from the picture rail and set them together on the table, side by side, and chatted to them while I began brushing them gently with the mixture: first Father, then Mother, admiring the way the artist had captured Mother's playfulness, and the witty way her mouth turned up at one corner. Perhaps he had been in love with her, for he had not reproduced my father's essence the same way. But there were things only I knew that no picture could capture: how he smelled of pipe tobacco, and hummed old sailors' songs when he climbed the staircase, smoothing the banister with his large hand.

Watching the house being packed had been excruciating; I had stood in doorways as dust sheets were thrown over busts and tables, while indifferent men combed the rooms to value our home and our lives, directed by Aunt Cassandra. Worse, though, was the way these men looked at me, as though I was damaged, for at the time I could not speak, and walked about the rooms like a shadow.

Years later, Ambrosia told me a rumor she'd heard from the village: that I had died, too, and the young girl with the flour-white face and haunted eyes was a ghost. I was envious of my sister, not for her smart brougham, nor her house, nor even for her confidence and the easy way with which she moved through the world. No, I was envious only of the way she saw the fourteenth of June as an ordinary day on the calendar, perhaps with a fleeting sadness at our parents' passing, if she remembered at all. The significance of the day might enter her head and leave just as quickly, for she had no memory of it to linger, or stain, or poison. To change the course of her life.

Once Mother and Father were clean, I sponged them down with wood ash, and Agnes brought up a little dish of nut and linseed oil, which I dabbed lightly all over with a feather to make them shine. While I worked I glanced here and there out of the window at the street below, noticing nothing unusual, apart from a man who stood for five or ten minutes on the opposite site of the street against the railings, smoking tobacco. He was sallow-skinned, with very dark hair and eyebrows, wearing a black coat and cap, but what made him unusual was the unlit torch in his hand. Clearly he was a linkboy waiting for someone, or else waiting for darkness, though it was a few hours off yet.

With every draw from his pipe, he held the smoke in his mouth for so long I began to think he'd swallowed it, but then it would tumble from his lips in a cloud. After two or three or these, he must have sensed he was being watched, and looked up, finding me in the window. I did not move, but he did, drawing the pipe from his mouth, pulling his cap down and ambling lazily away. I could not think of a worse job than his, creeping around in the darkness, not knowing what lay ahead or behind.

By the time I hung my parents back again, an hour and a half had passed. I put away the cloth, apron and gloves, suddenly feeling very tired. I told Agnes I would not have tea that day, because my stomach would not take it. I sat in the withdrawing room, looking at the newly varnished pictures, and waited. The brandy had lulled me. With the small fire burning the air was still and warm, and I felt my eyes closing, and let myself be carried to sleep.

A disturbance. I felt the air stir, and opened my eyes to dimness; night had not yet fallen, but the drapes had been drawn partway across the windows.

Three figures were crouching over me,

wearing masks.

I came to consciousness slowly and then all at once, feeling as though a pistol had gone off inside my chest. Terror flooded me, pinning me to my chair and tipping the room upside down, spinning my head in dizzying circles. I opened my eyes again and found I was not dreaming; they were there still, leering, waiting, grinning behind their dreadful disguises, like ravens' beaks. Three men, ready to kill me. Someone was screaming, and I tried to get up, the room bouncing around me like a ball. They had come back for me. They had returned. It was happening. I had no faculty of my limbs, did not know if I was sitting or standing or falling or rising, but suddenly they were grabbing at me, and I was tearing at them, clawing and screaming and dying. The shot would sound any moment; I knew it was coming, and every line in my body was primed for the fire. I was pinned to a carriage seat, stiff and wet from my own piss, as my parents lay on either side of me as the life bled out of them, thick and red and staining everything, leaking over their clothes from the holes blown into them: Mother's head and Father's chest. My face was warm with their blood; it was in my eyes and mouth, and tasted salty.

The men: there were three of them. One had climbed into the carriage, filling it with his dark bulk, combing my parents' bodies, unfastening rings and necklaces, even my mother's hairpin. I felt her hair tumble downward and brush my shoulder. He took Father's buckled shoes from his limp feet, and Mother's dainty slippers, and the pocket from her dress, grunting and cursing from behind his black mask and throwing things out of the door to the others. All the while my parents leaked and leaked, their blood pooling in the footwell, running beneath our feet. Their eyes were open and glassy.

My ears still rang from the shots, louder than anything I'd ever heard, filling my whole head. Distantly, a child was crying. But that was not part of the memory; I had not cried, and Ambrosia had been at home with a cold. Who was weeping, then? They had not shot me yet, and perhaps they wouldn't, if only I could — "Mrs. Callard!"

They had seized me, and I fought with all my might. I kicked and bit and punched and tore, and then I was on the floor, my cheek pushed into the carpet. I could see nothing, but then my arms were released, and in a moment I was crawling and reaching, finding the poker before the fender and gripping it hard in my palm. I began swinging and jabbing, roaring for Agnes and Maria at the top of my lungs.

"Alexandra, no!"

The poker crashed into an almighty fist, and was wrenched from my hand. I clung and pulled, but he was stronger. All I saw in my blind, sick panic was the terrible black mask, and a man's hat and a green coat. And then the poker was being flung to the floor, and my arms forced against my sides, and I realized two of the figures were wearing skirts. My eyes grew more used to the darkness, and I could see the taller one had her arms wrapped around a girl, who was crying.

"There's a child in there," one of the men had said, thirty years ago on that road in Derbyshire, which wound like a river through green peaks and gorges. And now there was a child here, in my withdrawing room, and the mask was being pulled from her face, and it was Charlotte. The woman holding her was Eliza, her nursemaid, and the man grasping me was my friend Doctor Mead.

I looked at each of them in confusion, in terror. Were they changelings, or was I? Was I a child of ten, or a woman of forty? Their faces darkened as the light faded, and the room began to turn once again, and I felt myself falling, falling, falling.

I woke in my bedroom, as Doctor Mead was lowering me onto the bed. He removed my slippers, attending to the task with great care and attention. He had not realized I had woken and was watching him, and when he saw me his face was so full of sorrow it broke me in two. I began to cry: great, howling, racking sobs that came from somewhere deep, deep down — that chink, that keyhole of grief that I could never open because who knew where it ended and I began?

"Mrs. Callard," came his gentle voice. "Here." He passed something beneath my nose and told me to sniff, and an icy wind blasted through my senses, cleansing my mind and making my eyes water. He was sitting on the side of the bed with a warm hand on my forehead, and gradually my dreadful choking noise stopped. He cleaned my cheeks and nose with a handkerchief, then put it in his pocket. When I had finished, I could not look at him. He was sitting too close; his presence was invasive, cloying. I wanted him out of my room, and my house.

"Leave," I told him.

He stiffened, and the bed creaked beneath him. I turned and stared at the wall on my left, at a picture of two milkmaids on a lane.

"Mrs. Callard." He spoke quietly, passionately. "I am deeply troubled by —"

"Leave now," I whispered, staring hard at the milkmaids' pails, their dreamlike expressions. "Now."

He remained sitting for a moment or two, then stood shakily, his hands dangling at his sides. "I will come back with a tincture," he said.

"You are a cruel man." I turned to look directly at him. His face was more awful than it had been after his grandfather died. His hair was messed, his collar torn, as though he had been in some common tavern brawl. I realized with horror that I must have done this. His pea green frock coat was nowhere to be seen, discarded, no doubt, to lift my body upstairs. I blushed with shame and revulsion, and his mouth opened noiselessly.

"W-we thought we might surprise you," he stammered. "We bought masks at the gardens; it was my design."

"You know, do you not, that my parents were murdered before me by highwaymen? Three of them, in fact, wearing masks, who pillaged their bodies while they were still warm. I was sitting between them."

His face collapsed, written all over with sorrow and regret. "I did not," he said thickly. "Daniel did not tell me."

"Really," was my sour reply. "How regrettable. If only he had, we might have avoided this experience altogether."

"He told me they died in a carriage accident."

My hair had fallen down from its pins. As if I was not humiliated enough, I was lying in bed, with it all about my shoulders, and my gown rucked up around me, with a man in my room. Only hours before I had told him our friendship was cast in marble, injuries in dust. I had tried to lift his spirits by letting him go out with my nursemaid and daughter. And here I was, washed up like river debris, empty and hollow and drenched in shame. Icy anger coursed through me, and I bade him leave again. He tried again to remonstrate with me, but I remained silent, and finally he left with a humble bow. I heard the door close softly behind him, and the pain of my past lapped gently at my feet, inviting me to bathe in its tempting waters, and I sank back into it, and let it carry me down.

CHAPTER 14

Doctor Mead tried to visit five or six times over the next few days, but I would not admit him. I stayed in my bedroom, moving in an unhappy triangle from the bed to the chair at the window and sometimes the floor, looking at the things in my ebony box, reading old letters or sleeping. Sometimes I looked at the sky, and did not move until the light faded and the windows of the houses opposite lit up, their shadowed occupants moving unguardedly. I ate in bed, and got through a bottle of brandy, which Agnes refilled discreetly when my bed hangings were closed. At night, I heard men on the stairs. I saw them at the window in black crow masks, their beaks tapping the glass as they peered in. Once I woke in the night convinced someone was under my bed, and lay in the darkness, weeping like a child, too afraid to check the black space beneath. When all I found was dust clumps that clung to my fingers, I did not know whether to laugh or cry harder.

Thirty years had dissolved in a matter of days, casting me back to that windy morning when my life had ended with three bangs. Now I was stuck like a fly in wax. Each time I looked down at my nightgown I expected to see a rose-pink silk dress with little black boots sticking from my skirts. The dress had been drenched with blood, as though a carriage wheel had torn through a great puddle of gore while I'd been standing by the roadside. In my fitful sleep I heard the gunshots and the horses neighing, and felt the wind whistle in from the peaks.

On the fourth day, I slept till noon. My room was stale, and I threw the window wide to let the air in. It was a thick, heavy sort of day, with rain in the air and no breeze. Agnes brought me a breakfast tray, and I asked her to send up a bath and water so I could wash. I took my time soaping my hair and skin, and rinsing it clean, and I sat in the tub until the water turned cold and I was shivering. I eyed my nightgown on the bed. The idea of putting it on again depressed me.

By now it was late afternoon, and I could smell food from the kitchen. That made my mind up: I was ready to leave the fug of my bedroom and sit straight-backed at a table, instead of eating in bed slumped like an invalid. I dressed and went downstairs, passing the dining room to do a cursory check of the front door before I ate. The candles were lit on the hall table, and the door was indeed locked. All was in order, but something was different. I glanced up and found myself looking into a great big pair of eyes. On the wall, above the hall table, was a large portrait, framed in gilt, of a woman in a red dress petting a dog. I moved very slowly toward her, trying to recall how she came to be there, and failing. Her expression was vibrant and playful, and she had a scroll at her right elbow, as though she had at that moment been interrupted reading a letter. A large cross sat at her neck, almost Catholic in its lavishness, and she wore a white indoor bonnet. Then I noticed something else, which at first I thought part of the painting: a note was tucked inside the frame, wedged between canvas and wood. I took it out and unfolded it.

Dear Mrs. Callard,
You spoke of a desire to adorn your hallway with a painting of my choice from my grandfather's collection. This,

of the late Mary Edwards, by William Hogarth, is my favorite, and I believe she will feel much at home with you. Something of her manner reminds me of yours. I sincerely hope you will admit me presently. I wish more than anything to offer my deepest apologies in person, because a letter — and indeed a painting — just won't do.

Yours faithfully (in marble),

Elliott Mead

So, he had given me a Hogarth. Removing a work of that value from his grandfather's estate would have been no small matter. I imagined his mother alone would have put up an enormous resistance, matched only perhaps by the auctioneer. Yet here it was. I examined the subject, whom Doctor Mead had compared to me, yet found no similarity between us. I did not even like dogs.

At the dining table, Eliza and Charlotte looked up in alarm as I entered the room. They were hunched over their plates, knife and fork in each hand like a mother and daughter in a chophouse. Charlotte was speaking quietly, a small, easy smile on her face, which vanished when I came in. I took my usual seat, and waited for Agnes's idle hum in the hall, knowing she would be carrying my dinner tray upstairs. When I heard it I called her. There was a short silence, followed by: "Madam, is that you?" A silver tray appeared at the door, bearing a bowl of broth and a bit of bread and cheese — a servant's meal, which I had been eating for days, and quite unlike the hearty liver and onions Charlotte and Eliza were enjoying.

"Madam!" she crowed. "You are better. I'm very glad to see it. Let me set these down for you." She began arranging my place with the napkin and bowl.

"I am not an invalid, Agnes, nor do I wish to eat like one any longer. I will have some liver, if you would be so good as to fetch the china."

She began taking up the things at once, a blush spreading up her neck. "Right away, madam. Glad to see your appetite is restored." She hurried from the room with the broth rattling on the tray, and the three of us sat in unpleasant silence until she returned with the dinnerware, setting it out around me in a fussy little ceremony. I sat stiffly until the final spoon was placed, and she closed the door very quietly behind her in the manner of someone leaving a sickroom.

"Are you better, madam?" Eliza asked

gently. Her eyes were solemn.

I said nothing, and began spooning cabbage onto my plate. I had not yet looked at Charlotte, afraid to see myself reflected in her eyes. She had knocked gingerly on my bedroom door once or twice over the last few days, no doubt encouraged by Eliza, but I had not admitted her.

"Madam," Eliza spoke again. "Forgive me if I'm speaking out of turn, but I'm sincerely sorry for the other day. We didn't know it'd cause such distress."

I looked sharply at her. "What did Doctor Mead tell you?"

A little frown pulled at her eyebrows. "Only that you thought we was intruders, and that's why you . . ." She swallowed. "It was thoughtless of us. We didn't know we'd frighten you so."

I stared hard at her, and wondered if Elliott had told her the truth. From the corner of my eye I saw Charlotte's pale face and wide, dark stare.

"This cabbage needs more cream," I told Eliza. "Would you take it back to the kitchen?"

I could not bear the force of her abject pity. It was worse, even, than the fear I'd seen when she took off her mask. I felt the smallest tug at my seams, as though I might unravel again. Eliza got up and left with the platter of cabbage, closing the door behind her.

I heaped food onto my plate, though I was thoroughly unappetized, and said: "Tell me, Charlotte, how did you find the pleasure garden?"

Sitting opposite me in her snow-white dress, she kept her gaze on the tablecloth. Her hair tumbled in a braid down one shoulder, a pink ribbon woven through it.

"Was it not pleasurable?" I prompted. Her jaw hardened, and she glanced at the door. I threw my fork down.

"Do not look for your nursemaid; answer me."

"Yes, Mama," she said miserably.

"What did you like about it, exactly?"

She stared at her lap. "I liked being outside. There were lots of people there."

"And were they all wearing masks?"

"No," she whispered.

"What else did you see?"

Alarmed by the direct questioning usually reserved for lessons, Charlotte rubbed at a stain on the tablecloth. "Lots of things," she said. "I saw a funny dog, like Aunt Ambrosia's. And there was an orcha . . . orchist . . ."

"Orchestra?"

273

"Yes, playing music, like at church. And people were eating food *standing up*."

That's when I noticed it: the gap at the front of her mouth. Her pink tongue poked through like a reed, softening her speech. A cold shard of terror spiked through me from the head down as I remembered the poker, and grabbing it, and smashing it . . . where?

"When did you lose your tooth?" I spoke harshly, and her apprehension turned to terror. At that moment Eliza returned, and the way Charlotte's expression plunged into relief . . . She was afraid of me now, and always would be.

"Charlotte's tooth is missing," I said, trying to sound calm. "When did she lose it?"

"Oh, only yesterday, madam. It was wobbly since Monday, wasn't it? And last night it jumped out by itself." She was bright and cheerful, as though relieved to be talking of something else, and came to stand behind Charlotte and hold her shoulders. "We saved it — didn't we? — to show you. We thought you'd like to see it, as it's her first one."

I had not struck her in the face with a fire iron, then.

"Charlotte was telling me about the pleasure gardens," I announced dryly. "Tell me, does everybody there wear masks?"

"No," said Eliza.

"I find masks dangerous things. They conceal. Concealment is a very dishonest thing, don't you agree? Why might a person hide who they are, unless they were up to no good?" I chewed a mouthful of liver, finding some gristle and removing it with my fingers. "I have no idea why they are worn at balls and the like. Surely one would prefer to know whom one was addressing."

"I have never been to a ball," Eliza said.

I could imagine the parties typical of her kind: like servants let loose, with beer spilling on the floor, and maddening fiddles, and girls flashing their petticoats as they danced barefoot. Eliza began fishing in her skirt pocket, bringing out what appeared to be a coin. It was bronze, emblazed with a fiery sun and the year 1754, and she passed it across the table to me.

"What is it?" I asked.

"A ticket," she said. "Doctor Mead bought us a year's entry, in case we want to go back."

I looked at Charlotte. "And you have one of these?"

She nodded.

"Well," I said, picking up my fork, and allowing a beat or two of silence. "You can forget that notion at once."

After dinner I went to sit at my writing desk, and an hour went by with only the words Dear Doctor Mead atop the page. I put down the quill, then picked it up again, and licked it along my wrist. I went to fetch my map, and found on it Bedford Row, and stared at it until the sky began to darken. I had never been to his house, never seen it, even. Had never sat in one of his chairs, or drunk from his china, or heard his clock chime the hour. I did not know the layout of his rooms, or how he moved about them. I willed him to knock at the door so that I could refuse him again.

There was a scuffle at the parlor door.

"Madam?"

It was Eliza's voice. I admitted her, and with her came Charlotte in her nightdress, her pretty plait falling down her back. She grinned, showing the gap in her smile, and held her palm out to me. On it was the missing tooth, tiny and white, like a shard of china. I took it from her and said thank you, and set it before me on the table.

"Charlotte," Eliza said. "Kiss your mother good-night."

I held my cheek to her and said good-night, and the two of them left, closing the door behind them. I lit a candle and took up my quill.

Dear Doctor Mead,
Thank you for the portrait, though I cannot accept it. I am unused to gestures of such grandiosity; the sum token of Daniel's affection, in all the years we were together, was a heart made from whalebone, and only half of that. I would be a hypocrite to leave our friendship in dust, but I should be grateful if you would allow me to lick my wounds for another week or so. Then you may come in peace.

Your friend (in marble),
Alexandra Callard

I left it on the hall table for the morning's post, and took the candle up to bed.

It was the wind that woke me, rattling at the sash. I turned over and tried to ignore it, but it persisted, and at some point I realized it was coming from inside the house. I sat up in alarm, frowning in the darkness. Floorboards creaked upstairs, and I opened my curtain to look at the yard, lit dimly in the moonlight. It was empty. I must have left my room at the same time as Agnes, for I found her coming down the stairs with a candle in her nightdress, her eyes wide behind the flame. The noise started up again, and at the same time we realized it was the doorknocker.

"Who in heaven's name is that at this time?" she asked.

Whoever it was would not stop pounding and pounding. I was equal parts curious and frightened, and hovered for a moment at the top of the stairs as Agnes went down, tidying her shawl about her shoulders. The sound became more urgent, and I heard Agnes muttering that it was likely a drunk swell come back from his club to the wrong house.

I decided that the likelihood of somebody about to rob or murder us doing so by announcing themselves loudly at the front door was small, and intrigue got the better of me, so I followed her, hanging back in the dark hallway to let her answer it, thinking of what I could take hold of if we were attacked: the brass candleholders on the hall table? And there was a dagger locked somewhere in a drawer in Daniel's study. But where was the key? I was entirely surprised to find that I did not need it, because standing on the doorstep in the moonlight was not a brandy-soaked neighbor, or even the nightwatchman with news of a crime, but Doctor Mead.

He was utterly disheveled, with the troubled look of a madman, and he pushed past us into the house.

"Doctor Mead! What is the meaning of this?"

"I got your letter," was all he shouted over his shoulder before barreling up the hall, taking the stairs two at a time. Agnes exclaimed, closing the door behind her, and we stared at one another in mute horror.

"What did you put in your letter, madam?" she whispered in the darkness. "Is the child not well?"

"What letter?"

"The one you left on the table this evening."

I felt my forehead pucker in confusion. "Only that I could not accept the portrait. But how has he read it? And why would he come so suddenly?"

"I had it delivered, madam; the post boy was walking past as I was drawing the curtains."

What was happening? The Scarlet Lady on the wall looked down upon us with her quiet eyes. Something was wrong. Fear soaked me all over. Clumsily I locked the front door, then groped my way through the velvet dark to the staircase. Moonlight shone in from the fanlight above the door, revealing the first few stairs, and with Agnes and her light behind me I climbed upward, feeling as though they were made of sand, until I reached the first landing.

"Doctor Mead?" A moment later I heard his feet pummeling the stairs, and he appeared on the first floor.

"Alexandra."

That he had said my first name made me go cold. He was taking me by the arm now, and leading me up to my bedroom — no, to Charlotte's bedroom — and I felt once again as though I was in a strange dream, one which made no sense and perhaps never would. And then I saw.

The curtains in Charlotte's bedroom were open, and moonlight flooded in, casting its silvery glow on the beds, which were empty, and neatly made, with the pillows soft and plump. Care had been taken; urgency had not been at play. I stood numbly in the doorway, swaying slightly. I tried to understand what I was seeing, for my eyes were working, but my mind was not.

Doctor Mead fled again, tearing around the house like a bloodhound, looking in every room, searching the parlor, the study, the kitchen. I heard him banging doors and thudding on the stairs, and felt a tiny gnawing inside my mind, a worm turning in an apple.

Presently he was back, breathless beside me, and I could not see his face. I could not see anything; we were in near total darkness, though Agnes's candle burned on, trembling in the shadows.

"It's Eliza," he said.

"Where is she?"

He seemed more worried than he should be, at a servant fled in the night. If only I could see his face! Then: a glimmer of revelation, like the first sliver of dawn.

"Where is Charlotte?"

He came to me then, and took my hands in his. Only then did I comprehend the terror in his eyes. "Charlotte," he said, and his voice was pleading. "Is she yours?"

I had never felt shock like it.

"Answer me!" he pressed. "Is she yours?"

I pulled my hands from his. "What is the meaning of this? Where is Charlotte?"

"Alexandra, you must answer me! Is Charlotte your —"

"Why are you asking me this?" I screamed. My ears rang with distant bells, warning bells. A slow sort of horror began to drench me.

"Eliza left a child at the Foundling Hospital six years ago. The token she left was half a heart, made of whalebone."

I began to shake.

It's not possible.

Blindly, I pushed open the door to my room, which was lit by moonlight, and took out the little ebony box. The painted figures knew as well as I what would be missing, for they had seen it happen. Perhaps I had known since I saw the empty beds — no, before that — since Doctor Mead began pounding at the doorknocker. Perhaps before that, even; the tiniest part of me had known this day would come, and yet I was not prepared for it. Their wide, dark eyes, the reddish tint to their chestnut hair, their freckles. The way they giggled behind doors like lovers, and danced like sisters. The night she had looked for Daniel's picture with her secret flame. The way she blanched when I came in the room. The way she lit up when Charlotte did. Eliza. Bess. Elizabeth. The knowledge grew and bled like ink in water, like blood. I was water; she was blood.

My hands fumbled in the box for the two halves of a white bone heart carved with lovers' letters, for the little leaden tag on a string, bearing the number 627, but of course they were gone.

"Kiss your mother good-night," Eliza had said to Charlotte.

Her mother had been here all along. And now the bitch had taken her.

■ ■ ■ ■

Part Three:
Bess

■ ■ ■ ■

CHAPTER 15

"You're all right with me, girls, long as you stay close. I'll light my torch just as soon as we're south of Holborn. Then we're gonna crisscross down so quick you'll get dizzy. How's about that?"

We clung like shadows to Lyle, the link-boy I'd befriended in my time at Bloomsbury, who led the way through the black streets. I had one arm around Charlotte's narrow shoulders; in the other I held the canvas bag I'd arrived with, packed differently now, with underclothes, a spare dress, stockings and shoes, and the things I'd taken from the larder — bread, a cold pork pie, a bottle of beer and two apples, and some gingerbread wrapped in paper.

The night was cold, the streets empty. Not one to leave the house after dark, when London's nocturnals came creeping from their holes and peril hummed down every alley, even here on these wide, fine streets my skin prickled with fear. Especially here — the few lonely shapes were likely to be valets fetching tobacco for their masters, or men coming home from their clubs, but there was something unsettling about the silence that made me eager for the bright, open doorways and unquiet streets of Ludgate Hill. We would soon be there; Lyle was taking us, and with every step we drew closer, and farther away from Devonshire Street. The only sound was our feet pitter-pattering in the road, and our breath in our throats. The windows watched us blackly, their dark glass like blank eyes.

"You reckon she's got you licked yet?" Lyle asked, his voice bouncing into the road.

I shushed him. "Not here," I said.

I had known him only a few weeks, and yet here we were, putting our trust and our liberty in him. I'd met Lyle one night soon after I arrived at Mrs. Callard's, when the strangeness of the house had pressed down on me in my bed and I had the overwhelming sensation of being buried alive. I'd taken the key from the jar in the scullery and gone to stand on the steps up to the street just to feel the cold on my arms and the night air stirring my hair. Sitting on the top step, looking at the empty road, a voice had called out: "Need a glim?" and Lyle had appeared, brandishing his unlit torch like a sword. I'd jumped, and clapped a hand over my mouth, knowing a scream would wake the house, and the ones on either side of it.

"No," I'd said. "Now push off."

He ignored me. "Blower?" He offered his pipe, and I shook my head, shivering. I wanted to go back in but knew that when I did the coffin would seal behind me for another day. He was dark — foreign-looking, with sallow skin and a heavy expression, but his accent was like mine. He wore a black cap, pulled low over his face, and a slim black coat that fit him well. Everything about him was shadowlike, as though he had been created by the night, and could melt back into it at will.

He'd leaned idly against the railing, and regarded me over his pipe. "I suppose you ain't no Covent Garden nun waiting for a swell, from the way your nightgown's poking out beneath your cloak." Blushing furiously, I'd wrapped it tighter around myself, and he threw his head back and laughed louder than he ought. "Besides, we're a long way from Covent Garden. And that's a rum ken —" he nodded at the house "— but you don't look like a miller, either."

"I ain't a thief."

"So my reckoning," he went on, "cos it's

dark, you see, and I can't make you out proper, is that you're a mop-squeezer, and you're waiting for someone."

"I'm a nursemaid," I said hotly. "But you're a man of too many words is what you are, and I wish you'd shab off."

"Who you waiting for, then? Fancy man, is it?"

"No."

"Husband, then?"

"I wouldn't be here if I was married, would I?"

"Then it's my lucky evening."

And with that, he'd given me a wink, and gone striding off without looking back.

I saw him again a few nights later, waiting for me across the street, leaning against the railings, and smiled despite myself. His name was Lyle Kozak. He never lit his torch when we were speaking, should searching eyes find him. He'd been a linkboy — a moon curser, he called himself, for work was hard to come by on a clear night — since he was ten or eleven. He was twenty-three now, and bringing home as much money as his father, a tailor.

Lyle and his mother and father had come to London twenty years ago from Belgrade, and he lived in St. Giles with them, three sisters and four brothers. There were nine

Kozak children altogether, with the eldest sister living out. He was the oldest at home, and worked at night so he could look after the children in the day. He told me he only needed three or four hours' sleep, and could kip on a washing line, what with having such a large family, and the chaos and noise that came with it. They spoke Serbian at home, and he had learned English in the streets, copying the accent and making it his own. What he liked best was Cockney, and he collected words and phrases like a magpie. He carried two pistols, both cheap, and likely to explode if he used them, but he'd never had to, because drawing them out was usually enough to make rogues turn on their heels. ("And if they're no good for shooting, they'll do for a crack on the custard," he added good-naturedly.) All this I learned on our moonlit meetings. We'd sit on the steps, most often at no. 9, whose tenants, Maria told me, were on the continent. We shared his pipe, and sometimes I'd bring us a bit of something to eat: a bottle of beer from the back of the pantry that afterward I'd fill with water so Maria wouldn't notice, or a breakfast muffin that I'd break in half.

I told him about Alexandra Callard, and how she stroked the pictures of her dead parents but could not touch her daughter. I told him about Charlotte, how she loved animals and reading stories and eating oranges in cream. I told him about Ned coming to the backyard and asking for money, nearly losing me my job. One night we'd decided to walk around the square, having seen a light in one of the houses, and that was when I told him my plan to steal my daughter and bring her home.

He told me I was dicked in the nob. And when he offered to help, I said yes.

And then Mrs. Callard had attacked us. The butterfly had turned into a beast. She'd the same look in her eye as the Smithfield cattle driven to the slaughterhouses; I'd seen the whites of her eyes. She was a dangerous woman; that was certain. What sort of mother could take a poker to beat her child? She was not safe, and neither were we in that tall prison, that dungeon above the ground with its sleeping dragon inside. Who knew when it would wake again? Charlotte, terrorized, trembling Charlotte — for though she would always be Clara to me, I had called her Charlotte a month, and was used to it now — had left the mother she knew and returned to a monster. The poor thing had cried herself sick, and sobbed in my arms until she fell asleep, her quivering, damp little body clinging to mine. In the morning, I knew we had to leave; the hand had turned full circle, and our golden hour was up.

The trouble was life at Devonshire Street had grown comfortable. I'd grown comfortable: my figure was thicker from all the cream, my hair shinier from the soap. My hands were softer, the smell of brine gone. I'd grown used to the carpets beneath my feet, the overheated rooms, the groaning dining table. I was content in that little bedroom, where we lived and played and slept and sang. I could have stayed forever, locking the door and swallowing the key. But there were things I still did not know: how Charlotte had been plucked from the Foundling and come to live in that house. How Mrs. Callard had known of her existence, but did not know me. Somebody did, though.

I had been so anxious she would recognize me when I stepped into her home. The withdrawing room, she'd called it. The withdrawing house, more like. I had not known it was possible to live that way, choosing to shut out the world, never going out. Her food came to the street door, her money from a lawyer. Tea from China, brandy from France. She had no family that I'd seen, no friends calling of an afternoon.

Yet she seemed . . . *satisfied.*

Charlotte, however, was not. The day I met her, I sensed she wished for a different life. She knew French, and music, and could read words longer than my arm, but she did not know what it was to push a hoop down a street, or feed a horse an apple, or make a ball of snow. She had been shy, at first, and lived in her books, asking me if I had seen forests and rivers and boats. For a child of London not to have seen a boat! Sometimes I found myself paralyzed with doubt that this soft, floury thing might hawk with me in the streets, a little basket of lemons at her arm. It seemed like something from one of her stories. More than once I'd resigned myself to staying her nursemaid until she grew older, so that we could live out our days in bliss and comfort on Mrs. Callard's tab. That way, when we left, Charlotte's Bloomsbury voice and pretty face would get her a position as a lady's maid. That was the best she could hope for with me.

But then the walls would close in on our striped prison, and she would grow irritable and teary, attaching herself to me in a way that made me sick to my heart, for this was no better than a gaol, no kinder than an asylum. It was enough to send you mad. I could not tell if Mrs. Callard herself was mad to begin with, or if she'd made herself that way. She certainly seemed to occupy herself, with her letters and her newspapers. But what good was paper, with a world outside? Her only companion was Doctor Mead, who overlooked her strange ways, but I think she amused him.

Poor Doctor Mead; how I had hoodwinked him. If there was space in my heart to regret pulling such a filthy trick, I'd feel it. But there was no room, because my heart was filled with my daughter. My daughter, who I had dreamed of these six years, and loved even more than I knew I could. My daughter, who I had made and who'd grown inside me, who walked around, pulling my soul everywhere she went. Her dark hair that twisted down her back, her warm hands, finding mine, the way she yawned when reading made her tired. The fact that she *could* read — I shouldn't have been prouder if she flew. How could there be room for sorrow, or regret, or pity? I had never been in love before, until now. When she laughed, or showed me a drawing, or led me to a mouse hole in the kitchen — it almost choked me. "You are mine," I'd wanted to tell her from the very night I'd moved in. "I am your mother."

And then, just like that, the opportunity

presented itself. At bedtime, a little over three weeks after I had arrived, we had finished our game of cribbage and got her into her nightgown. I sat beside her on the bed with a candle as she read me her favorite story, a pious tale from a children's magazine about a spoiled little girl called Biddy Johnson. She'd read it to me once before, but I had been tired, barely listening as she recited the adventures of a young girl who ran away from her nurse and became lost in London. After accepting an orange from a stranger, spoiled, stupid Biddy was kidnapped by a gang of thieves, who took her to the countryside and tried to kill her. But she was saved at the last moment by the heroic Master Tommy Trusty, who spirited her back to London and returned her to her family. Charlotte did not know all the words and had to miss some parts out, and when she had finished she put the magazine on the coverlet and nestled closer to me. I had sat in deep thought, and she tugged my sleeve.

"Do you like oranges, Eliza?" she asked. "I think they are my favorite because Biddy Johnson has one."

I stared at the square of dark sky in the window, and hoped she could not feel my heart thudding. "I do," I said.

"I like them with cream," she went on sleepily. "And when they are cut you can put them in your mouth and it looks as though you are smiling. Like this." She used her fingers to pull the corners of her lips into a grimace, and I smiled, and wondered if the moment should be now, or if there would be a better one.

"Charlotte," I said, and it came out in a whisper. "Have you ever thought of running away?"

Our faces were close, her breath sweet on my face. Her eyes were very dark, and shone with alarm. She shook her head ever so slightly, and I could smell the soap from her hair, which I'd washed the night before. Then she nodded gently, and plucked at my sleeve, but would not meet my eye.

"I have, too," I whispered.

"Please don't go," she said in a small voice.

I shifted on the narrow bed, and breathed in her warm, sleepy smell, and put an arm around her. "If I was to go, would you go with me? We could go together." *I am your mother.* How did you say it, if not in those words?

She looked thoughtfully at me. "Like Biddy Johnson and Tommy Trusty?"

"Just like them." My voice was so quiet now I could hardly hear it. "Charlotte, what if I were to tell you that . . ." I got up from the bed and knelt on the floor so as to see her better. She lay against the headboard, her face turned toward mine, clean and white in her nightdress. She knew I had something very important to say, for her little face was serious, and dreadful, as though in some way she understood that what I was about to tell her would change her life.

"Do you want to hear a story?"

She nodded, and I took her hand in mine.

"There was a little girl," I said, "who lived in a big house on the edge of London. There was a meadow at the end of her street, with cows in it, and at the other end was a square, with black railings and tall trees. She had everything she ever wanted: servants, silk dresses and ribbons in her hair. She had a turtle, and a bird in a golden cage. She drank chocolate for breakfast and had marmalade every day. She lived like a princess, but she was lonely, and she never left the house. She sat at the window and watched people go by in the street. She wanted to be among them, and she dreamed that one day her real mother would come and rescue her.

"One day, her mother told her she would have a nursemaid. And the woman who came to look after her had dark hair like her own, that went red in the sun, and she had brown eyes, same as hers. They ate every meal together, and played with the dolls in her room, and the little girl read to her, because, the nursemaid, she couldn't read herself. And one night, as they was tucked up in bed and the little girl was falling asleep, the nursemaid whispered to her: 'I am your real mother, and I've come to take you away.' They made a plan to run away together, and then one night they tossed their things into a sack and left. And only the stars saw them, and the moon told the stars not to say a word."

The silence was deep and instant. She did not move, or breathe, her dark eyes fearful, her lips pursed in a question. I waited, and watched, resisting the urge to reach for her.

"I am your mother," I whispered, finally. "I left you at a hospital when you was a baby, and Mrs. Callard took you home to take care of you. For me. I was always coming back, you see? And now I'm here."

She blinked once, twice. A little frown had begun to knit itself across her forehead. "Is it true?" she asked.

I nodded. She needed something else I realized; she'd had a story, and now she needed the truth. I climbed back on the bed and held her, and she let me, resting her head on my chest. My heart still banged furiously, and I whispered over the clamor of it.

"When you was born," I said, "I wrapped you in a blanket and walked from my house with my pa — Abe, I call him, your grandpa — to the Foundling Hospital, where we go to church. They look after babies there, until their mothers can fetch them back. So when you was born, on the twenty-seventh day of November, I wrapped you up in a nice warm blanket and took you there, for them to look after you. And I left with you something that was very special, that your father gave me: a white heart, about this big." I drew it on her palm. "He'd cut it in half, with a crooked line like this, and he gave me one of the pieces, and kept the other for himself. And on it he carved the letter B with his penknife, for my name, Bess. I carved a C underneath, for your name, which was Clara then."

She was like a baby owl, made of eyes. "Your name is Bess?" she whispered.

"It's Elizabeth. But some Elizabeths are called Eliza, and some are called Bess, and some are Liz, or Lizzie, or Beth, or Betsy. There's lots of names that come from Elizabeth. But you must call me Eliza here. Do you promise? I'm Eliza now."

She nodded, and I hugged her fiercely.

"Is my papa the same papa?" she asked, and I told her yes, he was, and that he'd love her if he knew her. She'd listened solemnly, and then said: "What happened next?" I stroked her thick, dark hair and told her how the hospital promised to keep her safe for her mama, until she was ready to be collected.

"And now here I am," I said. The words fell between us, landing on the bed like stones. "I know you like stories, but that's the truth."

She had gone to bed that night seemingly unchanged, though thoughtful, and a little while after I'd closed the curtains, when I lay wide-awake in my bed, mulling over what I'd done, I heard her quiet voice from across the room.

"Eliza," she whispered.

"What is it?"

To my surprise, she told me to stay where I was, and I was too shocked to do anything else as she climbed out of bed with quick, easy limbs and darted to the door. I lay there, listening for her feet, and not even a minute later she was back, closing the door and holding something behind her. She stepped toward me, and her face was shining with bright, uncomplicated triumph.

"Where did you go?" I whispered.

"Mama's bedroom."

"Where is she?"

"In the parlor."

She held her hand out, balled in a fist, and I put mine beneath hers, and something fell into it — hard, and small, and sharp. It was a flinty object, like a shard of china, and it took me a moment to realize what she'd given me. I could only stare at it, and then at her, and again at the crooked shape I held between my finger and thumb. It was just as I remembered it — the looped B, and the crude C I'd made with a shelling knife at Billingsgate, when my belly was big.

I said nothing, but felt, finally, as though I had been put together again.

Charlotte returned the token before Mrs. Callard missed it, but knowing it was in the house was like an itch, a craving. It sung to me from her room, as though my own bone had been cut out and hidden. That it was locked away made me want it all the more, and finally the time had come.

I'd been surprised to see Mrs. Callard glide into the dining room, stiff and proud after the sequence of events a few days before. The house had been holding its breath with the mistress out of sorts, and her presence righted the balance again, though she simmered with fear and dignity, clearly afraid of how we saw her. When she set me on a pointless errand to the kitchen, my opportunity arrived. I crept up the stairs and quietly made my way to her bedroom, which was mercifully unlocked. I had been inside it once before, when she made me lock Charlotte in her room, but that day it was a different place altogether. Now her things lay all about in a mess, her bed unmade and drawers and chemises cast all over. A crystal decanter sat on her vanity with an inch of brandy inside, and scrunched paper and ink bottles littered every surface. It was a chamber of waste and indulgence: pear cores turned to mulch, and soap melted on a dish by a copper bath. The straight-backed, orderly Mrs. Callard she presented to the world was privately a sloven.

Charlotte had told me about the ebony box, and the key that unlocked it that she kept on her vanity. Briefly I wished I could sit at her looking glass and hold her pearls to my neck, but there was no time. I found the key in a velvet-lined caddy that smelled faintly of sponge biscuits and went to her bureau, taking out the ebony box painted with Japanese figures and opening it, feeling my breath coming quick. I scrabbled through her keepsakes, feeling only a distant pang of guilt, looking for white among the gold and enamel. But first I found something else I had not been expecting: the tiny leaden tag, with the number 627 stamped on it.

I squeezed it in my hand, felt it real and hard in my palm, and that's when I saw the counterpart: the left-hand side of the heart, pale and shining, like a fragment of the moon.

I traced the shape engraved on it with a finger and knew it to be a D from Charlotte's books, the ones she was too old to read now, which lay untouched on the shelf: D for dog. D for diamond. D for Daniel. Alexandra had it. He had given it to her.

Then something else in the box caught my eye: the glimpse of a face, looking into mine. I frowned, and moved the trinkets around, and could not believe what I saw. As though I'd conjured him, an oval miniature of Daniel, the size of a small pebble. I took it out to look at him properly, and though I would recognize him anywhere, I realized I had not really known him at all; this was not how I remembered him, though the winning expression was there.

He was younger here, wearing a uniform,

looking as freshly minted as a new coin. I could not help but smile, and for the first time felt his presence in the house he had lived in and died in.

I thought back to the brightly lit doorway beside Russell's coffeehouse, the way he'd looked at me across the street. Had I taken a left and not a right that day, walked on down the wide thoroughfare of Fenchurch Street and not turned left into Gracechurch Street, I would not be standing here in a quiet bedroom in Bloomsbury, about to become a thief. The last seven years had led me to this moment. All the things I needed were in this house, and now I'd found them. I put both parts of the whalebone heart in my pocket with the leaden tag and closed the box quietly, and went downstairs for more cream for the cabbage.

"You ain't scared of the dark, are you, girl?" Lyle asked Charlotte.

We were moving east through narrow streets somewhere around Gray's Inn. Being so unused to strangers and walking outside, Charlotte had closed up like a mussel, and did not reply. I'd seen her eyeing Lyle's unlit torch, which towered above his head like a club. I hadn't taken a link before, sticking only to the streets I knew after dark, when I had to go out at all. The night watchmen — Charlies, Lyle called them — would be about with their sticks and lanterns, calling out the hour and the state of the weather, plodding up and down like overfed cats, before retiring to their boxes for a game of cards and a nip of brandy.

Lyle was avoiding the thoroughfares and their slow, dark figures moving without a glim or torch. He knew all the streets and passages, living as he did in the darkness; his feet were his eyes and ears.

"Who's the cove, then?" he had asked on one of our moonlit meetings.

I'd taken a swig of beer and passed him the bottle. "The mistress's husband, but he's dead now."

He let out a long, low whistle. "And how'd you meet him?"

"Russell's coffeehouse, near the Exchange. Do you know it?"

"Not in the daytime I wouldn't. What's a giggler like you doing in a coffeehouse? They don't let women in. Ahh, was it one of *them* coffeehouses? With the hand on the pot, keeping it nice and warm for the swells?"

I knew he was teasing me and stuck him with my elbow. "Shut it, or I'll find a place for your torch so dark it'll never light again.

No, he was coming out, and I was walking past."

"And that's how you got poisoned, is it? Just walked past? That's a new one."

"I didn't know he was married. I didn't know anything about him, other than his job. Still don't, living in his house. There ain't a picture of him, none of his things nowhere. It's like he was never there."

"Did you try and find him?"

"No."

"A merchant, eh? He might have helped you, if he'd known."

"I think we both know he would not."

The night had been cold, and I thought he would go back to work, but he said: "Do you know what I would have been, if I weren't a moon curser?"

"What?"

"Well, I like growing things, you see. Which ain't easy on the fourth floor, but on the sills we have basil and sage and thyme. I even tried tomatoes last summer, but they never turned red. I want my own garden outside the city. Lambeth, perhaps, or Chelsea. Somewhere green and spacious, where I can grow things for the markets: apples, cabbage, carrots, turnips. I'd love that, taking 'em in a cart to Covent Garden."

"I've never had a tomato. And I've never known anyone dream of working on the markets, neither," I said. "It's early mornings and cold winters, outside all the time."

"Well, I'm late nights and cold winters, ain't I? Same difference."

I shrugged. "I wouldn't care if I never saw a shrimp again."

"I'd sooner smell of a tomato than a shrimp. Not that you do. You're a bed of roses, you are."

But I knew that I was not, and though the Billingsgate smell had faded in place of the starch and lye of service, and we'd both escaped our lives for a short time to imagine ourselves a nursemaid and a market gardener, I was still a shrimp girl, and he a linkboy.

The next time he came he brought out his hand from behind his back, and on it sat one of the bright, round fruits that had more color in its flesh than the whole street, than the whole of London. I bit into it and wet, cold sweetness flooded my mouth. I do not know how he had found a tomato in London in winter, but that was Lyle: he brought light, and he brought tomatoes.

"Stop." I put a hand on his arm, and we paused in a narrow street high with cramped

306

buildings: warehouses or store rooms, shut up for the night.

Lyle had lit his torch once we'd crossed the Holborn thoroughfare, and it threw light in a shallow pool around us. I expected we were somewhere south of Clerkenwell, from the way we'd come. This was not the city I knew, the London of night; I had joined the shadow dwellers, the criminals. I peered into the darkness behind us, thicker than tar. Had I heard footsteps?

"We ain't stopping," he said, pulling us along. We came to the mouth of the alley onto a wider, quiet street with a few windows lit in the upper floors, distant but reassuring.

"How'd you do, angel?" I whispered.

Charlotte was tired, her eyes dull. She was too big for me to carry but I wished I could.

"We'll be home soon," I told her. "And you'll meet your granddad, and I'll put a nice warm brick in your bed, which is right beside mine. Then tomorrow morning we shall go and find a new house, just the two of us. How does that sound?"

She was silent. A few minutes later Lyle's torch showed the sign of the Drum and Monkey, and I looked for the spire of the church down the lane, and knew that we were only a few streets from Ludgate Hill. I told Lyle he could leave us.

"I ain't doing my job if I leave you," he replied.

"Oi!" came a cry out of the darkness, sending me cold with fear. "Oi, you."

The slim frame of a man appeared. I gripped Charlotte's hand so tight it might have snapped, and prepared to run.

"Need a glim for a sedan going to Soho," the man said, his shoes echoing on the cobbles.

"I got someone," Lyle said.

"Oh, is that right?" The man peered at us, his face solidifying before the flame. He was old, with baggy skin and a foul-looking wig. We passed by him, and I kept my head down, catching the sharp whiff of brandy.

A merry fiddle was playing in the tavern at the end of the street — and inside people were whooping and stamping their feet. I had no idea what time it was. We crept in single file through Bell Savage Yard and onward into Black and White Court. Lyle's torch burned white, and we came to a stop at the mouth of our lodgings. All was quiet; a dog barked distantly, but the building looked to be asleep. I breathed out, a long, low sigh that I had not known I'd been holding. Lyle had a triumphant look, a smile curling the right side of his lips.

"What do I owe you?" I asked him.

"How about a kiss?"

The torch choked and spluttered. I drew Charlotte into its pool, and she stood, statue-like, her eyes serious. I leaned down and spoke into her ear. "Charlotte, what do we say to Lyle for bringing us home safe?"

Lyle gave me a look, removed his cap and crouched to Charlotte's level, but she said nothing. He grinned, and straightened. "It stings a man to be rebuffed," he said. "First your mother, now you."

Your mother. I had not heard it before, and it felt strange, and wonderful.

"Thank you, Lyle." We stared at one another for a moment in the black mouth of the court. "You won't tell a soul, will you?"

"I ain't leaky. You have my word. Bess who?" He winked. "Right. I'm off to find an old boozy who'll snore all the way home in his sedan. Until next time, I wish you bene darkmans, Misses Bright."

"Good night, Lyle. Thank you."

I did not know when I would see him again, or how he would be able to find me. Perhaps it was better that way. I stood on my toes and kissed his cheek, and breathed in his smell: of pipe tobacco, and something sweet, like herbs, or soil. Before I could draw away, he took my cheek in his hand, bringing me toward his face. His lips were inches from mine.

"*Laku noć,*" he said, and with that he dissolved into the night.

CHAPTER 16

The court was empty, and we scuttled across it to the main door, which opened easily into the pitch-dark hall. Though I could see nothing I knew instinctively the distance toward the stairs, and found them with my foot. Holding Charlotte's hand, I felt our way to no. 3, set the sack down on the floorboards and fingered for the key inside it.

"Eliza?" came a whisper in the dark.

"Yes, my love?"

"Where are we?"

"I told you, we're at my house now. This is where I live."

"Why is it so dark?"

"There's no oil lights, we use candles here, and I ain't got one. We should have asked Lyle for a rush, shouldn't we? You ain't scared, are you? Remember Biddy Johnson. She wasn't scared, was she, even when that gang of ruffians came after her."

The terrified silence that followed told me I'd said the wrong thing. "Only there's no gangs here," I whispered. "Everyone's asleep, that's why it's so quiet and dark. You won't believe the noise in the morning, with everyone fetching water and bumping about. You won't be able to hear yourself think! Thank heavens . . ."

I found the key and groped for the lock, and held my breath until I heard the familiar clunk, then picked up our things and ushered Charlotte inside.

The sitting room was freezing cold. The thin curtain was open, and moonlight soaked the floorboards. The fire was out, and dirty pots and pans littered the fireplace. The faint smell of day-old fried fish turned my stomach. I glanced over at Abe's bed, at first thinking it empty. He barely made a shape under the blanket, hunched on his side in his nightcap, facing the wall, snoring gently. I decided not to wake him, and crept with Charlotte through to the bedroom.

"Here we are," I whispered, setting down the sack. Charlotte swayed slightly on the sunken floorboards. I had a month's wage from Mrs. Callard to add to my savings, and knelt beside my bed to feel under the straw mattress for the domino box.

It was not there.

I hauled the mattress off completely, exposing the ropes beneath. There was nothing on them, or under them. I did the same with the other bed, listening for the clatter of wood falling to the floor, but there was only straw and rope and the wooden bed frames, which were bare. I looked desperately about, for the curtain was open here, too. That's when I saw it, on the dresser beneath the window, next to the chipped jug I used for washing. Lying open, the lid pushed all the way out. I knew it was empty from across the room.

My breath came out in quick little clouds. Abe still snored in the other room, and I heard the creak of floorboards as Charlotte shifted uncomfortably. A cold, sick panic began spreading from my stomach, and made me lower myself down onto the mattress. I was oddly clear-headed. The box had been here when I came on my half day a little over a week ago; I had checked. But had I opened it?

That morning I'd been happy and distracted, and impatient to get back to Devonshire Street. I'd gone, too, to Ned's, but he was out, so I'd spent a half hour with his wife, Catherine, and the children, holding the baby while Catherine chopped vegetables for a broth. Her face was drawn, her jaw a tight line, as she told me he had not been home since two nights ago. I was worried but not frantic, in a vague, manageable sort of way, like hunger before it slides into starvation. I'd told her he would be back, and she nodded, because he would be, but we both knew the problem was more serious than that.

I went into the other room to wake my father. "Abe," I said, shoving him firmly.

He woke instantly, midsnore, pushing himself up in bed and frowning in the darkness. "Bess, is that you? What you doing here?"

"I've come home," I said. "When was Ned here?"

"Ned?" He took a moment to respond, his voice cracked and growly. "A week, p'raps? But why are you home? I thought you was —"

"Did he go in my room?"

Abe's face was scrunched in confusion. "He might have, I don't remember rightly." He gave a great yawn and sat up straighter. "He's in trouble, Bess."

"The filthy cheat! What do you mean? What kind of trouble?"

The bed creaked beneath him. "He has the body snatchers after him. He might be

314

in the clink now, all's I know. Or the pillory. I've no way to help him and he's past helping himself."

I had the sensation that, one by one, the floorboards were vanishing beneath me. Charlotte stood watching from the bedroom doorway, stiff and mute, out of Abe's sight. I knew I should have comforted her, brought her to meet her granddad, but I couldn't move an inch.

Sleep did not come that night, but guilt and fear nestled on either side of me and rested their heads on my pillow. With the money gone, it was impossible to pretend I wasn't done for. In the morning I'd have to tell Abe what I'd done: thieved a child, who I planned to hide with at some shabby lodging in the lawless burrows between the Fleet Ditch and St. Paul's. But now, with my savings gone, I could barely afford that. That money had meant I didn't need to find a job straight away, but now we both would. And staying here at Black and White Court was not an option, for as soon as the magistrate was told.

I shuddered. The bedroom was icy cold, and I'd put Charlotte to bed on the narrow mattress beside mine. She was used to feathers not straw, and the single, clammy blanket hadn't been washed in a long time. She was pretending to sleep, her dark hair falling over the pillow, her white face still. I lay next to her in my dress and boots, watching her closely, rubbing her arms and legs and singing to her, and breathing in her soapy smell. I held her lily-white hands and wondered how I could send them to work, those hands that had only ever tied silk ribbons in her hair and turned the petal-thin pages of books.

I shifted onto my back, and my breath clouded in the moonlight. It was too great an effort to close the thin curtain, and I looked out at the rooftops and wondered if Mrs. Callard was awake, or if she would not realize we were gone until the morning. I could not imagine how she would react: with white, silent astonishment or violent rage, now that I had seen her tidy disguise slip. My taking Charlotte would tip her orderly life into chaos. No doubt she would tell the servants first, and send Agnes to fetch the watchman, who would in turn tell the magistrate. But how was I to escape an enemy I did not know? The search would spread in an inky pool through the city, starting in Bloomsbury and leaking out, east, south and west, filling the alleys and parks, whispered over gloved hands and gossiped about by laundrywomen pegging out sheets. She had the money to spread the news to every inch of the city, and comb it, too. It was the greatest difference between us. To her, money was a pool to drink deeply from. Me, I was parched.

I felt a stillness beside me, and turned my head to see Charlotte watching me in the darkness. We stared at one another, and her eyes were unreadable.

"Are you really my mother?" she whispered.

"Yes," I whispered back.

"Is that my grandpa?"

"Yes," I whispered. "You'll meet him tomorrow. Now, it's time you shut your eyes, and in the morning I'll go and get us a fresh loaf, and some milk we can warm in the pan. You'll like the milkmaids. They carry it on sticks over their shoulders, and wear frilly caps the color of cream."

She complained she was cold, and I rubbed and rubbed her arms again. All that wood and coal at Devonshire Street and now we'd none of it. She closed her eyes, and I hummed her gently to sleep, like when a bad dream woke her. Now she lived in one. From Devonshire Street to Black and White Court; Bloomsbury to the Fleet. It was like something from one of her children's books. But it went the other way, in the stories.

By the time dawn broke over the rooftops, the other room was silent; Abe had left for the market. I decided he was better off not knowing Charlotte was here, that way he had nothing to hide. Once he returned we'd be gone with our things to a new lodging, and there I could invent a plan. Guilt tugged at me; there was much that needed doing here and nobody to do it with me gone. The floors and hearth were thick with grime and coal smoke, the windows, too, and a new bucket of lye needed making for Abe to clean his clothes. But there was no time, and he would have to do without me.

"I'm cold," Charlotte said again, moving next to me in bed. I dropped a kiss on her head and threw my blanket over her, tucking her in tightly.

"Oh," I said suddenly, remembering. "I've been saving clothes for you all this time. Do you want to see them?"

Only half-curious, she watched me go to the chest in the corner of the room and unload piles of linen and cotton and wool. It did not take long to empty, and I held up the nicer things to show her — an oat-colored gown that nipped beautifully at the

318

waist; a smart felt jacket with only one small hole beneath the armpit.

"Do you like them?"

Her face was smooth as marble. Of course she did not like them. She was used to Spitalfields silk, and here I was showing her linsey-woolsey worn by someone else: a child that had died, probably. The clothes felt heavy with their old lives, and I folded them and put them away. She looked as though she might cry.

There was a banging at the door, and our eyes met in mute shock. I had not told her we were hiding, but somehow she knew. The knocking came again, rapid and impatient.

"Abe, you in there?" It was Nancy Benson from downstairs. I held my breath, not daring to make so much as a floorboard creak. "Abe? I thought I heard feet on the dancers last night; jess thought I'd look in."

The door to the other room was closed, but what if she had a key? If she walked in here and saw us . . . I felt her presence behind the wall, imagined her plump fingers on the handle, and willed her away. After a minute or two she gave up, and the stairs creaked as she shuffled back down. That put paid to me fetching water from the pump in the court; I couldn't risk it with Nancy sniffing around like a bloodhound. We would not wash, then, so there was no point building a fire.

I dressed quickly and threw the windows wide to let out the stale air, thinking of Agnes, who said a ventilated house was a healthful house. With a twist in my stomach, I realized no. 13 Devonshire Street would certainly be awake now. No doubt Agnes would be wringing her hands, her kind face made simple with confusion. She would not believe me evil enough to take the child. Only weeks before we had sat at the kitchen table long after everyone had gone to bed, a single candle between us and a glass of sherry at our elbows.

"The child ain't hers," she'd whispered, her lips glistening with liquor.

I'd been very silent, and listened to the wind sigh around the yard outside. When I trusted myself to speak, I tried for a mixture of astonishment and disbelief. "Why do you say that?"

"She weren't big," she said. "Her belly was tight as a drumskin. Her appetite was the same. And —" She shifted her light blue eyes to the room's black corners, as though Mrs. Callard might be folded into them. "She bled every month. Then, one day, a few months after the master dies, a cradle's delivered and put in the nursery. It weren't a nursery then, of course; it was a bedroom. The master used to sleep in it sometimes if he'd been out late, and he was staying in it more and more afore he died — if he came back at all, that is." She paused, relishing her diversion, enjoying her audience. Maria was not one for gossip, and Agnes was pleased she had someone to chew the fat with. It had not been hard to get her to speak.

"Where was I?"

"The cradle," I said.

"Oh, yes, the cradle. I says: 'Who's that for, madam?' And she says, clear as a bell: 'My child. I am expecting a child.' Well, you could have knocked me down with a feather. At first I thought — and don't tell Maria I said this — I thought she'd met someone else, so soon after the master's death. Terrible of me to think that, I know." Delicately, she took another sip of sherry and grew confiding, leaning in so I could smell it on her breath. "I didn't expect she meant it would arrive the same day."

I arranged my face into a picture of surprise.

"She sent us out on errands — me to the haberdashers, though we had plenty of everything, and Maria to pay a bill. And then, when we got back, there was this strange noise. At first I thought a cat had got stuck somewhere. But I goes upstairs, and there it is, lying in the cradle. A baby. Now, I don't know how all that works; I don't have children myself. But I'm sure as my name is Agnes Fowler that babies aren't born in the amount of time it takes to buy buttons. If I didn't know any better, I'd have thought she'd bought it at Fortnum's emporium."

"Perhaps she did," I said, and we'd laughed. I poured us another measure from the bottle, though Agnes pretended to resist. I was growing fond of her, with her bright blue eyes and white hair, her gentle, powdery skin. She was plump as a cushion, and indiscreet as a bawd. A throwaway "good morning" could fix you in a room for fifteen minutes while she made her way through some tale or other, and a "good night" could leave you in deep admiration at how two words could lead her to a story about a Newcastle sailor who tried selling her a goat in Spitalfields.

"She didn't feed the child herself, then?" I asked.

"Heavens, no," said Agnes. "Swells don't, of course. A wet nurse arrived later that night and stayed about a year. Belinda, her name was. A young thing like yourself."

I'd heard of wet nurses, but didn't know anyone who used one or, more likely, anyone who was one, as the rich sent their babes outside the city for suckling. I watched the candle dance in the darkness and imagined another woman feeding Charlotte, and rocking her at night. And then Mrs. Callard had interrupted us, drifting into the kitchen like a rain cloud.

The next day, I asked Maria what she knew about Charlotte's birth. From behind a veil of flour, she gave me a searching look. "No different to any other, I should imagine," she'd said, and picked up her rolling pin.

I had been glad Agnes hadn't minded her business that day, for she was a trusting lamb. With a pang of shame I wondered what she thought of me now.

"Where are we going?" Charlotte asked weakly as the clock struck eight.

"We," I said, pulling up her drawers, "are going to find Uncle Ned, to get our money back. Hold your stampers, and we'll put them on at the bottom of the stairs." I handed her a pair of sturdy boys' boots that were well worn in, and would not hurt her feet.

"Where does he live? I'm cold."

"Not far from here. Now, don't you look a picture in your new things?" I had dressed her in a brown printed cotton dress, with a warm wool shawl and gray wool stockings. With her dark hair tucked into a white cap, I had wiped every trace of Bloomsbury from her, and made her a child of the courts.

Together, we went silently down the stairs, passing Nancy's door with our fingers over our lips before hurtling out of the back entrance of the court into Fleet Lane. Making our cautious way north and avoiding the thoroughfares, I told Charlotte to keep her eyes on the ground as we walked, but she gazed agog at every man, woman and child we came across. And not just the people: every painted street sign was stared at, pile of horseshit examined and hawker looked in the eye.

Nobody wanted to live somewhere worse than where they came from, but that's what had happened to Ned. Three Fox Court was half a mile north, on the edge of Smithfield meat market, a place so dank and narrow the sun never reached it. Trapping the fearful stench of cattle and backing onto a slaughterhouse, it was rich with rats and flies, and the ground washed daily with blood. It made you feel drunk to stand in, with all the buildings leaning, threatening to topple over. A litter of children crouched in the darkest corner, barefoot despite the cold puddles. Their wizened faces gave them the look of organ-grinders' monkeys, and among them, the most pinched and sour of the lot, was Ned and Catherine's eldest, Mary.

"Mary Bright, what are you doing down there?" I said, approaching their hostile little party.

They had been playing with bits of rubbish they'd collected: fish bones and what looked like a rabbit skull. One of the smallest girls lifted her skirts and began pissing. I moved so it wouldn't touch my boots and took Charlotte by the shoulder. Mary stared at her, her expression pure spite. Named for our mother, she was four years old, but looked forty. She wore no cap, and her mouse-brown hair was cut blunt like a boy's. She had none of Ned's smooth features, nor his carrot pate; she was all Catherine — narrow eyes, a long, pointed nose and freckles. Her shapeless dress was the same color as the wall. She might have been born of the grime and shadows of Three Fox Court, a creature of Smithfield, made of leftover bones.

"I'm here to see your pa. Do you know where he is?"

Her eyes were like two slits, and she jerked her head at the house with a wariness beyond her years. The others watched with suspicious eyes. I let myself in the door at the bottom and climbed the two flights of stairs to Ned's rooms, ducking under mildewed washing and passing a child of two or three, sitting on a stair and screaming fit to burst, its face the violent purple of a turnip. A rich black bruise blossomed beneath one eye. Charlotte clung to my skirts as I banged on Ned's door. From behind it came the sound of shouting, and the baby crying, then an urgent shushing.

I banged again and Catherine's voice came: "Who is it?" I told her and banged again, and the door flew open.

Catherine barely registered who we were before pulling us inside. Her thin hair was falling out of her cap, and the baby in her arms was a scarlet ball of fury. Ned was slumped at the table with his shirtsleeves rolled up, as though he was ready to fight. His face was gaunt, and there were shadows beneath his eyes.

"We thought you was the bailiffs," said Catherine, putting a hand to her hip. But it wasn't a defiant gesture; she appeared to be holding herself together at the seams. "Who's this, then?" she asked, noticing

Charlotte, who, despite every effort to blend in, still gave off the air of a child in disguise.

"I want my money," I said to Ned, moving toward him with an outstretched palm, Charlotte's hand in the other. "Come on, Ned. You stole it when I was out, like the coward you are, and now I want it back. Don't tell me you've spent it."

"You stole from Bess?" This was Catherine. "How could you do that, Ned?"

Ned was silent, and stared hatefully at the table. Baby Edmund had stopped crying at the sound of my voice and sat in Catherine's arms, looking from me to Ned and back again, his cheeks damp with tears.

"He's gone and sold everything," Catherine said. "The cupboard, the bed, the pans. The sheets. Even the pissin' chamber pot."

The room, I noticed, was almost bare. What little food they had sat on a shelf to keep from the mice, and there was a lumpy mattress in one corner, made of straw wrapped in blankets. Along with a little pile of folded linen on a broken stool and a bowl so chipped it wouldn't have held soup, these appeared to be the sum of Mr. and Mrs. Bright's belongings.

Finally Ned looked up, and nodded at Charlotte. "That your broken leg, is it?"

"Don't call her that. Don't even look at

her. *I'm* talking to you."

"Found her, then, did you? Don't tell me, you've brought her back here to save her from a life of wealth and privilege."

"You're a thief."

"I ain't the one who's snatched a child. You think you're doing her a favor, taking her out of that house I saw? She'll be dead in a week."

I pushed her behind me. "If she does it'll be your fault," I roared. "You stole my savings! What did you do with them, Ned? Because if you've spent all that down the gin shop I'm amazed you're still alive, and disappointed, frankly."

"Go and swim in the Thames, Bess."

"That was mine and Charlotte's. I bet your children haven't seen a penny of it."

"Ha," Catherine laughed darkly. "Ain't that the truth."

Quick as a flash, Ned leaped from his chair and sent his fist across her face. The sound of it cracked across the room, and plunged us into silence. Then several things happened at once: the baby began to roar again, Charlotte pressed into my skirts and started to sob noisily, and Ned spread his hands over the table and rested on his wrists. I noticed he was shaking, but perhaps not with anger. He was damp with sweat. A powerful need to escape overcame me; I could not bear to stand in that miserable little room another minute.

"If Mama could see you now," I said, at a loss for anything else. Ned did not move, and I looked at the familiar way his hair curled over his ears, and wondered where my brother had gone.

I took Charlotte and led her from the room.

CHAPTER 17

The entrance to Black and White Court was a passage, no more than two feet wide, a quarter of the way up Ludgate Hill between a victualler's and a cooper's shop. The passage led to Bell Savage Yard, which was long and narrow, strung with laundry between the buildings, and Black and White Court was beyond that, at the end of the yard on the right. With Charlotte ahead of me, we came into Bell Savage just as a tall, well-dressed man in an ink-black hat reached the far end and disappeared around the corner. Bell Savage Yard and Black and White Court joined as a thoroughfare to Fleet Lane and the Old Bailey, but not a well-trodden one. In short, you only went there if you had to.

The man, I told myself, might well have been harmless — a visitor, a bailiff, an inspector. I knew, though, that he was not. I swore under my breath and pulled Charlotte to a stop. She looked at me as if to ask what was the matter, and I dithered for a moment, hopping on my heels and turning once, twice, before cursing again, and finally deciding to leave like the chicken-hearted sneak I was.

"Leading a merry jig, are you?"

Half-concealed by a drying sheet, Lyle Kozak was standing against the wall of Bell Savage Yard with his arms folded, looking for all the world like he was watching a game of cock-a-hoop. He was quite at odds in daylight without his torch, though his features still had a shadowy quality about them, as though he had been drawn with coal. His black eyes glittered, even from a distance.

"You look better in the dark," I said.

He grinned. "You Billingsgate coolers know how to woo."

I jerked my head back toward the passage and he was alert at once, following me back into the tide of Ludgate.

"How goes it, miss?" he asked Charlotte, as we walked. He waited for the girl's attention before pulling a coin from his ear and handing it to her. She smiled and took it, and I realized I had not seen her smile since we left her house. "Go and buy yourself a currant bun from the baker's in there, you

331

see? Go on." After a moment's hesitation and a reassuring nod, she slipped into the open doorway we stood beside, and I looked hard at Lyle.

"Did you see that man just now, who came in before me?"

"The jemmy fellow? I saw him. Thief-taker, I reckon."

I swore and looked up and down the hill for his cocked hat. "All my things are in there! And Abe — he won't know I've gone again."

"Whoa, Nelly. He didn't find you, did he? There's nothing in there I can't get for you. You got some balsam?"

"Yes."

"How much?"

"About six shillings."

"Say it a bit louder, I don't think the deaf wench in Westminster heard."

"Oh, shut it, will you! Don't make out you're the only one who has your wits about you. I've got us this far, haven't I?"

"*I* got us this far," he said with a power-fully irritating wink. Charlotte came out of the baker's with a bun the size of her head. "That ain't all for you, is it?" Lyle teased when she'd reached us. "You won't need to eat till next Saturday."

At that moment, a woman stepped out of

the passage with two of her children, and I recognized her as Helena Cooke, a shy mother of five who lived with her husband and mother at no. 8. I pulled my cloak over my head and faced into the baker's window, and Lyle shifted immediately to cover me. I waited for Ludgate Hill to swallow them up.

"Are you peckish?" Lyle asked, once they'd gone.

"Yeah, I suppose so."

"Let's go to the beef house and I'll get you a chop. Oi, Tom Thumb."

He collared the first boy he could find, a dirty, idle-looking lad of about thirteen, and then two more, a wide-eyed child of around eight and a stocky thing who looked like a fighting dog, giving each of them a penny to watch the court's three exits. "Whoever sees him first, follow him to his digs," he told them, "then come back here and wait for us and there'll be a bit of balsam in it for you." They hurried off, each of them eager to win.

Fifteen minutes later, Lyle, Charlotte and I were seated at a bench in the dim, smoky basement of a beef house off the Fleet Market, each with a bowl of stew, a heel of bread and a cup of milky tea.

Since living at Devonshire Street my appetite had grown, and my waistline with it. My stays were pressing at my waistband, and Lyle watched me enjoy the food with a smug smile. He himself ate in a surprisingly delicate way, almost like a swell. He didn't put his elbows on the table or drink his stew from the bowl like some men did, chewing instead in thoughtful little mouthfuls as I told him about Ned stealing my money, and how I'd soon have nowhere to stay.

"So you need an escape," he said after the pockmarked serving girl had poured us more tea from the kettle.

I nodded, and wiped Charlotte's collar absently where she'd spilled her stew. She was shyly fascinated by the eating house, which was dark and loud and pungent, with the smell of roast meat from the kitchen, unwashed bodies and spilled beer. Almost every seat was taken at the long, scrubbed benches, and dirty plates covered every surface. Smoke clung to the low ceiling, and elbows bashed against one another as people laughed, gossiped and quarreled. The din rang in my ears, though it never used to.

"Here's what we'll do," Lyle said, leaning in. "My sister works in Lambeth, on a dairy farm by the marshes. It's only two or three miles from where we are now. I'll go and see her and ask if she can get you a position

— a dairymaid or summink — where Charlotte can go, too."

"I've never been to Lambeth. Ain't it countryside there?"

"That's right." Lyle turned to Charlotte, and realized she was listening. "Can you milk a cow?" he asked.

She looked so affronted we couldn't help but laugh.

"All right," I said. "But, Lyle, only if she can come. It's no good me finding a position and they won't take her in."

He waved a hand. "We'll tell 'em you're a widow; we can get you a bit of tin for your finger."

I sighed, rubbing my face, and tucked my hair in my cap. "Who sent you?" I said. "I must have done something right in a different life."

"Or summink wrong in this one."

"I suppose I'll have to hide till we hear from your sister. I'll go to my friend Keziah's. Can you come there when you know? She's at Broad Court, off Shoemaker Row by Houndsditch. Can you remember that?"

"Shoe Court, Houndsmaker Row, Broad Ditch."

"Lyle!"

"I know it, girl."

335

"I just got to hope that man don't find me in the meantime."

"You're golden. What's a thief-taker got to go on: a brown-haired woman and a little girl? There's ten thousand of them all over London. Now," he said, draining his cup. "I'll go and find out what them Tom Thumbs have to say for themselves, and I'll get your things. Where shall I meet you?"

I thought for a moment. "Paternoster Row, behind St. Paul's, where the bookstalls are."

He nodded. "I'll see you there in ten minutes, fifteen at most. Then you can get yourself to your friend's. But remember to keep your head down."

"Have you quite finished telling me what to do?" I teased, handing him my key, which he shoved inside his jacket.

"Nobody tells Bess Bright what to do, eh? Well, I'm looking after you. Sounds like you ain't used to it."

The streets off Ludgate Hill were quieter, and Paternoster Row was a prosperous, gloomy thoroughfare in the shadow of St. Paul's. Nobody would be suspicious of a mother and daughter browsing prayer books at the wooden stalls outside the printing houses, when the industry of pages and words was a world away from my own. I knew nobody who could read or write, nor any of the book printers, whose customers came for gold-edged bibles if they had money, and secondhand volumes if they did not. I told Charlotte we were to look at books, and she brightened at once. Lyle peeled off into the courts and we walked slowly up Ave Maria Lane.

"Charlotte," I said very quietly. "We need to seem as though we're out on an errand, but don't stop for too long anywhere, and don't look anybody in the eye."

"Why not?"

"Because we don't want to be seen."

The street was shady, and positioned in front of the printing houses were two dozen stalls heaped with books. Holding hands, we walked to the end before coming back down, and I nodded briefly at a stallholder, who tipped his hat, and shook my head at another one who proffered a cheap bible. A woman selling turbans wandered around, spinning them on her hands, and two priests in robes glided over the cobbles, talking quietly.

"Why don't we try and find some of your books here?" I said to Charlotte.

"*My* books?" She was confused.

"No, not your books. They're not here,

337

but the stories will have been printed more than once."

She frowned in confusion, and that's when I saw him at the next stall along. The thief-taker was moving idly up Paternoster Row, glancing at the bookstalls and stopping here and there where they caught his attention. I could only see the back of him, his cloak and hat, and a brief glimpse of the side of his wide, smooth face. I hadn't seen him properly before, but I knew instinctively he was the same man, as a rabbit knows a fox. I felt as though I'd been doused with ice, and gripped Charlotte's hand to move away, but she pulled back and reached for a little red book.

"What's this one?" she asked.

I tried to guide her away, every line of me ringing with fear and alarm, but she brushed me off crossly and said: "I am looking at this."

"Can I help you, miss?" The stallholder approached us, and I felt my insides turn to slush.

"Put that down," I said.

"I want it! It's red, like *Biddy Johnson.*"

"I haven't the money," I murmured. "Now put it down."

I felt the thief-taker's unbearable presence move closer, heard his shoes rap smartly on the ground.

I cast about wildly for something, anything, to make us invisible. If he moved around me, and saw her face, and then mine.

"Speak French," I hissed urgently. "Tell me the garden story, now, quick!"

Charlotte stared at me, wide-eyed, but was old enough and clever enough to sense unspoken danger. The thief-taker moved very closely behind us, and wordlessly I urged her to speak.

"Le jardin est magnifique en été," she said.

I nodded, and noticed that he had stopped behind us now.

I turned slowly toward the stall, trying to appear natural, and Charlotte went on haltingly, *"Les roses s'épanouissent sous le chaud soleil et les parterres sont un éclat de couleur."*

"Excuse me, miss?"

I closed my eyes, and felt the ground slide beneath me. Could I pretend not to have heard? Then I felt a hand on my shoulder, iron-like, and spun around to look into his face with an expression of confusion.

"Oui?" It was the only word I knew. He was peering at me very closely; his eyes were small, and sat in his large face like currants in a bun. He wore no wig, and his hat and

clothes were expensive. I returned his stare, praying with every fiber that Charlotte would stay silent.

"Do you speak English?" he asked me. His voice was Cockney, but smoothed at the edges; nobody would mistake him for a swell, though he wished to appear as one.

I frowned and shook my head, gesturing that I did not understand with one hand, and squeezing Charlotte's fingers hard with the other. She winced, and he looked at her. After an age of pure agony, he said "Good day," and, with a final long look, moved on, with his hands behind his back.

"Who was —" Charlotte asked not five seconds later, and I shushed her before she could finish, and turned back to the stall, moving my shawl over my head so it sat like a hood. I could sense the man had not left Paternoster Row, could feel him like a lump beneath the skin. When a minute or two had passed, I stole a glance down the street and saw him at one of the last stalls, weighing a volume here and there in his black gloves and putting them back. In case he was still watching us, I tried to look as though we had found nothing of interest, and moved very slowly back the way we had come. It felt as though we were turning our backs on a lion. There was no sign of Lyle, but I decided we could not wait.

"You were very good then," I told her, glancing here and there as we turned right instead of left, moving away from Ludgate Hill and Lyle. I realized I was trembling. "You did what I said and spoke beautifully. We're playing a game, you see, where we don't look at people or speak to them, and move as quickly as we can. If anyone talks to us we've got to talk French, and tell them we don't have any English."

"Why?"

"Because," I replied. "Those are the rules of the game."

"Where are we going? We said we would meet Lyle at the bookstalls." I realized with relief that she had no idea of the real danger we'd been in.

"We can't do that now, but don't worry. He'll find us."

Keziah's court was empty when we arrived. I hurried across to her window to knock, keeping my face hidden beneath my hood to avoid the attention of her neighbors who overlooked the dim yard. We had criss-crossed our way through the city to wring out the afternoon until I knew Keziah would be packing up her cart and trundling home, feeling all the time as though we were being followed, that the thief-taker would be around every corner, leaning languidly in a doorway, waiting for me to fly directly into his web.

Our tedious dance through the city, where I'd felt every pair of eyes upon us, had made us both tired and anxious, and then it had begun to rain. Somewhere around Cornhill, Charlotte had complained that she was wet, and her boots hurt, and she needed the chamber pot, so I'd lifted her skirts for her to go in an alley. She refused, white with dread, insisting she needed the pot, so I'd had to lift my own to show her how it was done. A spasm of something had crossed her face then, as if she was ashamed of me, but I'd brushed it aside.

Finally Keziah's face appeared at the window, and a moment later the door opened, and she hurried us inside and into her rooms.

The Gibbons boys were eating meat pies at the large table, their legs dangling inches from the floor. Keziah crouched before Charlotte and grasped her shoulders.

"You must be Clara! I've been so looking forward to meeting you." She pulled her into a hug. Charlotte was stiff as a broom handle, her dark eyes huge in her pale face.

"I'm Charlotte," she protested, and Keziah

laughed.

"So you are. Ain't you the little mort! She's the picture of you, Bess."

Charlotte moved away and attached herself to my skirts.

"Charlotte," I said, "this is my friend Keziah, and her sons, Jonas and Moses. She sells dresses to very fine ladies in the East End." Charlotte looked around at the shabby room and at the boys sitting at the table, who were watching her quietly. I pulled down her wet shawl and stroked her hair. "She's met a lot of people lately, haven't you? More today than in a year, I'd imagine. Here, you sit there with Moses and Jonas, while I talk to Keziah."

She shook her head, and I crouched down. "What's wrong?" I said. "You aren't shy! Remember Biddy Johnson. Why don't you tell the boys about her, go on." I tried to lead her to the table, but she shook her head again and looked ready to sob. I sighed. "All right, come and sit with me, then."

Keziah hung our shawls over the bar in front of the fire and we sat on either side, me in the rocking chair, with Charlotte on my knee. The solid chair with its steady rhythm had always comforted me, and I pushed on it now absentmindedly, as I told

343

Keziah of the events of the previous night and this morning. Her dark eyes were grave, and as she listened she took off her cap and teased at her little ropes of woolly hair.

"You can stay here, long as you need," she said when I had finished, and I thanked her. Charlotte felt heavy on me, and I realized she was asleep. Now I could talk freely.

"Mrs. Callard's got a body snatcher after me," I whispered. "I saw him at Black and White Court and he almost filched us earlier." I swallowed, as the question I'd been leading up to pressed at my throat. "Do you think they'd hang me, Kiz?"

"They can't hang you for taking back your own child!"

"They don't know that's what she is, though. Mrs. Callard'll swear she's hers."

Keziah bit her lip, and I could see the boys watching wide-eyed from the table. She glanced at them, then at Charlotte. "You're sure she's yours?" she murmured.

"Yes. Look what I found in her house." From my pocket I pulled the two halves of the little whalebone heart. Keziah took them from me, bewildered.

"Mine's the one with B and C on it. Mrs. Callard had it along with the other one. The D is for Daniel."

"Then this is all you need! There will be a

record of the token at the Foundling place?"

"Yes, they wrote it down. But I stole it from her house!" I shook my head. "I don't understand how she knew what the token was, but didn't recognize me. It doesn't make sense."

Keziah opened her mouth and closed it, and sighed. "I don't know, Bess. None of it makes sense."

I was suddenly deeply tired. The light was fading at the window, and I rested my head against the chair back, just for a moment, as Keziah left to wipe the boys' hands and build a fire. I let my eyes travel about the room, noticing the damp walls and the stains in the laundry hanging above our heads.

Keziah's bowls had always been chipped, and her chairs missing a spindle here and there, yet somehow my eye was now drawn immediately to all the faults and snags. If I had not been so tired, I would have felt angry that a woman who worked six days a week from dawn until dusk, and her husband dusk till dawn, had not even a scratch of Mrs. Callard's wealth. Mrs. Callard, who was irritable and proud and short with everyone she spoke to, when all she did was climb up and down stairs in her silk slippers and have tea brought to her on a silver tray.

There were footsteps in the court beyond, but a thin red curtain covered the window now. I realized that it served to hide me, too, and began to understand for the first time what Keziah lived through every day. She had to hide her sons, and now I had to hide my daughter. But the difference was I still had hope of an end to it: that one day, we would be able to move freely through the streets with our heads bare, and not be afraid of who we met.

There was no end to it for Keziah and her children; they would always live with fear. I'd known it, but never really understood how it felt until now. Why her ears were pricked constantly for her boys, and how her heart beat always for them. I watched her tidy the hearth, sweeping cinders into a pan, and felt a powerful rush of love and loyalty. I held my daughter, heavy on my chest, and I understood that love and fear were no different. Not really.

We stayed with Keziah all that week, trying to be helpful and not nuisances. I gave her a few coins toward food and rent, and made myself useful, darning her clothes for the market and looking after the boys when she went out to work. William kept his usual routine, sleeping or rehearsing during the day and taking his violin out before nightfall.

We slept in the big chair by the fire. Charlotte was withdrawn, and in quiet moments I would see her looking about the room with interest. She was unused to sleeping, eating and living in one room, but Keziah kept a warm, tidy home and cooked good, simple food from the markets. She had only ever lived with three people, two of whom worked for her, but she gradually began to relax in the Gibbonses' company, for theirs was a traditional home, with a mother and father and two children, like the ones she had read about. It was the reason I found comfort in them, and I think she did, too.

On the second night she showed an interest in Keziah's piles of clothes and frippery in the corner of the room. Jonas submitted good-naturedly as she began putting caps and coats on him while we watched from the chairs before the fire. His older brother decided they would open a shop, turning over an old crate to use as a counter and charging a penny an item. Keziah and I used thimbles and buttons as coins, and Charlotte played happily for an hour or more, wearing a striped gown that was ten sizes too big and a man's cocked hat, and handing over garments as we pretended to inspect them for fleas and stains. William brought home a bag of roasted chestnuts while they played, and we shared them before closing the shop and putting the children to bed.

In the morning Keziah went out to work and William left to rehearse with his quartet, and I played shops again with the children. The boys liked having Charlotte as a plaything; she grew less shy around them, and found a pack of cards and taught them gin rummy and patience. They told her about Mrs. Abelmann's canary, and she asked to see it, but of course the answer was no. She read to us while I yawned and closed my eyes for an hour, and I woke to find them on their bellies in the bedroom collecting bits of dust and seeing who could gather the biggest piles. The afternoon came and went, followed by night, and still nothing from Lyle. Long after we'd cleared the supper things away and everyone had gone to bed, I was woken from a fretful sleep by the sound of William letting himself in. He closed the door quietly, and sat on the bench to remove his shoes in the dark.

"William?" I whispered.

He paused, and I waited, pinned beneath Charlotte, who was breathing deeply, while he moved around to find a rush to light. In the paltry flame, I could see he was wearing a gray wig and a smart blue jacket.

"What time is it?" I asked him.

"Just after two," he whispered. He took the chair opposite, and glanced at the bedroom door but did not go inside. I rubbed my eyes, and though it was dark, I could see he was troubled.

"What is it?"

He seemed to weigh up what to tell me for a moment.

"Tonight I was playing at the Assembly Rooms in Piccadilly," he said levelly. "We were positioned by a large dividing door where people moved through the rooms. While we were changing our sheet music, I heard a conversation between two guests, standing just the other side. They were talking about a missing child."

The rush spat and flickered.

"One of the men — a lieutenant general, I think; I didn't catch his name — was telling the other about a little girl stolen from a house in Bloomsbury, the child of a rich widow. Every watchman in the area is alerted, and looking for her."

My heart was beating fast.

"They are looking for a woman of around five and twenty, with dark hair and eyes, and a printed cotton dress."

I shrank back into the chair, shifting beneath Charlotte, who was still asleep. We were silent a full minute while I let the enormity of what he'd told me sink in.

"Did you hear anything else?" I asked eventually.

He shook his head, and the rush sputtered.

I sighed. "Oh, where is Lyle? He said he would come soon. But even then, if they're looking for me all over, how will I get to Lambeth?"

William was thoughtful. Then he said: "They won't be looking for a little boy. Charlotte could wear Moses's clothes, and put her hair beneath a cap."

"Good idea. That's something, at least. Only thing is, what if Lyle's sister can't find me work after all? Oh, I hope he comes soon, else I won't know what to do."

I thought William would get up, but he looked grim and serious, as though there was something else.

"William?"

He shifted in his chair and looked guilty. "I don't know how to say this, Bess."

My mouth felt very dry, and a chill swept the room. "What is it?"

"Well, Keziah and me being who we are,

if somebody sees you here, they might think it odd. We can't pass you off as family, and if they were to look through the window and see a white child . . ."

I closed my eyes. "Of course. I understand. I'll go soon, I promise."

William nodded and went to bed then, leaving me in darkness, with guilt soaking me through. If I stayed, it would surely only be a matter of time before I was found; Charlotte would open the curtain, or tiring of the situation, scream to be taken outside. And all the while, I was putting my friend and her family in danger. I pictured a mob outside Keziah's front door with flaming torches in their hands, their faces masks of hatred. There was no appetite like that for a criminal avenged. I'd been myself to hanging day — Paddington Fair, they called it, which brought to mind garlands and picnics. Tyburn gallows was a minute or two's walk from Black and White Court, at the top of Old Bailey. The widow at no. 7 made ropes for the hangman.

I thought of Abe, asleep at home. Did he know I was a wanted criminal? He wouldn't read it in the paper but he could have heard it on the courts from Nancy, or any of the Billingsgate men and their wives, who might have heard there was a search for me. What would he think, when he heard his daughter was a child snatcher?

I hadn't told him the truth, of course, when I got the job at Devonshire Street. Abe had been bewildered when I said I was going to be a nursemaid, and even then didn't know the half of it. My loose design was to arrive back with Charlotte and say I found her and the position didn't suit me, hoping he wouldn't press for details. Abe was a man who kept to himself, and didn't pry. I knew I'd have to get a message to him once I was in Lambeth, and tell him not to worry, but Abe was the least of my troubles, and I thanked the heavens that he hadn't seen Charlotte the night before.

I slept in snatches that night, imagining the newspapers and what they said. They'd likely have printed my name, and where I lived. I'd convinced Doctor Mead my real name was Smith, telling him I'd come to collect my child under a false one, and that I went by Eliza, not Bess. He had believed me, familiar with the lengths women took to cover up an illegitimate child. To cover up their shame.

A broken leg, Ned had called her. I should like to give him two. It was because of him I was shut up in here like a stowaway, relying on my friends' kindness. Perhaps, though, it was safer here than in lodgings, with no landlady to grow suspicious or neighbors to avoid. I knew how quickly opinions were formed of newcomers, and how solidly they set in their molds. Well, here I was, and I had a comfortable chair to sleep in tonight, and a bit of money for when we had to find somewhere else to live.

I didn't have to wait long. Before daylight fully arrived there was a light tapping at the glass. I had been dozing, with a dead arm from Charlotte's weight, but I'd not wanted to move and wake her. The knock had been so soft I thought it might have come from the rooms above, but then it came again, unmistakably at the window. I was awake at once, and lifted Charlotte carefully, setting her down in the big chair with the blanket and going to lift the curtain. Dawn scratched at the court, and I peered out, seeing no one at first, then fear turned to relief as I saw it was Lyle, with his cap pulled down over his eyes. I hurried into the quiet hall to let him in, taking the front door key from the hook behind a picture. Neither of us spoke as he followed me inside and set his torch beside the door. Over one shoulder was a large sack that I recognized as mine, and he set it gently on the ground.

"You came," I whispered.

He removed his cap. It was a good-mannered gesture that made me like him all the more, and I realized then how much I'd been thinking about him, how much I'd wanted to see him. I knelt at the sack and began rummaging through it.

"You been carrying this all week?" I said pointedly.

"I hid it at a storehouse; pal of mine watched it for me. What happened at Paternoster?"

I told him about the thief-taker and our narrow escape, and he swore and put on his cap again, then removed it and scratched his head. I wanted to ask him what had kept him away this long, but felt powerfully shy, suddenly, and confused by it. I lifted our clothes from the bag and began folding them in a pile on the kitchen table with my back to him.

"In case you're wondering why I'm only coming now, I realized when I went to fetch your things there might've been a ware hawk watching the place. I dunno what I was thinking, walking in there, bold as brass. So I came out and trolled about a bit just in case, and went to a coffeehouse for an hour. I dunno how them swells drink it — horrible stuff. This your mate's gaff, then?"

"Keziah's asleep," I said.

"She's out for the count." He nodded toward Charlotte, who was wrapped in the warm blanket with her feet dangling above the floor. We both looked at her for something to do, and then I remembered why he'd come.

"Any news from Lambeth?" I asked him.

"Oh, yeah. You've got a position at the farm as a dairymaid. Well, Beth Miller and her daughter, Clara, have. We've told the farmer she's nine, so she might have to stand on her tiptoes. She'll work alongside you. You're a sailor's widow from Shadwell, and you'll share a bed in the farmhouse."

I felt weak with relief. I turned and thanked him, and he watched me closely, clinging onto his cap.

"No more hiding," he said. "You'll be golden with our Anna; she'll look after you."

"When can I start?"

"The day after tomorrow. Well, I suppose it's morning now, so tomorrow. I'll meet you on Westminster Bridge at midnight tonight, and take you there. Anna will be expecting us. It's not far from the river, two miles or so."

"Is it far enough?"

"A dairy farm in Lambeth? Put the Thames between you and you're as good as overseas."

"And what of the thief-taker?"

"Oh, him. He was after you. His name's Bloor; he works from a den at Chancery Lane. I staked him out to have a look; plenty of pork pies behind him, but he's a slick cove. You could outrun him, though, if it came to it." He smiled lopsidedly, and I smiled back. "Don't look so worried," he said softly, closing the space between us. "You're out of here."

The dim light from the red curtain fell on us, and threw half of Lyle's dark features into shadow. When he was silent, he looked so solemn, and he was looking at me now as though there was something else he wanted to say. I took an involuntary step toward him.

There was a cough from the other room; dawn was here now. I pulled my shawl tighter where it had fallen from my shoulders.

"Midnight," I said. "Westminster Bridge. I'll be there."

CHAPTER 18

Abe shut up the shrimp stall at three, and I knew the route he took home with my eyes closed: up Thames Street toward London Bridge, then north along Fish Street Hill to the Monument, before climbing west from Great Eastcheap to St. Paul's. Not wanting to be too close to either Billingsgate or Black and White Court, I settled for the middle, leaning against the railings of an untidy churchyard near Budge Row with my shawl around my head. I arrived at three, hoping he'd kept his usual hours and not gone to the Darkhouse tavern for an ale, or to the dockyard to hear the papers read. I kept my eyes on the steady flow of traffic going west, and at twenty minutes past the hour almost missed his old, defeated form trudging up the other side of the road. I ran quickly across, dodging a cart, and without greeting, pulled him into a shady passage. He shook me off, squinting in the dimly lit space. I put a finger to my lips, and his eyes widened. I pushed him along into the court beyond — a smart, cobbled place with a lone tree in the middle, lined with redbrick townhouses.

"Bess —" he began, but I shushed him and pulled my shawl farther over my head.

"I can't stay," I said. "I came to tell you I'm leaving tonight. I'm sorry it had to be like this and I've not been home."

"You've got the girl, then?"

"You've heard?"

"Me and everyone else. Bess, it's all over the newspapers, all over the courts, about Elizabeth Bright, the nursemaid what stole her charge. All over Billingsgate! I got the porters asking if it's true; they can't believe it. 'Your Bess, thieving a child?' I don't know what to tell 'em. I haven't been able to sleep. Where you been?"

"We're at Keziah's. But I'm leaving tonight, to go to Lambeth, to a farm there. My friend Lyle, he's helping me. I'm meeting him on Westminster Bridge and he's going to take me. His sister's a dairymaid and she's found us work, me and Charlotte."

He shook his head. "I hope you ain't caught, cos the watchmen, they been looking for you. And another cove, a thief-taker. He's been no less than three times, bashing at the door, wanting to know if you've popped in for a cup of tea. I've been dreading you coming back when he's there."

"I know he's been after me, and he shan't find me, with any luck. Here." I fished in my pocket for the remaining shillings I had, and gave him three. He began to protest, but we both knew it was in vain and he needed them. Wordlessly, he put them in his pocket with a sigh. "I'll send more when I can," I said.

"Jesus Christ, I wish you'd be careful."

"I am, aren't I? I had her with me that first night I came back, and you didn't even know. If only you could have met her, Abe. You'd love her, I know you would."

He looked very old then, and the lines around his eyes and mouth seemed to deepen. "This ain't right, Bess. I wish you hadn't done it. What a mess it is. Ain't she better off in that fancy ken where she came from? What kind of life can you give her? You should have left her where she was."

I felt a flash of fury. "She lived with a mother who didn't love her, didn't want her. It was like a prison there, Abe. She never went outside. I might only have a shilling to my name but *I'm* her mother."

"You might well be, girl, but a child needs a father as well. How do you expect to live?"

359

"I told you, we've got positions, both of us. She's old enough to work. Heavens, you had me on the stall after my old mum died; it ain't much different. I only had you, all this time. We done all right, haven't we?"

He shook his head again. At that moment one of the painted doors in the square opened and a housemaid stepped out with a dustpan. She gave us a hard look, emptied the pan onto the cobbles and waited. I could see how we looked, two shabbily dressed vagrants, who had no place in this handsome square. I glared back and turned away, moving into the passage.

"I have to go now, but I came to tell you I'm all right, and I'll see you . . . Oh, I don't know when I'll see you, but I will." I pulled him into an embrace. He smelled of the market, which to me was like home. The enormity of what I was doing, what I was leaving, hit me then, and I held him hard and tried not to cry as he squeezed back. We didn't need to speak, me and him. We woke together, walked to work together. I might've gone around the city, the coffeehouses and taverns and markets, but I always went back to him, and there'd be a fresh basket of shrimp waiting for me, like he knew I was coming. Our words were in the way he took my plate off my lap when

I'd fallen asleep, the way I passed him his hat before we left the house. The way we sat quiet on a Sunday when it rained outside, and brewed a pot of tea with the used leaves from the charwoman.

I didn't know when I'd see my home again, couldn't imagine a day when I'd be able to walk through the court and let myself in at the door. I'd never forget it, though: the floorboards where I learned to crawl, and the sloping ceilings. The pictures I'd pinned to the wall as a girl, faded now, of frivolous things like balls and lovers, and ballads I'd picked up off the street that I could not read but that showed girls looking out over fields, with long dark hair like mine. The dirty lace at the window, and the chair Abe sat in, with its old red cushion, and the door to the bedroom in which Ned and I dreamed and whispered and laughed, with the enamel jug on the side, and my mother's chest, carved with roses.

"Best of luck, Bessie," Abe said, and his voice cracked. "Watch yer back, won't you?"

"Thanks."

I pecked my pa on the cheek, trying not to cry, and could not look at him again: at the doubt and shame and fear in his milky eyes, for they mirrored my own. I embraced him once more, tightly, and let the crowd swallow me up.

By the time the clock struck half past ten, we were ready to go. It would take an hour or more to walk across the city to Westminster Bridge, and a light drizzle had begun to fall. We would go along the river, keeping it on our left and following the bend of it, like a tobacco pipe turned upside down. The canvas sack had been packed again, and Charlotte and I were wrapped against the wind and rain. William's idea to make Charlotte appear look like a boy had been a good one, though she had complained as we plaited her hair and pinned it beneath one of Moses's caps and dressed her in Jonas's jacket and trousers.

"Ain't you the little swell!" Keziah had exclaimed, and Charlotte had scowled, making us laugh. The boys watched with glee as I did up her buttons and laced her own boots. When the clock struck ten, my stomach had twisted itself into knots as I went over our things again: dresses, shawls and drawers, two blankets, a few candle stubs, two tin mugs and plates, a bottle of beer, and Charlotte's playing cards and her copy of *Biddy Johnson.* I had asked Keziah to buy her an orange as a treat, which I would save until it was needed. There was a dreadful finality to it all, as though we were going on a very long journey to a foreign land, and not a few miles from where we stood.

"Are you sure you don't want William to go with you?" Keziah asked.

"Thank you, but no. It has to be just us. You won't follow us, will you?" I asked him, and he shook his head. He had no work that night, and had gone out for some beer to go with our tripe stew. Perhaps sensing the atmosphere, Charlotte had been fussy with her food and refused to eat it, and I'd lost my temper, telling her she had to start work in the morning, and would not be able to on an empty stomach. Then I was angry at myself. I should have been tucking her into bed with a doll, not making her walk through London in the middle of the night. But climbing into bed seemed so distant; a simple thing I would never again take for granted.

Hatefully, shamefully, in the darkest part of my mind a tiny thought had burrowed and planted itself as she whined, to go not along the river, but into the city and up the thoroughfares, where the maze of little streets and alleys gave way to wide, empty roads with tall houses, and knock on the door at no. 13. I let the image take shape, picturing Mrs. Callard's white-faced shock, Agnes's trembling relief. And Charlotte, clinging to me, sobbing on the doorstep . . . No . . . No good. I could never do it. She was mine.

I had told her that our life would be hard from now, that she would have to work and rise early, and be very tired and hungry, but Mama would always be close by. I knew that she would find it tough, that she had been spoiled, and I would have to unspoil her. Churning butter, milking cows, lifting pails: I had prepared her for all these things in the stretching hours at Keziah's, but I could tell she was listening as if it was a story, not real life. And what if she refused to work? If she threw tantrums and made a show, and lost us our places, what then? *No, don't think on it.* All we had to do for now was get safely to Westminster, and stand on the bridge and wait for Lyle. I did not know if he'd hire a trap for the journey or if he'd come on foot. I would have to watch very carefully, and try not to draw attention.

We kissed inside the Gibbonses' door and said our goodbyes, and my stomach twisted worse than ever because I could see the fear in Keziah's face. I told her I would find a way to send a message, and she laughed then, and told me if I ever learned to write she'd frame my first letter on the wall, and we smiled at one another and hugged fiercely. And then the door was closing, and I saw the red curtain twitch as they looked out, and felt choked with emotion — and relief, too, that they were no longer in danger.

"Bye!" Charlotte called, and I had to shush her. She shrank away from me, frowning, as though I would scold her again.

I crouched down and tucked at some stray bits of hair that had drifted out of the cap. "We have a very long way to walk now," I told her. "I know it's dark and raining, but we have no choice. Will you stay close to me and try to keep going, even when you want to stop?"

She looked solemnly at me, and I rubbed at her cheek. She nodded.

"Good girl. Off we go."

We made our way to Westminster Bridge as best we could in the dark. We couldn't go along the river itself, as the Thames bank was filled with complicated little wharves and stairs and piers, and there was no path, but I was sure to keep it in sight as we traveled west. Knowing it was there, wide and glittering beneath the night sky, was a feeble sort of relief; I made my living from the water, and it was a comfort to have it there beside me like a faithful old dog.

I told Charlotte about the market as we walked, and where the ships came from and what they brought, and the characters who worked there. She liked hearing about the dead shark that was hung on the dockside like an ugly mermaid, which had its teeth pulled out one by one.

Around halfway the drizzle eased, but a dreadful knowledge set in as Thames Street tapered to an end and I realized why. We were approaching the Fleet Ditch, the river that sprang north of London and flowed beneath the city, reappearing again below Farringdon, where it funneled down and emptied itself into the Thames. There was only one way to cross it: over a bridge at the end of Ludgate Hill. The tight lanes and streets this close to the river were dark and quiet. Alehouses and taverns lined the riverbank that would be filled now with wharfmen, dockworkers and lightermen, but they were all I could hope to meet at this hour on their way home. I led us hurriedly north, telling Charlotte again not to look at anyone, and wrapping my shawl more firmly around my head. The narrow bridge and the streets on either side were mercifully empty, and we crossed at speed without looking back.

It was a quarter to midnight by the time we drew up at the northern bank of Westminster Bridge, damp but triumphant. A few torches burned here in the smarter part of town, and the river gleamed blackly beneath us, stretching and yawning around its curve. The moon was behind cloud, which had served us well, for we had not been noticed. I put my hand on the balustrade and finally allowed myself to relax. Lyle would be here in fifteen minutes. We had done it: we had got here.

"That's the hard part over with," I told Charlotte, lifting her up and setting her on the low stone wall. "Now, what do I have in my bag of tricks for a good little girl?" She watched, her little pink tongue darting through the gap in her front teeth. I brought out the orange and joy broke over her face, and she asked me to peel it. "Let's get to the middle of the bridge and I'll do it while we wait for Lyle."

There were one or two people about: two men in conversation striding across the other side of the bridge, and partway along, a vagrant-looking woman bundled against the balustrade, heaped with rags. I took Charlotte by the hand and walked with her over the river, pointing at the dozen or so boats going their different ways, for the traffic was quieter at night.

"That's a trawler, see, like I told you fetches the shrimp from Leigh," I pointed out. "And do you see those little ones, going between the big boat and the quay? They're lighters, what carry the cargo to shore, because the boat's too big to get up alongside it, you see? It looks like they're carrying timber, look."

We walked farther along and came to a stop in the middle. A coach-and-two passed by us. The mail coaches would be leaving London now, starting their long routes into the country. I told Charlotte we could write Moses and Jonas a letter once we'd arrived for their father to read to them. I rubbed her hands with my own, for the rain had made the air cold. After a few minutes, I saw Lyle approaching from the north bank, hunched against the wind, with his cap pulled low. My heart began beating fast, and I smiled, standing away from the balustrade so he could see us better. But he gave no sign of recognition, and did not slow down to approach us, nor did he break into a smile. As the distance closed between us, I realized it was not Lyle. The man's face was pale, and he was taller, and leaner, with wide, clear eyes. There was a flash of red hair at the sides of his cap.

"Ned," I said in surprise. "What are you doing here?" I was smiling, but frowning, too, and felt strange, as though I was seeing him in a dream. And then I understood.

Another man was gliding toward us, from the direction Ned had come: a tall man, with a black cocked hat and thick cloak. He wore leather gloves. He and Ned were the men I had seen on the opposite side of the bridge five minutes earlier.

The fox had found the rabbit. I felt as though an ice bucket had been tipped down my back as the thief-taker regarded me coldly, seeing the recognition in my eyes mirror his own. I was clutching Charlotte's hand very tightly now, and she winced. I pushed her behind me, and hoped she would not feel me trembling.

Ned would not look at me, and turned to the thief-taker.

"This is her," he said flatly, nodding once at Charlotte.

"We've met before," the man said softly. His voice was deep and cracked, like leather.

"No —"

He darted toward her. Ned took my wrists, restraining me as I cried out, as the thief-taker gripped Charlotte by the shoulders, making her sob and cling to me. Our hands were ripped apart, and hers flailed through the air, reaching for me.

"Ned, no! Don't do this!"

A carriage had been waiting at the north end of the bridge, and it drew up beside us, slowing to a stop. In a flurry of darkness, like shadows wrestling, the thief-taker bundled my screaming child inside, and her cries tore through the air, tore through my very soul. In a moment the reins were shaken and the horse pulling. The wheels turned, and the carriage moved in a wide circle across the bridge, going back the way it had come. At the same time a figure was hurrying toward us from the north bank. There was a long instrument in his hand, like a baton, or a torch.

"Lyle!" I screamed. "He's got Charlotte!" Ned held my wrists still, too tightly, and I spat in his face just as Lyle reached us and landed his fist in Ned's face. But Ned had been prepared and swerved the impact of it, dropping me from his grip and swinging back at Lyle. Before I knew it the two of them were grappling in the road. The torch had been dropped somewhere nearby, and I almost tripped over it as I went hurtling after the carriage that cut sleekly through the night and was swallowed at the end of the bridge. It was no good running after it;

I knew where it was going.

I stood numb, shattered, looking at the place it had disappeared, trying to put together in my mind what had happened. Behind me, grunts and blows carried over the lonely cobbles as the two men tore at one another. Lyle had begun using the torch as a club, and I heard the dull thud of it cracking into my brother. I wanted Lyle to kill him. If I'd had a pistol, a knife, a bludgeon, I'd have done it myself; I'd bash and stab and blast the life out of him until he leaked scarlet and his glassy eyes no longer saw the stars. No, his blood would not run red. His blood would be black as his soul.

■ ■ ■ ■

PART FOUR:
ALEXANDRA

■ ■ ■ ■

CHAPTER 19

The red-headed man came that afternoon. I'd been sitting in a chair at the window beneath a blanket, looking out at the street. This was the sixth day, and it had rained all morning, hissing at the windows and making them slick. When the doorknocker sounded in the hall I had left my mind again, going into that distant place I seemed to exist in now. But its rap jolted me back to my seat, and I was instantly alert. There was no carriage in the street; someone on foot, then. My heart thudded briefly, and then as quickly as it arrived the spasm of intrigue passed, and I sat back as dullness consumed me again. It was most likely Doctor Mead, who had attended me these past days with the dedication of a dutiful nephew, and I his invalid aunt. I had not wanted his tonics or snuffs; did not care for food and drink, even, taking bits of meat and the odd bread roll in this chair, when I ate at all, and remaining until the small hours in the darkness with no candles lit, to better see the street. None of my clothes were warm enough, even with the fire piled high, so I'd taken to wearing one of Daniel's old greatcoats around my shoulders, like a general in retirement.

I waited for Agnes to announce whomever it was, and a minute later the door pushed against the carpet, and I felt her presence in the room. I had not turned from my chair, and when she told me a gentleman was here to see me, at first I did not recognize his name. She showed him in and closed the door, and I turned, finally, to look into the face of Bess's brother. I knew him at once as the lean, pale-faced man who had looked over the yard wall all those weeks ago.

Agnes had been wrong: he was not a gentleman. Shabbily dressed, he did not quiver so much as jerk, and his gaze was very intense; it felt as though he was touching me all over, and his fervency repulsed me. His manner was the least repulsive thing about him, though, as it turned out. When he offered me information on Charlotte's whereabouts, or rather, where she *would* be, at first I thought he was playing a trick. I said nothing, as he told me in a stammering voice that for a fee, he would reveal Bess and Charlotte's location. He knew they were fleeing the city tonight, and could bring me the child. He'd stumbled over his words and shook so badly I thought him ill, but then I noticed the slight slur, and the gray pallor, and though he could not have been out of his twenties, there was already a purpling map of blood vessels beneath his skin. *Oh,* I thought, with detached interest. *He's a drunk.* It went a way to explaining why he would betray his sister, and I believed Bess was his sister now, for they had the same small nose, and large, slightly bulging eyes, which she had passed to Charlotte. Which meant, then, that this man was a relative of Charlotte's, too.

I listened to what he had to say, then asked what fee he commanded. At this, he went very still and thoughtful, then regained himself, clearing his throat and announcing with false bravado that a hundred pounds should cover it.

After a long silence I said: "Very well."

He had pulled a face then, and I realized he was smiling. He said: "Thank you, miss, much obliged to you, you shan't regret it, miss, very much appreciated," and passively I wondered if he was here under someone else's design. By that time I wanted him from the room: I could smell drink on him, and there was something deeply unsettling about his desperation, and the deferential way in which he treated me. But he hesitated, and I sensed there was something he wanted to ask me. I waited.

"Only thing is, miss," he muttered, shuffling his feet, "as it's me sister, what took her, and I'd hate to see her in gaol, 'specially if it's at my hand, you understand. As it's me sister, I was hoping you'd let her go. In exchange for the little one."

"Ah," I said, understanding. They had come up with the scheme together, then. All this time I'd fastened locks to my doors and windows, thinking I'd keep out the thieves that way. Instead I'd invited one to live with me in my home, and was now offering my legacy to another. "Very well," I said again. "You'll take a man with you: Mr. Bloor, at Chancery Lane. His office is at the sign of the falcon. Tell him to take a carriage."

He nodded, his mouth working all the time, as if he was chewing tobacco, and as soon as he was gone I shuddered, overwhelmed by a desire to open the windows and air the room.

The carriage clock ticked faithfully on the mantelpiece in its mahogany case, and I watched the slim gold hand travel around and around as the light left the room.

Doctor Mead did not come, nor did anybody else.

On a table next to me were a pile of newspapers, in each of which I'd placed daily notices for Charlotte's safe return, as well as the details of Benjamin Bloor, the private thief-taker Doctor Mead had found in the *General Advertiser.* There had been an engraving of him, wearing a cloth cap and holding a mace as he professed his services of investigation and reprimand.

Doctor Mead had arranged it all: the commission, the fee. Mr. Bloor had come to the house to take everything down, making large, looping notes in a leather-bound book. I'd been overwhelmed by the size of him; his hands were like small frying pans. His skin was smooth and tanned like leather, and he had small, piggish eyes sitting close to his misshapen nose. I had no likeness of Charlotte to give him: no miniature, not even a sketch. He'd advised we place our own advertisements in the newssheets, and Doctor Mead had taken care of that as well: twelve in total.

"And the girl, Bess," Mr. Bloor had said. "I assume you want her apprehended?"

I had been silent for a minute. The carriage clock ticked, and Mr. Bloor and Doctor Mead waited, watching me intently.

"What would that entail?" I asked.

"Well. I'd inform the magistrate, and when she's found she'd be held in a cell until her trial."

"And then?"

"And then either she would be acquitted." There was an idleness to his tone that implied that would not be likely. "Or she would be charged. In which case: Newgate, most likely, if she's sent to gaol. Or she might be transported to the colonies. Or hung. Depends who's got the gavel on the day." He smiled at this, as if he'd made a joke.

I swallowed, and moved in my chair. "Then don't inform the magistrate," I said. "Just bring the child."

The thief-taker had raised an eyebrow at that, and made a discreet note in his book. Doctor Mead had taken my hand, and squeezed it.

And who had come forward but Bess's brother. I did not trust him an inch, and wasn't certain he would return with the child. At a quarter after midnight I decided I had been proved right, and began to move up to bed, gathering the greatcoat around me and taking up my brandy glass. But before I set foot on the stairs, the doorknocker banged again through the house like a hammer.

I froze with one hand on the banister. The servants were both asleep, and I had not told them what the man, Ned, had promised. Made bold by the liquor, I went myself downstairs, hearing the creak and murmur of Agnes two floors above. The hallway was pitch-black, and I shuffled in Daniel's coat to the door, fumbling at the locks and opening it to find two people on the doorstep: the powerful presence of Mr. Bloor and, struggling in his arms, weeping openly, a small boy. Behind them, a two-wheeled carriage was parked at the railings. I stared at them in confusion, and wondered how this smooth, idiotic man had mistaken this boy for my Charlotte.

Then Mr. Bloor tugged the cap from the child's head, and I saw a mass of dark hair, pinned in an elaborate plait, and the eyes, large and frightened.

I fell to my knees, and reached for her. She shrank away from me, but was stuck fast in Mr. Bloor's strong grip, and protested loudly. We brought her inside just as Agnes appeared at the foot of the stairs with a candle and gave an almighty cry, and my legs gave out altogether.

"Miss Charlotte," Agnes was braying, over

381

and over, and it *was* Charlotte; she was here before us, flushed and dirty and coughing. Agnes was beside herself, sobbing and hugging the child, and Maria arrived a moment later, shrouded in a blanket, and their presence and the fretful noises they were making confirmed it: Charlotte was home, and the six long days and nights of hell were over.

I'd been assisted to a chair, and sat helplessly, watching the two women murmur and paw at her, taking off her wet jacket and wiping her nose when she sneezed. Mr. Bloor towered above this sentimental scene like a Pall Mall statue, while Charlotte wept and coughed and spluttered, and in a whirlwind of activity she was carried upstairs for a bath.

"She will need close attention," he was saying. "I would advise you send for a doctor."

My foggy mind tried to make sense of his words. I could hear Charlotte crying upstairs, sobbing fit to burst, and the sound was unbearable, like a fiddle played wrong. Mr. Bloor announced his departure, replacing his hat with black-gloved hands, and said he would call tomorrow. I did not move, was still clutching the sides of the hard-backed chair in the hall, rubbing the smooth wood with my thumbs. I did not ask what Mr. Bloor had done with Bess.

I'd had to tell Doctor Mead everything, of course. That Charlotte was not mine — Daniel's, but not mine — and I had retrieved her, like Moses from the reeds, and raised her as my own. That dreadful night, when Bess took her — for now I knew who she was I could not think of her as Eliza — we'd sat in Charlotte's room in the moonlight, me on her bed, him on Bess's, and the whole sorry mess had come unspooled. He'd listened in silence as I told him of that winter night all those years ago, when Ambrosia came tearing into the house as I'd been readying for bed. I'd not been a widow long; Daniel had been dead seven months. The landscape of my life had been rubbed away and painted over anew, and I was only beginning to grow used to it.

My sister had appeared in my bedroom in a gust of ribbons and skirts, bringing with her briskness of a November night. Her cheeks were pink, and her eyes shining.

"Daniel has a daughter," she'd said.

I'd stood before her, barefoot in my nightgown, my hair falling down my back, failing to understand her. She'd said it again, and I asked if she was sure, and she said yes, yes, she was, and what did I want to do about it.

"Do about it?" I'd asked in surprise.

"The child is at the Foundling Hospital, not half a mile from here. Will you make her stay there, in a nursery of sick children, until she is old enough to work as a maid?"

"A maid?" I'd said, as though that was the most shocking thing of all. I'd felt for the edge of the bed and sat on it, taking Daniel's pillow onto my lap and listening in disbelief as Ambrosia told me how, months ago, in January or possibly February, she went to one of the more raucous taverns near the Exchange, where women were allowed, and where whores roamed the tables. She had gone with her friend and her husband, a sergeant, who brought a pack of soldiers in high spirits, and sitting there at their crowded table, among the smoke and the sawdust she'd spotted Daniel across the room. It was too noisy to call out to him, and besides, a moment later he got up to go, but he led by the hand a woman — a girl, really — who she took to be a whore. She took her drink and followed them, stopping at his table to ask who the pretty girl was. His companions had shrugged, and she'd stepped outside to find him, and turned a corner to find them moving together in the dark.

She had gone back to her table and not told a soul about it, then Daniel died, and she forgot it altogether, until that cold night later that year, when she was invited to the lottery at the Foundling Hospital to watch women leave their babies. She told me about the colored balls and how they saw the women draw them from a bag; a dreadful sport, but it brought a tear to the eye, and the guests paid handsomely for it. But *there,* she went on, she had seen the same young woman, dark-eyed and frightened, standing with her father, holding a baby in one arm and reaching with the other into the cloth bag.

From behind her fan Ambrosia had watched the young woman draw one and be shown into a side room, and ten minutes later she emerged with empty arms and a shocked white face. The woman's father had led her gravely from the grand room, where trays of punch circulated among the guests, and the tinkle of glasses and laughter drowned out the pleading from the new mothers, and the occasional cry of the babies.

Ambrosia had closed her fan and marched into the side room and asked the clerk very sweetly the name of the dark-haired girl in the gray dress, and was told that the mothers' names were not recorded. Then she had asked, even more sweetly, with a flutter of her fan, about the tokens she had heard of, and what sorts of things they left, and could he show her one, so that she could describe it to her friends outside?

With his breath smelling of coffee and decay, the clerk explained how the unmarried mothers left parts of themselves, cutting their dresses to pieces and scratching their initials into coins to leave with their children, should they ever return. On the table by his elbow was an odd, little jagged piece of carved whalebone that looked like a gambling token or a small brooch. When she gestured toward it, the eager clerk was more than happy to oblige, placing the strange object into her gloved hand, which turned out to be half a heart, scored with initials: B and C.

I was glad to have been sitting then, because whatever doubt I had — that this girl was a whore, that it could have been any man's child between Westminster and Whitechapel — evaporated as I brought out my little ebony box, and showed Ambrosia the polished whalebone heart half, and watched her face turn white to match it. I had known, of course, that Daniel took women; I asked him to, the third or fourth time he had come to me at night. It always made me rigid and afraid, and I'd closed up like an oyster shell, before finally, gratefully, sealing off that part of myself.

That night, Ambrosia had gone after the dark-haired woman in the gray dress, who had come with her father. She followed them discreetly in her carriage to a crowded, festering part of the city, where tall houses gave way to leaking courts and dark alleys. She'd expected to arrive at a brothel and that would be the end of it, but the driver pulled up on Ludgate Hill at the narrow entrance to a court, and she had asked him to wait as she slipped in behind them and followed them to a door that seemed to be ordinary lodgings.

She'd waited until someone appeared, aware she might be robbed of her things at any moment, and asked them who the dark-haired girl was who lived with her father, who had been in childbed. The neighbor had been surprised, but said it sounded like Bess Bright, who lived at no. 3, and confirmed the name of the court. And no, she was not a whore — she worked as a shrimp girl. That was enough for Ambrosia to come straight to me at Devonshire Street.

I listened to all of this in my nightgown,

feeling as though my head was stuffed with wool as she told me she would arrange everything, and send one of her servants to claim the baby, telling her to give Bess's name and address, so that if she did come back the child could never be traced. As well as claiming her being the charitable thing to do, Ambrosia said, a child would be company, and besides, it was unlikely I'd have any of my own, with me a widow and my thirty-fourth birthday a fortnight before. She insisted that not only did I owe Daniel this, for taking me away from Aunt Cassandra's miserable mansion, but that I could give the child a comfortable life. She made the whole affair sound like a stray dog had turned up at the kitchen door.

By the time I finally climbed into bed that night, somehow I had agreed to be a mother, with a daughter arriving the next day. A polished wooden cradle belonging to Ambrosia arrived that morning, along with piles of snowy gowns and blankets and caps and sleeves, and printed cotton outfits for when the baby grew. I had to find space for them all, and sent the servants out in the midst of it, losing my temper when they asked where I wanted them to go. And before the afternoon was out, when the house was silent and lifeless, the doorknocker pounded once more and Ambrosia was on the steps with a soft, pink creature in her arms, like one of Maria's flayed rabbits. When she handed her to me, I took her stiffly, looking at her eyelashes, fine as silk threads, and her tiny nose. She was the same size as a bag of flour, and I felt, then, the enormous weight of how my life had changed irrevocably, from order to chaos.

"What shall I call her?" I had asked in the dim hallway.

"How about Marianne, for Mama?"

I shook my head. It had not been a lucky name for her. I thought about the token her mother had left, the B for Bess, and C for . . .

"Charlotte?" I said.

"Charlotte Callard." Ambrosia had beamed. "How splendid."

I think she thought Charlotte would be the making of me, or perhaps the undoing of the person I'd become. I would disappoint her on both counts.

Doctor Mead had listened to my story in silence, his jaw tight and pulsing, his eyes never leaving my face. In all the years we'd known one another, he had been ignorant of so many things about me — my parents' murders, Daniel's infidelities and the fact that I had not given him a child, but that he had given me one from beyond the grave.

By the time I had finished, daylight was deepening over the rooftops on the houses beyond. He sat in silence, touching his lips, painted with concern in a most familiar way that I longed for even as I saw it, fearful I'd never know it again. When he did not speak, I could not bear it.

"Am I despicable?" I asked.

His brow had furrowed. I'd hoped for an immediate reply, and did not get one.

"No," he said after a while.

"Do you think me selfish?"

Again he said no, but sighed very deeply, and took up a toy of Charlotte's, a spinning top, which had lain discarded on the floor. I saw in his face a reckoning, a dawning understanding, of the lukewarm affection I'd always showed Charlotte, and why I did not take her on my knee like the mothers in the pictures. Finally he looked at me, and asked a question so simple I had not been expecting it.

"Why did you not tell me?"

I opened my mouth and closed it, and looked beyond him at the striped wallpaper.

"I suppose," I said slowly, after a short silence, "I thought you might find me weak."

"Weak how?"

"A failure, then. The purpose of women is to become wives, and the purpose of wives is to become mothers. What woman would wish to raise a child who is not her own?"

"But children are brought up by women who are not their mothers all over London, all over the country. Men remarry after their wives die; relatives take children in. Some women do it very well, others not so, but you and Charlotte are mother and daughter in every way but blood."

"Charlotte was illegitimate; Daniel and I were married. You must see why I did it this way: she could never know she was not mine. Ambrosia knew, of course, and the servants would have guessed because one day a baby arrived and I had not been expecting one. But if I'd told anybody else — not that I have many to tell — it might have got back to Charlotte."

"I understand why you did not tell her. But I feel now as though I've been deceived, not once but twice."

"Twice?"

"By you and Eliza. Bess, whatever her name is. She told me her name was Bess, you know, in the beginning. Then she said it was false, and she'd invented it because of the shame. I believed her. I sympathized with her."

"Do *not* put me with her. She lied to you for her own gain; she played a devilish trick on both of us. More than that, she was deceitful, over and over, every day. How can you compare us?"

His eyes were glassy with defeat. "I wish she had been honest, but of course she had to hoodwink me. Imagine if she had come to me and said you had her daughter! I would have thought her crazed. At the very least I would have sent her away." He rubbed his knuckles against his mouth. "And now I feel wholly responsible for inviting her into your home and your life. But I do feel sympathy for her."

"How can you say that? She has *stolen* my child from me."

"She could say the same about you!"

There was no mistaking the hardness in his voice. Immediately he apologized, and, I think, meant it, but it was too late — he had said it, and could not take it back. "Of course," he went on, "this is much more complex than charging her as a thief, for she is the child's mother."

I glared at him. "I'm not sure what you mean."

"The courts will not prosecute a woman who has stolen her own daughter."

"Of course they will," I snapped. "*I* have

raised her, fed and clothed her. I have taught her lessons and nursed her when she was sick. *I have more of a claim to her.* I am not the whore who abandoned her at some pox-ridden baby farm."

He had winced at that.

"Besides," I added, "beyond her word, there is no proof the child belongs to her."

He stared at me. "Will you deceive the magistrate, and say that she is the liar?"

"I have not thought that far ahead."

"Well, think on it now, Alexandra, because the theft of a child is a serious claim! Would you see her hanged?"

I sat silently, feeling he was testing me, watching me closely with a twitching anticipation. A shadow passed briefly over his face, and he nodded warily and stood.

"I will ask the watchman if there is any news," he said, and went from the room without looking at me.

There had been a coolness between us ever since, packed like a layer of ice over what was already a wholly nightmarish business, and through it all I could not decide which was the worse experience: grief or shame.

I found Charlotte alone in her bedroom, lying facedown on the bed and weeping as if her heart would break. She was unclothed from the waist up, wearing a ragged pair of boys' trousers, and looked as though she had been scraped from the gutter, which I supposed she had. I went to kneel at her bedside.

"Don't cry," I said. "You are home now. What's there to cry about?"

She sobbed harder. Where was Agnes? I sat back on my heels, entirely at a loss for how to comfort her. I moved about, lighting candles and wishing anybody else was here — Ambrosia, Doctor Mead. They would know what to do.

Bess would know what to do.

The bed she had slept in was still there, neat and conspicuous in the corner. I could not look at it.

A moment later a flustered Agnes appeared in the doorway with the copper bath that hung in the kitchen, and a pail of heated water. I helped her set it before the fireplace and she emptied the steaming pail into it.

"Come on, Miss Charlotte," she said. "Let's get you in here and you'll be right as rain."

Charlotte sobbed and sobbed, resisting the maid with an iron will. Agnes and I looked at one another helplessly, as if the other might have a better idea of how to tame her. Maria arrived with a tray of hot buttered crumpets and a cup of chocolate, setting it on the little table beneath the window, but Charlotte ignored it. I went to take the dreadful flea-bitten trousers off her, and she smacked me away, her small fist meeting my face.

I held my cheek in shock, and felt a flash of fury. "Stop crying this instant!"

She did, for one second, two at the most, and there was such hatred in her eyes I felt as though I'd been hit again. Then she began roaring so hard she began to choke, and several dreadful, primal noises came from her dirty, bare little body before she bent double and vomited on the carpet.

Who was this changeling? The placid, good girl who'd been taken from me had been utterly defiled. Her hair was coming down from its pins all knotted, and her face and neck were streaked with dirt. She looked as though she'd been crawling through coals. Why did it feel now as though she was the captive and we the thieves? None of us knew what to do with her, but Agnes knelt to wipe the contents of her stomach with her apron, while Maria clung in pale-faced shock to the doorframe.

"Maria," I said calmly, "please go to Bedford Row to Doctor Mead's house, and have his housekeeper wake him. Tell him to come at once with a tonic for shock, and something to help her sleep."

Maria gaped and nodded, then fled downstairs. I approached Charlotte as one might a rabid dog, and told her she must have a bath to wash off the disease. She cowered away from me, and before I could get hold of her she dashed past my skirts and ran naked from the room.

"Charlotte!"

We found her just as she was about to slip like an imp before Maria into the street. The cook caught her at the last second, dragging her back inside by her armpits and slamming the door before collapsing against it. "Oh, oh!" she cried, clutching her chest. "Oh, Miss Charlotte!"

"Get to your room," I bellowed, pointing at the staircase, and she leaped past me with the most almighty screech and ran up them as if they were on fire. "Maria, go now to Doctor Mead, *go!*"

The cook gasped and panted her way from the house. Hearing Charlotte's unbearable cries, and feeling quite terrified of her, I had no choice but to find the key and lock her in until she'd calmed down. I told her through the door that she was to bath herself and eat the crumpets, and only when she was quiet would the door be unlocked.

I waited until the noises she made subsided to a stubborn, exhausted whimper, and fetched a chair from my bedroom, placing it outside her door to sit and wait for Doctor Mead, and shivering so hard my teeth chattered.

He arrived half an hour later, at half past one in the morning, striding upstairs in three leaps. When I finally unlocked the door Charlotte had not bathed herself or eaten a mouthful; she was sitting in her trousers on the bed, with her arms wrapped around her knees, shuddering violently. I waited outside while he looked her over, spending almost an hour in the room with her, and giving her a draft of something. I watched through the gap in the door as he sat with a cool, clean hand on her forehead, waiting for sleep to arrive, but before it did she spoke from her pillow.

"Where is Mama?" They were the first words she'd spoken since arriving home.

"She is just outside," he murmured. "You can see her in the morning. She is very glad to have you home."

"Not *her*," she spat. "My real mama. I want my mama." Tears came again, silently this time, from her, and also from me.

I wiped my eyes, and a minute or two later, Doctor Mead blew out the candle and closed the door, finding me in my chair on the landing. I felt very cold still, and he suggested we go down to the kitchen for something warm to drink, and gave me a draft to sleep, too, slipping a little bottle into my hand.

"She will be better in the morning. You must be so relieved," he whispered, as the long-case clock ticked from below.

"Yes," I said.

Maria and Agnes had a sherry to celebrate her return, clinking their glasses together in triumph, but I shook my head when the bottle was offered. I wished I felt the same straightforward relief, as if the whole matter was no different from a favorite necklace being found down the back of a cupboard. But for me it was much more complicated. They had not seen the way Charlotte shrank from me, as though I was the Devil himself.

CHAPTER 20

She was not better in the morning. Agnes brought me breakfast in bed, and I asked if she had been into Charlotte's room yet.

"She ain't in plump currant," was her reply. "I expected that draft the doctor gave her would have knocked her into next week, but she's awake."

"Is she ill?"

"She's stopped crying, but there's a warmness to her I don't like. I opened the window for some air, but then she seemed cold, and pulled the coverlet up to her chin."

"She might have a fever; it would not surprise me with her being dragged through all manner of filth in the streets. Doctor Mead is working today but said he would call later."

Agnes nodded, and appeared withdrawn.

"Is that all?"

"It's just," she began with uncertainty, "the little girl's been asking for her mama."

"I shall go in once I've eaten."

Agnes nodded, both of us pretending she had been referring to me. I busied myself with the breakfast things and she left, closing the door quietly behind her. Charlotte was just across the hall — I could move the tray from my lap, put on a bed jacket and pad across to her room in a matter of seconds. Instead I sat gazing into the middle distance as my eggs and coffee went cold.

As I was dressing, the doorknocker rapped downstairs, and I heard a male voice, and Agnes's. Then the voices turned urgent and firm, and there was the sound of the front door closing; no, it had *slammed.* A moment later a great racket began outside the house: a man shouting in the street. I expected a beggar or a drunk had come calling — sometimes the farm boys passed along Devonshire Street, laced with drink after an evening's diversion in the city, but it was not eight o'clock in the morning. I tugged at my sleeves and went downstairs to the withdrawing room to look out.

Bess's red-headed brother was bellowing obscenities at the house. I had forgotten him entirely, remembering suddenly his presence in this very room the night before. He saw me at the window, and his fury grew more focused.

"Oi, thornback!" he bellowed. "I want my money!"

His voice cut through the glass like a hot knife through butter. A bruise purpled at his eye that had not been there before, and his lip had been cut and dried. There had been a fight, then, in the hours between him leaving my house and coming back. I realized, with interest, that I was not afraid of him. The idea of him breaking into my house or threatening me did not send me into a dizzy panic. If, I decided, he forced his way in, I would kill him dead with whatever was to hand: a poker, a knife, a bottle. I felt quite calm about it, and drew the curtain.

"Mort bitch!" he yelled. "Give me my money. We had a deal. A hundred pounds and she's yours. You got her, ain't you? I want my hundred quids, you hear me?"

There was a short silence, and then a chink as something small and solid hit the window glass, followed immediately by a disruption as what sounded like more than one person apprehended him. Ned: that was his name. How changed my mind had been these past days; it was as though all the anxiety and dread of the last thirty years had lifted, like a pair of boots being removed after a long day's walking. And it had happened not through Charlotte's return, but when she had disappeared. In a way, this trauma had cauterized the other, sealing it in a way I'd never expected it could be.

Ned came again a while later, hammering at the doorknocker, and then went around the back, jumping over the wall and doing the same at the kitchen door. Maria chased him off with a meat cleaver, like a character in a comedy. I watched her brandish it at the gate, howling at him to stay away, and then I went in to Charlotte. I had expected to find her in a similar state to when she'd arrived, distressed and hiccuping but made more docile, perhaps, by Doctor Mead's draft. This Charlotte was worse. She was vacant and vapid, with a despondent gaze and utter disinterest in her surroundings, least of all me. A child-sized chair had been placed facing her bed, and I settled myself and my skirts on it with some difficulty.

"Are you feeling better?" I asked.

She was pale, with violet shadows beneath her eyes, which rested somewhere in the middle of the room, as though she was watching something particularly dull. I moved, and the little chair creaked.

"I am so glad Mr. Bloor found you. You had us quite worried."

Silence from Charlotte; there was no noise

even from the street below. No gin-addled man bellowing obscenities. I wondered if she had heard Ned; if she knew him. He was frightening. Perhaps she did know him, and he had terrorized her. Perhaps he'd done something terrible to her: scolded her, or hit her, or worse. I tried to recall if Doctor Mead had examined every inch of her for marks and bruises. But then there were the type of bruises that could not be seen, that bloomed inwardly — had they been looked for? He said she would not speak of where she had been or what she had seen there, and potential horrors began to appear to me, as though I was flicking through pictures in a magazine: Charlotte left abandoned in a freezing garret with no food; Charlotte forced to beg for money on the streets; Charlotte sitting in a corner as Bess and some faceless lover fought or fornicated in front of her.

"Did . . . did anyone hurt you?"

She might have been asleep, if her eyes had not been open.

"Was there a man there? Did anybody frighten you?"

Her arms were locked beneath the counterpane. Agnes had been right: there was a sheen of sweat on her forehead, and her hairline was damp.

"Would you like to play a game?" I looked around for a means of distraction, but all her books and magazines and toys had been tidied away.

"Or a lesson, perhaps?"

If she would not respond in English, I doubted she would in French. I sighed, feeling helpless. Why after six years did I not find this any more natural? When she had been a fat-cheeked baby she had not rejected me, and I longed for those simpler days when the wet nurse brought her to me. I had thought taking in a baby would make me maternal, forcing me into motherhood in the way that a dog thrown in a river will swim. The ease with which Bess had attended to Charlotte, the beatific indulgence that Ambrosia bestowed on her children, even the mothers at church, who so clearly existed in tandem with their children — they were all like pairs of wheels on a carriage, moving together in unison. I knew I would never be like them, even if Charlotte lived with me the rest of her life.

"I wish you would speak, Charlotte."

Silence.

"Charlotte.

"Charlotte.

"For heaven's sake, look at me!"

Then I noticed something: her fist was

closed tightly, as though she was gripping something.

"What is in your hand?"

She gripped tighter. It was the only signal she had heard me.

"Charlotte, what's in your hand?"

I did not know why I cared so much, why the only impulse to touch her came not from sentimentality but suspicion. I prized her fingers open, though she resisted, and made a noise akin to a protest, a whimper, which made a crack inside me but did not make me stop. A coin fell onto the bed. I do not know what I'd been expecting, but it had not been this; a letter, perhaps, or a token of sentiment. The coin was bronze and dull, the size of a crown, but I pounced on it a second before Charlotte did, pushing her hot little hand away. It was not a coin after all, but a ticket to the Ranelagh Pleasure Gardens.

"Why do you have this?"

She had fallen mute again, but it was a hostile muteness this time: her black eyes burned with fury.

I got up to go, dropping the coin into my pocket.

"I hate you."

I had one hand on the doorknob, and stopped. She was looking directly at me with a loathing more clear and intense than I could ever have expected from a child.

"I beg your pardon?" I said.

"I hate you. I hate it here. I want my mama."

I thought about slapping her, about dragging her from her narrow bed and hitting her legs or her palms. I had never done it before; had never needed to, but now a clear venom rose in me, tingling my fingertips, burning my neck. The last time I'd felt it come was the day I'd attacked them in the withdrawing room, and since then it had lain dormant, it seemed, until now. It cared not what twig it was poked with, just that it had been poked. I let it raise its stupid head and look around, and I kept very still, and when it realized the deep emotion it had been woken by was fear — yes, the same as before, but not the life-threatening kind — it yawned and curled again, sinking into slumber.

I closed the door and left her.

Her crying woke me that night. The sound of her sobbing spread over the surface of my dream, and lifted me from it. I lay in the thick dark listening to her, and wanting to go to her, but her disdain for me was like a wall of fire outside her door. I heard feet creaking the boards above me, and shuffling down the stairs, and Agnes — sweet, faithful Agnes — going in, already shushing and murmuring as she opened Charlotte's door, and for a moment the crying escaped into the house. I gathered myself and got out of bed, and waited at my bedroom door for Agnes to come back out. I heard her comforting the child, and Charlotte's guttural, wretched sobs.

"Mama," she cried, over and over. It died gradually, and Agnes hummed and soothed, and five minutes passed, then ten, then the door opened.

"Agnes."

The older woman yelped like a kicked puppy. "Oh, madam! You did give me a fright."

"Why is she still crying?"

Her white cap bobbed in the darkness.

"Do you think something happened to her when she was away?"

"I don't know, madam," she whispered.

"She is not the same child."

Agnes did not speak.

"Has she told you anything about where she was?"

"No, madam."

I waited. The clocked ticked in the hall. Doctor Mead had come again after supper with a little case of bottles that tinkled as he carried them up the stairs, like Agnes bringing the decanter. Perhaps Charlotte would be like me now.

Winter showed no sign of giving way to spring, and the next morning dawned cold and gray. Charlotte's condition worsened. A fever took hold, soaking her nightgown and the bedsheets, and she lay wilted on the mattress with the window open to the street. I was anxious about letting miasma in, but Agnes said fresh air was the only thing for a fever, and began making poultices for her chest and soaking rags for her forehead. She had been ill before, but only once or twice, caught both times from Maria, who suffered colds. This time was different, like the grief and unhappiness had curdled inside her and mutated there. Doctor Mead had called it shock. I sat beside her bed on the tiny chair, or else on the landing outside her room with the newspaper.

Shortly before noon I went upstairs to fetch something from the withdrawing room, forgetting instantly what it was, because to my great surprise a man was sitting in my chair.

I did not know him, but something told me I'd seen him before. He was quite at ease, with one ankle resting on his knee, tossing a paperweight from one hand to the other. He was perhaps twenty-two or three, with a shock of dark hair and serious black eyebrows. He was frowning, but there was something nonthreatening about the way he did it: an intentness, a curiosity, perhaps, almost like a scholar puzzling at an equation. I froze in the doorway, but before I could open my mouth, he held up a hand as if in greeting.

"Mrs. Callard," he said. "Just the person I wanted to see. Rum ken you got here." Before I could open my mouth, he went on: "I know you're handy with a poker, so before you empty your lungs, I'll level with you. I ain't weaponed." He held out his jacket, which hung empty on either side of him.

"Who in heaven's name are you?" My voice was more assured than I felt. "How did you get in my house?"

He made a self-deprecating gesture. "It was the work of a minute. Them window locks you got, they'll bend over for anyone with a crowbar. They should be lead, really; I'd have them changed if I were you." He said this conversationally, and I gaped in speechless horror.

"What do you want? Let me guess: you

are another acquaintance of Bess's."

"Another?"

"Or Ned's, rather."

The playfulness vanished from his face, and he gave me a hard look. "Not his, no."

"Who are you, then?"

"A friend of Bess's."

"Why do I know you?"

"I'm a Glim Jack. A linkboy. So unless you can see in the dark, I doubt you do."

"You've been here before. Standing there, outside. I saw you."

He raised a full, dark eyebrow. "You don't miss much."

"Why are you here?"

"I have a proposition."

"If it's money you're after —"

"It's not." He spoke harshly, and I fell into silence. "Please." He gestured for me to sit opposite him, and slowly, with trembling legs, I moved across the room to take the chair before him, noting the absurdity of how he treated the house like his own, and me a guest. I was utterly powerless. I let my eyes slide briefly around the room; the poker was in its stand, and a porcelain vase sat on the table beside us. He would move quicker, though.

He saw me look around, and said: "I promise I ain't gonna pink you."

The idea of him picking the window lock and slipping inside . . . it was as though he had seen my nightmares, and come to Devonshire Street to use them against me.

"Listen, Mrs. C," he said genially, relaxing back in the chair. His fingernails, I noticed, were very dirty, and he smelled of tobacco, like Daniel used to. "You have your reasons for wanting the child. I understand. I do. She's been yours these past years, and you've cared for her splendidly. The shine on her! She's like a fresh conker. And I can see you in her. I have to say, I imagined you different." To my mortification, I found myself blushing. "And the fact that you spared Bess, and didn't have her thrown in the clink . . . you have an heart, Mrs. C. And a conscience. But that child . . . Bess loves that child. Worships her. She has no reason to live without her."

I swallowed as my nose stung, and tears pricked my eyes.

"How is she, the little girl?" he continued.

"She is unwell. She has a fever. I don't know where you took her, you and Bess, but she arrived filthy and shivering, in hysterics that she hasn't recovered from."

"That's because Bess's brother shopped her."

"Ned?"

411

"I have another name for him, myself. Several, actually." He examined his nails. "I imagine he had a deal with you."

It was not a question. I colored again, and felt embarrassed, then indignant. "He came to me the night before last, and said he knew where she would be. I haven't paid him."

"And will you?"

"I haven't decided. I feel no remorse in swindling a crook."

There was the trace of a smile. "You and I both, Mrs. C."

"What's your name?"

"Lyle."

"Am I expected to believe that? Bess came here under a false name; I see no reason why you wouldn't, too."

"My name is Lyle Kozak. Well, my real name's Zoran, but I go by Lyle, see, cos it's more English. Only my old *majke* calls me that."

"And you're a friend of Bess's, you say?"

"Bess, Eliza, Ebenezer, whatever she goes by these days. Yeah, I knows her."

"At least one of us does," I said. "It's become quite clear I did not know her at all. Where is she?"

"Lying low. That's what I've come to speak to you about: she wishes the pleasure of your company."

I stared at him.

"Now, she knows you don't go outside, so naturally she hasn't suggested a Clerkenwell chophouse. Nor does she expect you to invite her in for tea. She will be at the Foundling chapel today at three o'clock, and hopes most sincerely to see you there."

"Does she. Well, you can tell her, Mr. Kozak, that I shan't go, and that I am astounded she expects a reconciliation when she has deceived me so. She stole my child, if you remember."

"She stole *her* child."

"As I said, I shan't go. And if you enter my house again, you will feel the watchman on your back."

"Ooh, which one? I know 'em all." His eyes shone with mirth. He was infuritating — a conversation with him was like a racket sport.

"You forget I hired a thief-taker. I can commission Mr. Bloor again; he has ties with the magistrates."

"Ha! Captain Queernabs? He couldn't catch a cold. You might as well have hired a blind beggar. Besides, he didn't catch her, did he? Her white-livered brother nosed her."

"Are you telling me they were not in

413

league together?"

"Do you really think she'd give her back, after all the trouble she took to get her?"

"So her brother betrayed her. I'm sure it's all she deserves."

"You have left her with nothing. And even with nothing, she is ten times the woman you are."

Fear and fury coursed through me. "You do not know a single thing about me, Mr. Kozak. I can change my mind, you know. One word to the magistrate and I'm sure they will find room in Newgate for a child snatcher."

"You might be more careful with your intimidations, Mrs. Callard," he said quietly, a malevolent sneer on his face now. "You gentry morts have no clue. You sit in your drawing rooms and bury your heads in your cushions, cos prison don't happen to the likes of you. You read about it in the papers, but it's just a story to you. An idea. I can tell you what it's *really* like, though, what it'd really be like for Bess. Well, to start, she has no money, and prisons are businesses, you see. They want to make a profit. You wouldn't go to an inn and demand supper and a room if you had no money — you'd get off to a bad start with the old bluffer, wouldn't you? Now, our friend Bess would have to cough up to enter the prison —" he began counting on his fingers "— then there's bed and board, food and drink, oh, and if you don't want your chains to rub you raw, they charge you for the pleasure of removing them. She can't afford none of that, you see, so like the other sad souls in that lice-ridden saltbox, she'd have to eat the rats and mice what she shares her cell with. It's a death sentence, you see, just a crueler and more undignified one than you get at Tyburn.

"It might not be the vermin what gets her, though," he went on, growing genial again, as I listened in horrified silence. "I reckon you're in there a week afore you're that desperate, and perhaps the sweating sickness will get her first. Or, I don't know, I doubt those sacks they give 'em to sleep on have been cleaned since the plague, so she might even catch some of that down there and be dead by teatime. And all because —" he slammed his hand on the table, making me shudder "— your husband made a duchess out of her. Now, that don't seem right, does it? I know he was put to bed with a shovel himself, rest his soul, but it don't make sense that Charlotte's made an orphan, if it can be avoided. Do you agree?"

My voice shook. "If only she had come to

415

me in the beginning, and told me who she was . . .”

Lyle hooted with laughter. “You would have handed over the child, would you? ‘Excuse me, miss, may I trouble you for my daughter back, what you have cared for these past years? Thank you for your generosity, we’ll be going now.’ Oh, why didn’t she think of that? If only she’d rapped your brass knocker! You wouldn’t have sent her away; I bet you’d have invited her in for tea and cake and a sit-down!”

I closed my eyes. “I am not a monster. Whatever you think of me, I am not cruel. I would not have turned her away.”

“Turned her away? You wouldn’t even have come to the door.”

The truth of his words struck me dumb. Then the withdrawing room door opened, startling us both, and Agnes gave a yelp upon seeing us.

“Agnes,” I said calmly. “Mr. Kozak is just leaving.” I turned to him, and said coldly: “Good day to you.”

I remained seated, and after a long look at me, he stood, setting the glass paperweight down gently on the table.

“Three o’clock,” he said.

I put on my cloak and took it off again, and

went to look at Charlotte, who had refused first her breakfast and then the tea Agnes brought in a steaming cup.

Since she had returned, I only saw Bess in her. There was nothing of Daniel, with his fair hair and gray, feather-colored eyes. She was all Bess. In her manner, too: inquisitive and stubborn, and sly as a fox. She had stuffed that morning's toast down the side of the bed and moved to Bess's bed, which had until now been neatly made. She waited for my reaction, but I did not betray it.

"I want my mama," she said upon seeing me, and when I did not respond, she reached for the saucer on the little stool by the bed and flung it at the wall, where it shattered, and cried: "I want my *mama!*"

I scolded her, and swept up the shards of china with my hands, feeling very weary then. Going from the room, locking her inside once more, I felt as though I could curl up on the carpet and sleep for a week. Her fever had broken, but for how long would she be like this? The child was willful and vexed, and I knew exactly how those two things could mature into something even more powerful, remembering the key turning on me at Aunt Cassandra's in the years after my parents died, when I'd thrown one of my *peformances,* as she called them.

Now I was the one holding the key. I found it endlessly surprising, how history would repeat itself, despite a person doing everything in their power to make it otherwise.

Her whole life I had kept Charlotte safe and healthy, away from pain and grief. In knowing only a few people and going nowhere, she would have nothing and no one to miss. I had been patted and preened by my parents, cosseted like a little lapdog. I'd known a dozen servants, and balls, and other children from large houses like ours, and been entirely unequipped for what happened to me. I'd not wanted to have a child at all, but the one I did have I'd reared to be self-soothing, clever and interested. And despite all that — because of all that — she was acting just like me in the months and years after my parents' deaths: violent, uncontrollable and full of rage. These feminine vessels we inhabited: Why did nobody expect them to contain unfeminine feelings? Why could we, too, not be furious and scorned and entirely altered by grief? Why must we accept the cards we had been dealt?

I heard the clock chime two in the hall, and attempted to drag myself from the past into the present. But perhaps we never could entirely. Perhaps we were always made up of both, and they fit perfectly together, like a jagged little heart.

The chapel was a different place on a weekday. I had not expected to find it open at all, but it was, empty and tranquil, like the first page of a new book, or a freshly drawn bath. I entered through the little vestibule and felt its significance dwarf me. I took a hymn book from the shelf at the side, as if anybody who might be watching from the balcony could possibly be deceived into thinking I had come to worship on a Wednesday afternoon. There was one other person in the chapel, sitting at the far end by the pulpit. The floor had been recently waxed and a great shining distance yawned between us. Daylight flooded in from the top windows, and without the congregation of three or four hundred, I allowed myself to look around, and take in the plaster ceiling rose, delicate as an iced cake, and the ornate wooden balustrades on the balcony. The pews were great wooden laps waiting patiently for bodies, for prayers.

The other person did not move, and kept their head bowed. Slowly I approached with the hymn book in my gloved hands, my slippers squeaking on the waxed floor. I had walked here, all the way. Up Devonshire

Street, right onto Great Ormond, passing the late Richard Mead's house, then left, where a mews, stable yards and allotments marked the edge of London, before it gave way to fields. I had not told anybody where I was going or who I would meet, slipping silently from the house, locking the door behind me, then dropping the key in my pocket.

Bess looked up before I reached her. She was wearing a plain brown cloak, fastened at the neck, and her head was bare. I noticed her eyes flick briefly behind me, at waist height, before she met my gaze again.

"I thought you wouldn't come," she said.

"Why did you think that?"

"Because . . ." She lowered her eyes. "Because I'm not sure I would, if I were you."

"You are not me," I said, taking the pew behind hers and sitting to her left. She turned her head slightly, but did not look directly at me. A pale pink ribbon tied her hair at her neck.

We sat still for a moment.

"You didn't bring no one with you?" she asked. "Doctor Mead?"

"I am alone."

I could see her working up to ask what she really wanted to, and waited.

"You haven't told the magistrate?" she said finally.

"No. Mr. Bloor was a private commissioner, not a law enforcer. If you think there is somebody waiting for you behind the chapel doors, I assure you there is not."

She nodded. "My brother gave me away. Did you know that? Oh, 'course you did. I know he came to you. He stole everything from me in the end." She closed her eyes. "We was so close growing up. Abe — that's my pa — he said me and Ned was thick as thieves. Turns out he was one all along."

"I have not paid him. I won't. Your friend, Mr. Kozak, the linkboy —"

"Lyle?" Her voice changed, growing warm and fond.

"I've never met anyone quite like him. He is very loyal to you."

"He was impressed with you, you know. He said you was like a tigress."

"Me?" I felt a stab of pride.

She turned then, and placed a white hand on the back of the pew, but still did not meet my eye. "How is Charlotte? Lyle said she had a fever."

"She is resting. Doctor Mead has been attending her. He says she is suffering from shock."

We were skirting around the heart of it,

the kernel, waiting to see who would seize it first. She lowered her head again, and a twist of chestnut hair slipped from the ribbon to fall down her cheek. The sound of children's voices outside played through the high windows; in the yards along the drive the Foundling boys had been busy making ropes, surrounded by straw-colored coils of twine. The girls were nowhere to be seen, most likely busy at their needles in the workrooms.

"I suppose you want to know," I said eventually, "how I knew about Charlotte?"

She nodded.

"I heard about her from my sister."

She looked sharply at me. "I did not know you had a sister."

"You would have met her, had she not been seeing out the winter in the north. But then, of course, the game would have been up. Usually she is at my house once or twice a week. Her name is Ambrosia. She was the one who saw you at the Foundling that night, and several months before, at a tavern in the city with my husband."

I watched her ear turn red. She was still, and then said: "I think I remember her. There was a woman looking at me strange that night. I thought it odd, but then I suppose everybody was looking at us strange.

She had a blue feather in her hair."

"That sounds like Ambrosia."

Another silence. "I want you to know . . ." she said after a while. "I want you to believe me when I tell you I didn't know he was married."

"I believe you."

Perhaps she had been expecting more resistance; her shoulders slumped, as though she had breathed out a great sigh.

"I don't want you to think I was in love with him."

"Why?"

"Because . . . because I wasn't. I only met him once before. And then afterward . . ." She swallowed. "After that night I never saw him again."

"It makes no difference to me," I said, realizing it was true.

"And how did you find out my name?"

"Ambrosia again. She followed you in her carriage."

She made a movement, and I realized it was an involuntary laugh. "You'd have thought I'd notice a great big carriage behind me. She must have acted quick to get her the next day."

"She did. She came to me that night, directly from following you. I didn't know whether to believe her at first, though I knew Daniel went with women, so I suppose it shouldn't have come as a shock. But to have her tell me he had a *child.* A living, breathing child. When she told me what the token was, I knew it to be true, because I had the other half."

Bess smiled then. "It's like Charlotte, isn't it? Half of me and half of you. That reminds me." She began rummaging beneath her cloak and drew something out, closed in her fist. She held it out to me, dropping it into my glove. "I wanted you to have this back."

It was my half, with the D carved in Daniel's sloping hand.

"It wasn't mine to take," she said.

I closed my palm over it and squeezed it tight.

"Mrs. Callard —"

"Please, let me speak." I said this thickly, feeling the emotion coming, and trying to hold it off. "I never wanted to be a mother. I was given a child by fate, not by God."

She was very still, and her dark eyes — Charlotte's eyes — were very grave.

"I read somewhere that being a good parent means preparing your child to leave you, and go into the world." I swallowed, and squeezed the heart, feeling my own squeeze in my chest, and tears sting my eyes. "I cannot say I have been a good parent. But I think . . . I think she is ready to leave."

Outside the gates, I drew the folded map from my breast pocket. The paper shook in my hands, and I traced my route with a finger, looking ahead at the empty lane. It was a cold, sunny afternoon, with a few clouds scattered here and there, and just as many cows dotted about the fields. Standing in the dusty lane with the green stretching on either side was a very strange feeling: I was exposed, and yet anonymous at the same time. I followed the dry stone wall south, passing again the allotments and stable yards, where liveried grooms walked over the cobbles with saddles and brushes, and did not notice me at all. I stood at the point in the road at which my carriage turned right each Sunday, going west. I turned left.

I walked down a narrow street of small townhouses, where the road was wide enough for a trap but not a carriage, coming out on a wider road by a modest chapel. There were a few people around: capped nursemaids with their young charges, and carmen with parcels. A crossing sweeper paused for a moment, leaning against his broom to catch his breath. Nobody paid me any attention as I moved south toward a large green square, planted with young trees. A coach and horse approached from the left, and I shrank against a tree as the wheels thundered past, closing my eyes against them for a second. My map, I held tightly in my gloved hand, and I drew it out again to look at it. The houses on the square were like mine, but lined on the first floor with little iron balconies, and had three slim windows on the upper stories instead of two wide ones. I walked along the path to the southeast corner and crossed the dusty road to better see the numbered doors, finding the one I needed was green, with a white brick pattern around it. The fan light above the door was two canes, crossed at the center.

I walked up the steps and knocked, and a moment later the door swung open, and the face behind it was too astonished for words.

"Good afternoon, Doctor Mead," I said, moving past him to step inside and closing the door gently behind me. The hallway was dim and quiet; outside another horse and cart passed, and farther away a dog barked. The doctor was in his shirtsleeves, and there was a smudge of ink at his neck where he had adjusted his collar. He smelled of wool and soap, and something else that no other

426

man shared: his skin, perhaps.

"Mrs. Callard." His voice was hushed, as though he did not dare breathe. At the foot of the stairs, a long-case clock ticked. "What are you doing here?"

I removed my gloves and put a hand to his cheek, which was warm. "Don't say anything."

"Is it Charlotte? Is she —"

I put my lips to his and kissed him, and moved my mouth to his ear. "You and I in marble," I said. "All else in dust."

CHAPTER 21

BESS

April 1754

We went straight to Bloomsbury from the church at St. Giles. It did not take long, being only half a mile from where Lyle lived in Seven Dials, though it felt a world away.

Lyle's family had come to the wedding: as many sisters and brothers as he could find when we arrived, spilling as they were out into the street, and his mama, a tiny, broad woman like a wooden doll, with Lyle's kind eyes and heavy eyebrows. His father was at his tailor's shop and Abe at the market, but both had given their blessing, and Abe had given me as a wedding present: a lace handkerchief I didn't know he'd kept of Mama's, with her initials, MB, on it.

It was a quick, happy service, with two pews of Kozaks, who whispered throughout in a unique blend of Slavic and English, shushed now and again by their mother.

Keziah and William came with the boys, and sat proudly across the aisle; my friend had given me a new dress to be married in, one of the most beautiful I'd seen, of palest blue, with a bonnet and matching ribbon.

One of Lyle's brothers, Tomasz, waited outside with the pony and trap we'd bought, and we emerged afterward to find him racing a crowd of dirty children down the street on the pony. We kissed all the Kozaks one by one, and Lyle's mother pinched my cheek and said something in Slavic, and Lyle thanked her warmly and kissed her on the forehead. Moses and Jonas ran around with the children as Keziah squeezed my hands and wished me luck, and William gave me a fatherly embrace and shook Lyle's hand. Then we went north, through the light morning drizzle.

The week before, we had moved our things to the Fulham countryside, where Lyle had signed a lease on three closes of land for growing vegetables: peas, turnips, parsnips and carrots, of which there'd be two or three crops a year, and corn and barley in between. A small cottage came with the tenancy — two rooms, with a dirt floor and large fireplace — and a fat pony, and the rickety old trap. I couldn't believe the silence out there, which fell like a curtain over the countryside. It was four miles from Covent Garden but might have been four hundred. Not that I missed it. It had not been a wrench to leave London. We'd had enough of selling shrimp and light.

We drew to a halt at no. 13, and a pale face disappeared in the first-floor window. The glossy black door opened before we knocked, and Charlotte flew out, barreling into us like a puppy in a petticoat. Lyle lifted her up onto his shoulders, and she swung her boots with glee. Several trunks were banked up in the hallway, and the painted woman in the red dress watched from her position on the wall as two figures glided from the shadows: Alexandra, and one I did not know, who was like Alexandra but larger, with a smile on her face that came easily and looked permanent.

"This is my sister, Ambrosia," Alexandra said. "Ambrosia, this is Bess Bright and Lyle Kozak."

"Actually, it's Bess Kozak," I said, and Alexandra's eyebrows lifted, and a smile broke her face as I showed her the slim gold band on my finger. "We just came from St. Giles Church."

She looked at him admiringly, as did Ambrosia, who gave a saucy wink. "At least you know what you're in for later," she told me. We'd all fallen about, apart from Alexandra, who looked so shocked it only made us laugh harder.

Charlotte pulled at my cap from Lyle's shoulders and said: "What are you laughing at?" which set us off again.

"Lyle!" she said suddenly. "Maria said I could give an apple to the horse. Will you take me to the kitchen?"

"By your leave, miss," Lyle said. "Watch your head!" He stalked off with her at a gallop down the hallway. We watched them go, and then it was the three of us.

"So you," said Ambrosia, "are the infamous Bess. I'd know you still, to look at you."

"And I don't know you at all." Something came to me then, which I'd wondered after I met Alexandra in the Foundling chapel, when we'd decided not to tear Charlotte in half anymore.

One evening the following week, like men drawing up military plans, we had spent the evening in Alexandra's parlor designing what Charlotte's life should look like. Alexandra had got a quill and ink and paper from the bureau, and I told her that I would have to trust her because I couldn't read. She'd put the quill down, then.

While we talked she told me about her past, and why she reacted with such fear and violence that night after the pleasure garden. I had felt powerful guilt then, and hot with shame. I thought I'd had the measure of her all along, but really I'd not known her at all. It was strange to see her so intimately, as an equal, almost. I had thought her so cold and unfeeling when I met her, with her straight back and stormy manner. I had thought her beautiful, too, but that word was too feminine, bringing to mind plump women and dreamy smiles. If she'd been a painting, she'd be a strong ship on crashing waves.

"Ambrosia," I said. "Something has bothered me since I learned it was you who saw me. How did you find out my name?"

"I went to the court you lived in and asked somebody."

"What did they look like?"

She frowned. "If I remember, a woman had seen me from a window and came out. She was large, very ordinary, though I couldn't see much of her as it was so dark. I think she was carrying a broom."

I almost laughed. Of course Nancy Benson the brush maker would have been beside herself to have someone so fine as Ambrosia arrive at our court and ask for me. She might have known it was something to do with the baby, who had been born that morning. She would have heard me in childbed; it would not have surprised me to know she'd placed a chair at the door and listened from start to finish.

Alexandra and I looked at one another. "What became of Ned?" she asked gently.

"He was arrested two weeks ago for robbing a goldsmith's. He'll be transported next month to the colonies."

Her face was very grave. "I'm not sure I'm sorry to hear that."

"I'm not," I said quietly, though I was, for the old Ned at least, who used to make puppets behind the red curtain.

Sorry, too, for the old Bess. But not this one.

Doctor Mead came carefully down the stairs with the final item — Charlotte's budgie in its cage, cheeping fretfully — and set it gently on the ground beside the turtle, which had been put in a fruit crate padded with straw. Charlotte came back then with Lyle and a shiny red apple and Maria following. She passed me a sponge cake wrapped in cloth, as a peace offering; I doubted she had truly forgiven me for stealing from her larder the night we ran away. I thanked her, and the two men began loading everything onto the cart. "Most of my books are there," she told me. "But I could not fit all of them. And my nicest clothes are here for church, because Mama said they are too good for Fulham."

Alexandra had blushed hotly then, and I'd smiled and said I thought that was very wise. And then it was time to say goodbye.

Alexandra knelt in front of Charlotte, her navy silk skirts rustling gently, and we all grew quiet. Charlotte drew something from her dress pocket — a drawing she had made, of a man wearing a tricorn hat and smart coat with buttons and buckled shoes, and a woman with a large skirt and neat jacket. She wore no hat, as Alexandra didn't, and her lips hinted at a smile. Between the pair was a love heart, with a jagged crack down the middle.

"It's you and Doctor Mead," she said.

"That's very good," Alexandra said. "You have a talent for drawing; I could never teach you."

Agnes appeared from somewhere, and put Charlotte into a wool coat — for though it was April it was not yet warm — and tied a straw hat with a blue ribbon beneath her chin. She was wearing a maize-colored dress and white stockings, and looked quite the little country girl.

"You will write, won't you?" Alexandra asked her. "I will make sure I always have coins for the mail boy, and I'll be waiting by the door for him every day in case he has something for me."

"Does the mail boy come from Fulham?"

"He comes from everywhere."

"How long will it take to get to you?"

"The same day, if you ask the mail coachman nicely."

She nodded.

"You must write in great detail about where you live. I want to know all about it. I want to know how many flowers you have in your garden, and what you can see from your window, and what the inside of your house looks like. I want to know what plates you eat from, and what you eat, and how many times you brush your hair before bedtime."

"That's too much to remember!"

"Just write what you can remember, then. And I will see you every fortnight, and you will stay Friday and Saturday, and then we will go to church in the morning."

"And have oranges and cream?" she asked, and everyone smiled.

"We will have oranges and cream."

"And Doctor Mead will be here?"

"He will be here, yes. Have you remembered your French book?"

She nodded.

"She's going to teach me," I said. "Aren't you, Charlotte?"

"Oui," said Charlotte, and everyone laughed again.

I was eager to be gone, and perhaps Alexandra noticed, because she came to me and pressed a silk bag of coins into my hand. "For this month," she said. "Think of it as a wedding present."

I thanked her, and looked at Lyle, and he winked at me, and nodded. We moved in a little chorus to the door, and the men loaded the last trunk onto the trap, and covered the budgie's cage with a cloth. Charlotte settled her turtle on her lap, and it lifted its head, as though to say farewell, before retreating into its shell. We were ready at last.

I looked up at the window where we'd slept, and at the withdrawing room window, where I'd seen Alexandra waiting fretfully all those weeks before.

I looked at her now, standing between Ambrosia and Doctor Mead in the doorway, and we smiled at one another in the way that people do who have been through something very significant, and come out the other side.

The rain fell lightly onto the trap, and Charlotte was settled beneath my arm under our canvas cover, and we had our backs to Lyle, who took up the reins. We waved, and they waved back, with Agnes and Maria peering out and beaming from the gaps in between.

"Bye!" Charlotte cried, waving very hard.

Alexandra had one hand fastened in Doctor Mead's and was waving back with the other. Her face was wet with tears, and alight with fear and love and pride.

"Are we ready?" I asked, and Charlotte cried yes. Lyle clicked his tongue, and the trap pulled away and we moved down Devonshire Street, toward the river, against the tide.

■ ■ ■ ■

THE LOST ORPHAN

STACEY HALLS

■ ■ ■ ■

READER'S GUIDE

QUESTIONS FOR DISCUSSION

1. The Foundling Hospital, established in 1740s London, was the first of its kind to take in babies at risk of being abandoned. What circumstances do you think would drive a mother or father to surrender the care of their child to an institution back then? While foster care has mostly taken the place of orphanages in the twenty-first century, do you think the reasons why a parent might give up their child have changed?

2. The benefactors of the Foundling Hospital thought it a good fund-raising opportunity to allow wealthy patrons to sip drinks and socialize while they observed desperate mothers face the harsh lottery system that would determine the fates of their infants. While such behavior seems particularly callous to us, can you think of

any fund-raising events in today's culture that might draw a rough parallel?

3. Bess and Alexandra both lost their mothers at impressionable ages and have lived without them for many years. How do you think their lives would have been different had their mothers still been alive?

4. Discuss the character of Daniel Callard and the feelings both Bess and Alexandra have toward him. Do you blame Daniel for taking lovers? Do you think he should have remained faithful?

5. Do you think Daniel's giving one half of a heart made of whalebone to Bess and one half to Alexandra had any sentimental meaning for him? Was it a token of his feelings or a mere gesture in the moment?

6. How do you think Daniel would have reacted to Bess's pregnancy and to having an illegitimate daughter?

7. Chance is at play throughout the novel and drives the narrative forward, but to what extent do you think Bess and Alexandra are actually masters of their own destinies? Are they passive or active?

8. Once you understand the circumstances that led to Alexandra's reclusivity, do you find her more or less sympathetic as a character? Did you think she would have had some empathy for Bess's predicament? Or is she a pure product of her time?

9. Do you think Bess is selfish to take Charlotte/Clara from the comfort of Alexandra's home? Or does Bess feel the need as her real mother to express her love for her daughter and raise her as her own?

10. Which do you think is more crucial for raising a child: love or money? If you had to choose between the two, which would you pick?

11. What surprised you most about life in 1750s Georgian London as depicted in this novel? The stark contrasts between the haves and the have-nots? The easy lifestyle of the wealthy and the harsh, unforgiving lives of the working class/working poor? The diversity of the life on the wharves?

12. In the end, what is the novel saying about the bonds between mother and

child, between husband and wife, among family? Do you think love, and our need for it, is the great equalizer among all classes? Or is it felt more among those who have less?

A CONVERSATION
WITH THE AUTHOR

What inspired you to write *The Lost Orphan*?

My inspiration for this novel came to me in the spring of 2017 when I visited the Foundling Museum, formerly the Foundling Hospital, in Bloomsbury. I was so moved by its purpose — the first of its kind, a place where women were able to leave babies they couldn't care for — and shocked and disturbed by lottery night, where London society would watch stricken mothers draw colored balls from a bag that determined whether or not their children were taken in.

Then I saw the tokens — scraps of love that they left with their babies. In a world before identification or widespread literacy, these ordinary objects — squares of cloth torn from their dresses, coins scratched with initials — were the only things linking the women with their children, whom some of them would have hoped to reclaim one day. *Immediately I thought, What if the system failed? That so many desperate souls went there hoping for a better life for their sons and daughters resonated deeply with me, and that was where the idea for Bess's story was born.*

What are you working on now?

My as yet untitled next novel will be set in Edwardian Yorkshire in the gloomy valleys and damp woodland of the north of England, where a recently graduated Norland nanny gets a position with the perfect family, who are hiding their own dark secrets.

ABOUT THE AUTHOR

Stacey Halls grew up in Rossendale, Lancashire, and has always been fascinated by history. She lives in London and has worked as a journalist for The Bookseller, Stylist, Psychologies and Fabulous. Her debut novel, *The Familiars,* was about the Pendle Hill Witch Trials. Her interest in London's original Foundling Hospital is the inspiration for her second novel.

The employees of Thorndike Press hope you have enjoyed this Large Print book. All our Thorndike, Wheeler, and Kennebec Large Print titles are designed for easy reading, and all our books are made to last. Other Thorndike Press Large Print books are available at your library, through selected bookstores, or directly from us.

For information about titles, please call:
  (800) 223-1244

or visit our website at:
  gale.com/thorndike

To share your comments, please write:
  Publisher
  Thorndike Press
  10 Water St., Suite 310
  Waterville, ME 04901